PAUL TEMPLE
and the
CURZON CASE

Francis Durbridge

WILLIAMS & WHITING

Applications for performance or other rights should be made to The Agency, 24 Pottery Lane, London W11 4LZ.

Cover design by Timo Schroeder

9781912582419

Williams & Whiting (Publishers)
15 Chestnut Grove, Hurstpierpoint,
West Sussex, BN6 9SS

Titles by Francis Durbridge to be published by Williams & Whiting

A Case For Paul Temple
A Game of Murder
A Man Called Harry Brent
A Time of Day
Bat Out of Hell
Breakaway – The Family Affair
Breakaway – The Local Affair
Death Comes to the Hibiscus (stage play – writing as
Nicholas Vane)
La Boutique
Melissa
My Friend Charles
Paul Temple and the Alex Affair
Paul Temple and the Canterbury Case (film script)
Paul Temple and the Conrad Case
Paul Temple and the Curzon Case
Paul Temple and the Geneva Mystery
Paul Temple and the Gilbert Case
Paul Temple and the Gregory Affair
Paul Temple and the Jonathan Mystery
Paul Temple and the Lawrence Affair
Paul Temple and the Madison Mystery
Paul Temple and the Margo Mystery
Paul Temple and the Spencer Affair
Paul Temple and the Sullivan Mystery
Paul Temple and the Vandyke Affair
Paul Temple and Steve
Paul Temple Intervenes
Portrait of Alison
Send for Paul Temple (radio serial)

Also by Francis Durbridge and published by Williams & Whiting:

Also published by Williams & Whiting:

This book reproduces Francis Durbridge's original script together with the list of characters and actors of the BBC programme on the dates mentioned, but the eventual broadcast might have edited Durbridge's script in respect of scenes, dialogue and character names.

INTRODUCTION

Francis Durbridge's *Paul Temple and the Curzon Case*, while it cannot be described as a lost radio serial, has certainly been elusive. It was broadcast on the BBC Light Programme in eight thirty-minute episodes from Tuesday 7 December 1948 to Tuesday 25 January 1949, and the episodes were repeated on Thursday each week. While this indicates that a recording was made, it was never broadcast again nor marketed on CDs or turned into a new production. So this recent discovery of the original script in Durbridge's own archives is something of an event.

Those not familiar with the career of Francis Durbridge (1912-98) might welcome a brief resumé. He began as a prolific writer of sketches, stories and plays for BBC radio in 1933, mostly light entertainments, but a talent for crime fiction became evident in his early radio plays *Murder in the Midlands* (1934) and *Murder in the Embassy* (1937). The Radio Times (11 February 1938) mentioned that Durbridge had by then written some one hundred radio pieces, and Charles Hatton commented in *Radio Pictorial* (28 October 1938) that "He is one of the very few people in this country who have succeeded in making a living by writing for the BBC."

Indeed, Durbridge continued to write plays and serials for BBC radio for many years, using his own name and the pseudonyms Frank Cromwell, Nicholas Vane and Lewis Middleton Harvey, while capitalising on a particular brainwave. In 1938 he had hit on the dream team of novelist/detective Paul Temple and his wife Steve, with the audience reaction to his radio serial *Send for Paul Temple* leading to Temple cases over several decades that built an impressive UK and European fanbase. So, following *Send for Paul Temple* in 1938, Durbridge responded later the same year with *Paul Temple and the Front Page Men* and continued with many more. From 1939 to 1968 there were another twenty-six Paul Temple cases, of which seven were new productions of earlier broadcasts.

Then in 1952, while continuing to write for radio, Durbridge embarked on a run of BBC television serials that attracted huge viewing figures until 1980. And additionally, from 1973 in the UK and even earlier in Germany he became known for stage plays that are still produced by professional and amateur companies today.

Paul Temple and the Curzon Case, with Temple played by Kim Peacock (1901-66), was the eleventh outing for Temple and Steve. Although Peacock had a long run in the role, beginning in 1946 with *Paul Temple and the Gregory Affair* and ending in 1953 with the one-hour *play Paul Temple and Steve Again*, he was then (to his great disappointment) replaced by Peter Coke (1913-2008) for *Paul Temple and the Gilbert Case* (1954). Coke then retained the role in all subsequent serials until the concluding *Paul Temple and the Alex Affair* in 1968.

Marjorie Westbury (1905-89), as Steve Temple, partnered both Peacock and Coke in all their appearances, and before Peacock she had played Steve opposite Barry Morse in *Send for Paul Temple Again* (1945) and Howard Marion-Crawford in *A Case for Paul Temple* (1946). In total she was Steve on twenty-three occasions until the final serial *Paul Temple and the Alex Affair* (1968) – which coincidentally was a new production of her first appearance as Steve in the 1945 *Send for Paul Temple Again*. But mention must also be made of Sir Graham Forbes of Scotland Yard, the role in which Lester Mudditt appeared on nineteen occasions from the original serial in 1938 until *Paul Temple and the Spencer Affair* (1957-58).

Paul Temple and Steve proved popular with cinemagoers - played by Anthony Hulme and Joy Shelton in *Send for Paul Temple* (1946), John Bentley and Dinah Sheridan in *Calling Paul Temple* (1948) and *Paul Temple's Triumph* (1950), and John Bentley and Patricia Dainton in *Paul Temple Returns* (1952). And happily these films have been preserved by Renown Pictures, shown regularly on Talking Pictures TV, and marketed as the DVD set The Paul Temple Collection Limited Edition, Renown Pictures, 2011.

Turning to Temple's popularity on the Continent, this resulted in the Dutch radio version of *Paul Temple and the Curzon Case* (Paul Vlaanderen en het Curzon mysterie, 1 October to 19 November 1950 in eight episodes), translated by J.C. van der Horst and produced by Kommer Kleijn, with Jan van Ees as Vlaanderen and Eva Janssen as Ina; and the German radio version (Paul Temple und der Fall Curzon, 14 November 1951 to 27 February 1952 in eight episodes), translated by Marianne de Barde and produced by Eduard Hermann, with René Deltgen as Temple and Elisabeth Scherer as Steve.

A paperback novelisation appeared as *The Curzon Case* (Hodder & Stoughton, Coronet Books, January 1972) and was later marketed as audiobooks – in two audiocassettes and two CDs in an abridged reading by Anthony Head as *Paul Temple and the Curzon Case*, BBC Audio, 2006; and a complete reading by Laurence Kennedy as *The Curzon Case* in four audiocassettes and four CDs, ISIS Audiobooks, 2007. And strangely, as Durbridge novels usually spawned many European translations, this book seems to have surfaced only in Germany as *Keiner kennt Curzon*.

Although the cheeky Charlie is as usual the Temples' factotum in the 1948-49 radio serial, the 1972 paperback instead features housekeeper Kate Balfour (a character from the 1969-71 Paul Temple television series). This, plus the use of a Francis Matthews photograph on the wrap, indicates that the book was a bandwagon spinoff commissioned while the television series was popular.

But now we can finally enjoy Durbridge's original script, perhaps while humming the familiar signature tune - Coronation Scot by Vivian Ellis – that was first used to introduce *Paul Temple and the Sullivan Mystery* in December 1947, then *Paul Temple and the Curzon Case* in December 1948 and every Paul Temple radio serial thereafter.

Melvyn Barnes
Author of Francis Durbridge: The Complete Guide (Williams & Whiting, 2018)

PAUL TEMPLE AND THE CURZON CASE

A serial in eight episodes

By FRANCIS DURBRIDGE

Broadcast on BBC Radio

Dec 7th 1948 – Jan 25th 1949

CAST:

Paul Temple	Kim Peacock
Steve	Marjorie Westbury
Charlie	Billy Thatcher
Sir Graham Forbes	Lester Mudditt
Inspector Morgan	Philip Cunningham
Diana Maxwell	Grizelda Hervey
Master John Draper	Peter Mullins
Dr Stuart	Duncan McIntyre
Peter Malo	Kenneth Morgan
Philip Baxter	Cyril Gardiner
Master Michael Baxter	Keith Lloyd
A waiter	Alan Reid
Tom Doyle	Hugh Manning
Carl Walters	Tommy Duggan
Lord Westerby	Leslie Perrins
Sergeant	Alan Reid
Porter	Ronald Sidney
Mrs Duncan	Ella Milne
1st Fireman	Frank Atkinson
2nd Fireman	David Kossoff
Lou Kenzel	Olaf Olsen
Inspector Vosper	Arthur Ridley
Major Browning	Tom Fleming
Pierre	George Owen
Sergeant Dawson	George Owen

Telephone operator . . . . .Denise Bryer
Other parts played by Diana King, Charles Maunsell,
David Kossoff, Alastair Duncan, Frank Atkinson,
Alan Reid

EPISODE ONE

THE BAXTER BROTHERS

FADE UP: *PAUL TEMPLE and Steve strolling along the corridor to the door of their flat: they have just seen a Musical Show and are in pretty high spirits. TEMPLE is attempting, somewhat unsuccessfully, to sing one of the numbers from the show.*

TEMPLE: (*Pleased with himself*) I think I should have done pretty well in musical comedy, Steve.

STEVE: What as?

TEMPLE: (*Taken aback*) What do you mean – what as?

STEVE: (*Laughing*) Have you got your key, darling?

TEMPLE: (*Surprised*) Isn't Charlie in?

STEVE: No, it's his night out. He's gone to the Palais.

TEMPLE: (*Searching in his pockets*) Yes. (*Suddenly with enthusiasm*) I say, that was a pretty marvellous show, wasn't it? I adored that number … (*Starts to sing*)

STEVE: Which number?

TEMPLE: (*Surprised*) Why this one! (*He half sings: half hums*)

STEVE: (*Laughing*) I suppose you mean … (*She sings the ditty in tune*)

TEMPLE: That's right. (*He sings out of tune*)

STEVE: (*Laughing at PAUL*) Open the door, darling!

The door opens.

CHARLIE:Oh, Mr Temple!

TEMPLE: I thought you were out.

CHARLIE:No. Unfortunately not. It was the cook that went out tonight. She's always forgetting things. If it weren't for me she would forget that she was born.

TEMPLE: Has somebody called for us?

CHARLIE:Yes, there was a phone call from a Miss – a Miss such-and-such. Now what was her name?

TEMPLE:	Ah, a Miss Such-and-such! Did she leave a message for me?
CHARLIE:	No, she said she'd call again later. If I could only remember the name. It's on the tip of my tongue.
STEVE:	You're a right pair you two – always forgetting things.
TEMPLE:	Is there someone in the living room, Charlie?
CHARLIE:	Yes, it's Sir Graham Forbes. He arrived ten minutes ago.
STEVE:	Sir Graham?
CHARLIE:	Yes. He's here with another man. They insisted they wait so I made some tea for them.
TEMPLE:	OK.
CHARLIE:	Was that allright, Mr Temple?
TEMPLE:	Totally all right, Charlie.

Door opens. TEMPLE and STEVE enter the lounge where SIR GRAHAM FORBES and INSPECTOR MORGAN are in mid-conversation.

FORBES:	No, no, no! It's not like that, Morgan. I think the important point in this story is Baxter and his brother –
TEMPLE:	Hello, Sir Graham!
FORBES:	Oh, here you are, Temple. Hello, Steve! How do you do?
STEVE:	Hello, Sir Graham. Why didn't you tell us you were coming?
FORBES:	We only decided to come at the last minute.
STEVE:	That sounds quite mysterious.
FORBES:	May I introduce you to one of my colleagues – Inspector Morgan. Mr and Mrs Temple.

4

STEVE:	I'm delighted to meet you, Inspector.
MORGAN:	It's my pleasure, Mrs Temple.
TEMPLE:	Nice to meet you, Inspector.
FORBES:	(*Pleasantly*) Well, you two look to me as if you've been celebrating?
TEMPLE:	We have. It's exactly ten years today since Steve came down to Bramley Lodge.
FORBES:	Ten … (*Staggered*) I don't believe it! I just don't believe it!
STEVE:	(*Laughing*) It's true!
FORBES:	You mean it's ten years since The Knave and The Front Page Men?
TEMPLE:	Exactly. Almost to the day.
FORBES:	Well, I'll … (*Still amazed*) By Golly, ten years! No wonder I'm going a bit thin on top!
TEMPLE:	1940 … Z4 … Remember, Sir Graham?
FORBES:	(*Thoughtfully*) '42 … The Marquis …
TEMPLE:	'45 … The Rex Affair …
FORBES:	(*Still thoughtfully*) '46 …. The Valentine Case …
STEVE:	And the Gregory Affair …
TEMPLE:	That was quite a year!
FORBES:	'47 … Dr Belasco …
STEVE:	'48 … The Sullivan Mystery …
MORGAN:	(*Slowly*) … and now The Curzon Case.
TEMPLE:	(*Looking up*) The Curzon Case? (*Suddenly*) What do you mean? What's on your mind, Sir Graham?

A pause.

FORBES:	(*Seriously*) Temple, we've got a case on our hands at the moment – rather a strange sort of case.
TEMPLE:	Go on …

5

A moment.

FORBES:	Do you know Dulworth Bay?
TEMPLE:	You mean the fishing village about two miles from Harwich?
FORBES:	Yes.
TEMPLE:	Of course, I know it!
STEVE:	As a matter of fact, we know it quite well.
TEMPLE:	Go on ...
FORBES:	There's a school at Dulworth Bay called St Gilberts. They have about a hundred boarders and fifty day boys. It's quite a good school and the headmaster – The Rev. Dudley Clarke – seems a very decent sort of fellow.
MORGAN:	He's certainly been extremely helpful.
TEMPLE:	What's happened at St Gilberts?
STEVE:	Don't tell me Young Woodley's run away with the housemaster's wife.
FORBES:	(*Laughing*) No, nothing like that.
STEVE:	Well, what has happened?

A moment.

FORBES:	Two of the day boys – two brothers – a Michael and Roger Baxter have disappeared.
TEMPLE:	Disappeared? (*Faintly amused*) You mean they've run away?
FORBES:	Whether they've run away or not we don't know. All we know is that they've disappeared: Suddenly – mysteriously – disappeared.
TEMPLE:	How old are these boys?
MORGAN:	Michael's the eldest, he's nearly seventeen. Roger's fourteen and a half.
TEMPLE:	What sort of boys are they?

6

MORGAN:	Michael's pretty clever. Roger's the sporty type; a useful little rugger player and a first-class bat.
TEMPLE:	Do they live in Dulworth Bay?
FORBES:	Yes, they live with their father in a cottage on the Westerby estate. Mrs Baxter died about two years ago.
STEVE:	The Westerby estate?
FORBES:	It's about a hundred acres of park land: belongs to Lord Westerby.
STEVE:	You mean Westerby Hall?
FORBES:	That's right.
TEMPLE:	Well, go on – what happened to the Baxter brothers?
FORBES:	About three weeks ago – on the afternoon of September 29th to be precise – Michael and Roger Baxter and another day boy called John Draper, left St Gilberts and strolled down the lane as far as the cottage. It's about three quarters of a mile. When they reached the cottage Michael suddenly remembered that he'd left a book at the school – a book he particularly wanted – and he told his brother and the other boy – John Draper – that he intended to return for it. He left Roger and John sitting on a fence in front of the cottage. Well, to cut a long story short, they waited for Michael for nearly an hour and then Roger decided to go back to the school and look for his brother .John went into the cottage, explained to Mr Baxter what had happened, then made his way home. Mr Baxter waited until nearly seven o'clock, then, since neither Michael

7

nor Roger put in an appearance, he went down to the school and saw the headmaster. (*A shrug*). The rest you can guess. The Rev Dudley Clarke hadn't seen the boys; he hadn't seen either of them.

MORGAN: As a matter of fact, from the moment they left Master John Draper, no-one saw them. They just vanished – disappeared …

STEVE: But they can't have vanished into thin air, Inspector!

MORGAN: That's precisely what they appear to have done, Mrs Temple.

TEMPLE: (*Quietly*) Tell me a little more about the Baxter boys. How did they get on with their father for instance?

MORGAN: Extremely well. (*Convinced*) Oh, there was nothing premeditated about this business, Mr Temple, of that I'm quite sure!

STEVE: Had they many friends in the village – apart from the boys at school?

MORGAN: A few. They were particularly friends with a Miss Maxwell: she's a niece of Lord Westerby's – lives at the Hall.

TEMPLE: Is that Diana Maxwell?

MORGAN: Yes. You've probably heard about her; goes in for writing poetry and that sort of thing. You wouldn't think so to meet her.

TEMPLE: Well – what did Miss Maxwell have to say?

MORGAN: She was obviously distressed by what had happened, but she certainly couldn't offer any explanation.

TEMPLE: M'm. (*Suddenly*) What about this other boy – John Draper?

8

A moment's pause.

FORBES: (*Hesitating*) Well, as a matter of fact, Morgan doesn't like Draper. He feels …

MORGAN: It isn't a question of not liking him, it's just that …

TEMPLE: Don't you trust him?

MORGAN: Oh, yes, I trust him all right. (*An afterthought*) At least, I think I trust him, but – well – I just don't like clever kids, Mr Temple.

TEMPLE: (*Amused*) I see.

FORBES: (*Slowly*) There is one point, Temple, rather a curious point, whether it means anything or not, however, we just don't know.

TEMPLE: Oh – what's that?

MORGAN: The two boys – the Baxter boys I mean – share a bedroom. It's a large, pleasant sort of room which overlooks the lane. I made a search of the room and in one of the cupboards I found a cricket bat. The blade of the bat had a lot of names on it – signatures – autographs – as a matter of fact, they were the signatures of the first eleven at St Gilberts. I made a check on the names and accounted for every one of them – with the exception of one.

TEMPLE: (*Interested*) Go on …

MORGAN: The name I couldn't account for was the last one on the list and oddly enough it wasn't a genuine signature. It had been written on the bat by Michael Baxter.

TEMPLE: Are you sure of that?

MORGAN: I checked it with his handwriting.

TEMPLE: What was the name?

9

MORGAN:	The name was Curzon.
TEMPLE:	Curzon? Just Curzon? No Christian name or initials?
MORGAN:	No – just Curzon.
TEMPLE:	Well, why do you think the name has any particular significance?
MORGAN:	I don't say that it has any particular significance, I'm merely suggesting that it's rather – well – odd.
FORBES:	You see, Temple, no-one at the school or in the village has ever heard of anyone called Curzon. We asked Philip Baxter about it – that's the father – and the name was completely unknown to him. Now, if the name was completely unknown not only to the boys' father, but to everyone else in Dulworth Bay, what made Michael Baxter suddenly think of it and write it down on the cricket bat?
TEMPLE:	Well, if it comes to that, what made you check the names on the cricket bat in the first place?
MORGAN:	(*Thoughtfully*) I don't know. I just had a curious feeling that I wanted to, that's all.
TEMPLE:	I see. (*Quietly*) Well, what is it you want me to do, Sir Graham?
FORBES:	I know what I'd like you to do, Temple.
TEMPLE:	What?
FORBES:	I'd like you to go down to Dulworth Bay for two or three days. Stay at the Inn. Mix with the local inhabitants. Keep your eyes open. You know the sort of thing.

A significant pause.

TEMPLE: Well – what do you say, Steve? (*Lightly: trying to persuade her*) It all sounds pretty harmless, doesn't it? A sleepy little village – two schoolboys disappear – a mysterious name on a cricket bat. (*A laugh*) Why, it's child's play! A push-over! Quite different from the Sullivan Mystery. (*A tiny pause*) Well – what do you say? (*He is very hopeful*)

STEVE: (*After a moment*) I'll think about it.

TEMPLE: (*Taken aback*) What?!

STEVE: I said – I'll think about it.

TEMPLE: (*Unpleasantly surprised and irritated*) By Timothy, why do women ALWAYS say – "I'll think about it"?

FADE UP of music.

FADE DOWN of music.

FADE in of STEVE speaking.

STEVE: (*Calmly: pleasantly: a little sleepy*) Now it's no good arguing the point, darling! I said I'd think about it and I will think about it!

TEMPLE: (*Still irritated*) But, Steve, there's nothing to think about! You heard what Sir Graham said: all we've got to do is to spend two or three days at Dulworth Bay and then …

STEVE: But I'm not so sure I want to spend two or three days at Dulworth Bay.

TEMPLE: Now, Steve, be reasonable! Just give me one good reason why we shouldn't pack our bags and …

STEVE interrupts TEMPLE with a gigantic yawn.

STEVE: (*Not having heard a word*) Gosh, I'm tired!

TEMPLE: (*Exasperated*) Really, Steve, you are the most exasperating woman.

11

The door opens.

TEMPLE: What is it, Charlie?

CHARLIE:I'm just off to bed. Anything you want?

TEMPLE: (*Still annoyed*) Yes. Mix me a whisky and soda.

CHARLIE:(*Taken aback*) O.K.

STEVE: Isn't it a little late for a whisky and soda?

TEMPLE: It is NOT late for a whisky and soda. As a matter
of fact, it's extremely early. I shouldn't be in the
least surprised if I didn't have four or five
whiskies and sodas.

CHARLIE:I would.

TEMPLE: (*Turning on CHARLIE*) What do you mean?

CHARLIE:There's no whisky.

STEVE laughs.

TEMPLE: (*Snapping at CHARLIE*) Very well, mix me a gin
and soda, a gin and orange, a gin and tonic, a gin
and lime, anything!

CHARLIE:(*'Keep calm'*) Okedoke, okedoke …

Silence.

Charlie mixes the drink.

STEVE: I'm going to bed, darling. See you later.
Goodnight, Charlie.

CHARLIE:Goodnight, Mrs Temple. (*Suddenly*) Oh! Oh, I
forgot! You know that telephone call. The party
I couldn't …

TEMPLE: Don't tell me you've remembered?

CHARLIE:(*Pleased   with   himself*) Yes! Yes, I've
remembered it all right! Knew I would. She said
'er name was Maxwell.

A moment.

STEVE: (*Surprised*) Maxwell?

CHARLIE:That's right. Miss Diana Maxwell.

TEMPLE: (*Quietly, sober*) What else did she say, Charlie?

CHARLIE:She didn't say anything. I told 'er you was out an' she said she'd ring later.

TEMPLE: What time did Miss Maxwell phone?

CHARLIE:Oh, blimey! What time is it now?

TEMPLE: (*Looking at his watch*) It's just gone half past ten.

CHARLIE:Oh – it'd be about nine o'clock. Perhaps a bit later.

A moment.

TEMPLE: (*Quietly, dismissing CHARLIE*) Yes, all right, Charlie. You can go.

CHARLIE:(*Surprised*) Here's your gin and orange.

TEMPLE: (*Thoughtfully*) That's all right. Put it on the side.

CHARLIE:O.K. Goodnight.

TEMPLE: Goodnight.

CHARLIE:(*To STEVE*) Goodnight!

STEVE: Goodnight, Charlie.

The door opens and closes and as soon as it does so Steve speaks:

STEVE: (*A note of excitement in her voice*) Diana Maxwell! That's the girl the Inspector told us about! Lord Westerby's niece!

TEMPLE: Yes.

STEVE: (*Tensely*) But what does she want? Why should she ring us up?

STEVE is interrupted by the ringing of the telephone. It rings for some little time before TEMPLE speaks.

TEMPLE: Go into the bedroom, Steve – listen on the extension.

STEVE: (*After a momentary hesitation*) Yes, all right.

The telephone continues to ring. A moment. The receiver is lifted.

TEMPLE: (*On the phone*) Hello?

DIANA: (*On the phone: tensely: a cultured voice*) Hello –
is that Circle 1789?

TEMPLE: Yes.

DIANA: Can I speak to Paul Temple, please?

TEMPLE: This is Temple speaking.

DIANA: Oh, Mr Temple – my name is Diana Maxwell. I
telephoned you earlier this evening but ...

TEMPLE: Yes. I got your message. What can I do for you,
Miss Maxwell?

DIANA: (*Hesitating*) Mr Temple, I know this must sound
a rather odd sort of request – especially coming
from a complete stranger – but I've simply got to
see you.

TEMPLE: (*Quietly*) What is it you want to see me about?

DIANA: (*Softly*) About the Baxter brothers. You know
what I'm talking about, don't you? You've seen
Sir Graham.

TEMPLE: I'm a pretty busy man, Miss Maxwell. I'm not so
sure that I'm interested in the Baxter brothers!

DIANA: (*Tensely*) Mr Temple, listen! I know what Sir
Graham told you about the Baxter brothers but
there's something he didn't tell you – something
he doesn't know. I want to tell you about
Curzon. I want to tell you why ... (*She stops*)

TEMPLE: Go on ...

DIANA: I can't talk now – not over the phone. Do you
know the Tabriz?

TEMPLE: Do you mean the restaurant in Greek Street?

DIANA: Yes. (*Quickly, about to ring off*) Meet me there
in half an hour. I'll be waiting for you.

TEMPLE: (*Interrupting her*) Just a minute! What do you
look like? What are you dressed in?

DIANA: (*Impatiently*) I'm wearing a blue costume – no
hat – blue handbag. I'm dark – about thirty-

14

eight. You'll find me all right. It's only a tiny place. I'll be at the table near the window.

TEMPLE: Yes, but just a minute! How do I know that you are Miss Maxwell? I've only your word for it.

DIANA: (*Surprised*) What do you mean?

TEMPLE: When I make a date, I like to be reasonably certain that I know who I'm making it with.

DIANA: Well – I'm afraid you'll just have to take my word for it. (*Urgently*) Please believe me, Mr Temple, I – Well – do I sound like an imposter?

TEMPLE: (*Slowly, smiling*) You know what Robert Browning said, Miss Maxwell. "The devil hath not in all his quiver's choice ..."

DIANA: (*Continuing*) ... "An arrow for the heart like a sweet voice" ... But for your information, Mr Temple, it wasn't Robert Browning, it was Lord Byron.

TEMPLE: (*Amused*) All right, Miss Maxwell. I'll be there in twenty minutes.

FADE UP of Music.

FADE DOWN of Music.
FADE UP the sound of a motorcar: the car is drawing into the side of the kerb. The car stops: the engine is switched off: the door opens: there are slight background street noises.

STEVE: Is this The Tabriz?

TEMPLE: Yes.

STEVE: Have you been here before?

TEMPLE: Once – a long time ago.

STEVE: (*Confidentially*) There's a girl sitting in the window. I can see her from here.

TEMPLE: Yes.

STEVE: (*Softly*) She's watching us.

15

TEMPLE: (*At the door of the car*) Is she dressed in blue?

STEVE: Yes, I think she is.

TEMPLE: (*Closing the car door*) Come along, Steve – let's go inside.

STEVE: Have you locked the car? I've left my coat on the back seat.

TEMPLE: Yes, that'll be all right.

They enter the restaurant: the door opens and closes. Fade street noises: The restaurant is nearly empty. Very faint background of chatter.

WAITER: (*An Italian*) Good evening, sir! Good evening, madam! A table for two?

TEMPLE: I think the young lady over there – in the window – is expecting us.

WAITER: Ah, yes, but of course! If you please …

TEMPLE and STEVE cross the room to the window. From the table in the window, you can hear the faint noise of the street traffic.

GIRL: (*Attempting to conceal a tense, desperate manner*) Mr Temple?

TEMPLE: Yes.

GIRL: I'm Diana Maxwell. It's awfully good of you to come like this, I do appreciate … (*She stops: staring at STEVE*)

TEMPLE: Oh – this is my wife. Miss Maxwell.

STEVE: How-d-you-do?

GIRL: Please sit down, Mrs Temple.

TEMPLE: Well, what's this all about, Miss Maxwell? You sounded pretty excited over the phone.

GIRL: (*She is nervous, over-wrought*) I suppose Sir Graham told you about the Baxter boys, about … their … disappearance … I mean?

TEMPLE: Yes.

GIRL: Is that all he told you?

16

TEMPLE: Miss Maxwell, I didn't come here to discuss what Sir Graham told me about the Baxter boys. I came because you said you had some information for me.

GIRL: Yes. Yes, I'm sorry I ... (*A note of urgency*) Mr Temple, tell me: are you going to investigate this case, because if you are then there's something you ought to know, something that ... (*She hesitates*)

STEVE: (*Surprised*) What's the matter?

GIRL: (*Frightened: staring out of the window*) I was watching that car. I thought it was going to stop. (*A tense whisper: obviously frightened*) Did someone follow you here? Did you see a large red saloon car?

TEMPLE: (*Stopping her: bluntly*) No. No one followed us! Now what is it you've got to tell me?

GIRL: Mr Temple, please don't think I'm out of my mind. I'm not used to this sort of thing. Six weeks ago, I was leading a perfectly ordinary respectable ... (*She stops: attempting to pull herself together*) My life's in danger. Twice they've attempted to kill me. Sooner or later they'll succeed, that's why ...

STEVE: Go on ...

GIRL: If you do investigate this case, Mr Temple, please go into it with your eyes open. Don't run away with the idea that just because two schoolboys have disappeared ...

TEMPLE: (*Interrupting her*) I should have thought it was perfectly obvious from our telephone conversation that I don't jump into anything without my eyes being well and truly open. Why do you think I quoted that poem of Shelley's? (*A

17

moment) Because I wanted to make certain that you were Miss Maxwell – the real Diana Maxwell. (*Slowly, watching her*) If you hadn't recognised that poem, I should have doubted you. (*A tiny pause*) Now what is it you want to tell me?

There is the sound of an approaching car in the street outside.

GIRL: I want to tell you the truth about Michael and Roger Baxter. I want to tell you why Michael wrote the name Curzon on the cricket bat and above all, now, before it's too late, I want to tell you the identity of … Curzon. (*A moment's pause*) Five weeks ago when I was staying at Westerby Hall – that's my Uncle's place at Dulworth Bay – I suddenly came across … (*She stops*)

STEVE: (*Quickly, alarmed*) What is it?

GIRL: (*A frightened scream*) It's that car! They're outside! They're watching us! They're …

TEMPLE: (*Suddenly, desperately*) Get away from the window! Get away, Steve! For God's sake get away from the window!!!!

As TEMPLE speaks, we hear the sudden revving up of the car engine and almost simultaneously there is a volley of fire from a sten gun. The window smashed to pieces: several people scream: Temple gives a quick cry of pain. There is general pandemonium both in the café and in the street. During the excitement, the car revs up and continues on its way.

WAITER: (*Terrified and bewildered*) What's happened? What is this? What has happened? (*Screaming*) Keep calm! Keep calm everybody! Look at the window! Just look at the window!

18

TEMPLE: (*In pain*) Telephone for an ambulance! Get the police ...

WAITER: But I don't understand, why ...

TEMPLE: (*Shouting at the WAITER*) Do as I tell you!

STEVE: Paul, look at your arm! Darling, look at your arm!

TEMPLE: (*Obviously in pain*) It's nothing. It's all right. Did you see the car?

STEVE: Yes. It was a red saloon. There were two men in it. I saw one man, but I wouldn't recognise him again unless ... (*She stops, horrified*) Paul! Paul, she's dead! Look! Look ... she's ... dead ...

TEMPLE: (*Softly*) Yes.

STEVE: (*Desperately: horrified*) Who did this? Who are they? Paul, who did it?

TEMPLE: (*Grimly: nursing his arm*) I don't know, but whoever they are, they've certainly made a first-class blunder!

STEVE: What do you mean?

TEMPLE: (*Unable to conceal his excitement*) This isn't Diana Maxwell. This isn't the girl I spoke to on the telephone.

STEVE: (*Staggered*) What!?

TEMPLE: They've murdered the wrong girl!

Quick, dramatic, fade up of music.

Cross-fade to less dramatic music.

Fade music completely.

STEVE: Is that all right, darling?

TEMPLE: Yes, just pull the bandage a little more to the left and then I can ... That's it!

STEVE: Comfy?

TEMPLE: Yes, that's fine. (*He sinks back into the armchair*) Now, Sir Graham!

19

FORBES: That looks pretty painful to me! Can you get
             about with your arm like that?
TEMPLE: Yes, I'll be as right as rain in a day or two.
             But by Timothy you should have seen it at the
             beginning of the week!
STEVE: You should have heard him at the beginning
             of the week! What a patient! Was he sorry for
             himself!

They all laugh.

TEMPLE: (*Quietly*) Well, what's happened, Sir
             Graham?
FORBES: We've had another interview with Miss
             Maxwell – the real Miss Maxwell – but we
             don't seem to be getting anywhere.
TEMPLE: She still insists that she didn't telephone me?
FORBES: She swears she didn't. As a matter of fact, she
             claims to have spent last Tuesday evening at
             Dulworth Bay – at Westerby Hall. Lord
             Westerby confirms this.
STEVE: Couldn't she have telephoned from Dulworth
             Bay?
FORBES: Yes, but she didn't, Steve – we checked all
             the calls with the local exchange.
TEMPLE: Then if Miss Maxwell did telephone me …
FORBES: I should say it's a pretty good bet that she did
             it from Town.
TEMPLE: And that makes our aristocratic friend …
FORBES: It turns Lord Westerby into a first-class liar.
             But you know, Temple, with all due respects,
             I'm not so sure that she did.
TEMPLE: You still think that the girl in the restaurant
             was the girl who telephoned me?
FORBES: (*Hesitating*) Yes …

20

TEMPLE: (*Shaking his head*) She wasn't, Sir Graham. Quite apart from the fact that as soon as I met her, I noticed a slight difference in her voice, don't forget she didn't pick me up when I deliberately made that slip about the poem. If she'd been the girl who had spoken to me on the telephone, she'd have spotted that I said Shelley instead of Byron. The girl on the phone very soon corrected me.

FORBES: (*Thoughtfully*) Then you think that the real Diana Maxwell telephoned you and then was deliberately stopped from keeping the appointment.

TEMPLE: Yes, I do.

FORBES: (*Almost a sigh*) Well, if only we could find out who the other girl is, we might get somewhere. So far, we've drawn a blank.

TEMPLE: What does Morgan think about all this?

FORBES: The poor devil's rather at sixes and sevens.

TEMPLE: M'm.

FORBES: I wish you'd go down to Dulworth Bay for two or three days, Temple, and take a look around.

TEMPLE: We're going down there tomorrow morning, Sir Graham – on the 12.45. We've booked a room at the Inn.

FORBES: (*Pleased*) Oh, good!

TEMPLE: I should prefer that you didn't tell any local people that I'm going.

Temple stops. A knock and the door opens.

TEMPLE: What is it, Charlie?

CHARLIE: I beg your pardon, sir, but Inspector Morgan's here.

FORBES: (*Surprised*) Morgan!

21

TEMPLE:	(*Suddenly: friendly*) Come in, Inspector!
MORGAN:	(*Entering*) Hello, Mr Temple!
TEMPLE:	(*Dismissing CHARLIE*) Thank you, Charlie.

Door closes.

MORGAN:	(*To STEVE*) Good afternoon, Mrs Temple.
STEVE:	Good afternoon, Inspector.
MORGAN:	(*To FORBES*) They told me at the Yard that you were here, Sir Graham, so I thought I'd …
FORBES:	(*Interrupting him*) Is anything the matter?
MORGAN:	No. No, nothing, sir, but – (*A moment*) I've got that boy with me, sir.
FORBES:	(*Surprised*) Boy? Which boy?
MORGAN:	Master John Draper, sir.
FORBES:	(*Very surprised*) You haven't brought him back to Town with you?
MORGAN:	(*Nodding*) Yes.
FORBES:	But why?
MORGAN:	(*Hesitating*) Well, I may be wrong, sir, but I've got a hunch that he's holding out on us. I somehow feel that he knows more about this business than we think.
FORBES:	But what excuse did you give to the boy's father for bringing him up to London?
MORGAN:	I didn't give any, sir – the Head made the excuse for me. He simply told young Draper to come into Town and collect some books. I'm taking him back on the 6.15.
FORBES:	I see.
MORGAN:	I want Mr Temple to have a word with him, sir. I've got a feeling that he might get more out of the boy than we can. (*To TEMPLE*) Apparently, he's read one or two of your detective novels.

22

TEMPLE:	(*Smiling*) Oh, I see. Where is he?
MORGAN:	He's in your study. I told him to wait in there until I'd seen you.
TEMPLE:	(*Quietly*) I'll have a chat to him, Sir Graham.
MORGAN:	(*Stopping him*) Don't underestimate him, Mr Temple. He's fairly intelligent.
TEMPLE:	Obviously. He reads my novels.

FORBES and STEVE laugh.

FADE Scene.

FADE UP on a door opening: MASTER JOHN DRAPER gives a sudden start of surprise.

TEMPLE:	(*Very friendly*) Hello, what's that you're looking at?
JOHN:	(*Faintly nervous*) It's one of your books, sir. It was on the desk. I hope you don't mind my looking at it, sir.
TEMPLE:	No, of course I don't mind. (*By JOHN's side*) Clayhanger by Arnold Bennett. Have you read it?
JOHN:	Yes, sir.
TEMPLE:	That's a first edition. They don't publish books like that nowadays, do they? Just look at the binding!
JOHN:	They don't write books like it either, sir.
TEMPLE:	What? (*Suddenly, laughing*) No, I suppose they don't. How long are you staying in London?
JOHN:	Only for a couple of hours, sir. I've got to collect some books for the Head.
TEMPLE:	Oh, yes, of course! The Inspector told me. (*Smiling*) The Rev Dudley Clarke. He's the big noise of St Gilbert's, isn't he?

JOHN: (*Laughing*) Yes, sir.

TEMPLE: What's he like?

JOHN: He's very nice, sir. Oh, he can be pretty foul of course, but – on the whole, he's quite decent.

Tiny pause.

TEMPLE: How long have you been at St Gilberts?

JOHN: Nearly seven years.

TEMPLE: That's quite a time.

JOHN: Yes, sir.

Another pause.

TEMPLE: Would you like some tea?

JOHN: Well – thank you, sir.

TEMPLE: (*Nodding*) We'll join my wife in a few moments. (*Smiling*) You know, the Inspector told me not to underestimate your intelligence. I'm not so sure that he hasn't done so. (*Smiling*) You know perfectly well why he brought you up to Town, don't you?

JOHN: Yes, sir.

TEMPLE: The books were just an excuse.

JOHN: (*Rather amused*) Yes, of course.

TEMPLE: They wanted us to have a little chat together.

JOHN: I've told the Inspector all I know, sir. I don't think he believes me, but – there's nothing else I can tell him, Mr Temple.

TEMPLE: Well, supposing you tell me what you've already told the Inspector.

A pause.

JOHN: What is it you want to know?

TEMPLE: I want to know what happened. (*Suddenly, very friendly*) You see, John, to all intents and purposes you were the last person to see the Baxter boys before they disappeared. Therefore, anything you say, anything you heard, anything

24

you even thought about, might quite possibly be
of importance.

JOHN: But I've already told the Inspector, sir. I saw
nothing. After Roger went in search of his
brother, I went into the cottage and told Mr
Baxter what had happened, and then went home.

TEMPLE: Did you walk home?

JOHN: Yes, sir.

TEMPLE: How far would that be?

JOHN: About half a mile, sir.

TEMPLE: Straight down the lane?

JOHN: Yes.

TEMPLE: You didn't see anyone – in the lane, I mean?

JOHN: No, sir.

TEMPLE: Did you hear anything?

JOHN: (*Puzzled, and a little surprised by the question*)
What do you mean, sir – did I hear anything?

TEMPLE: Well – did you hear anything?

JOHN: You mean anything suspicious?

TEMPLE: No, not necessarily suspicious, John. Anything
…

JOHN: No, sir. (*A moment*) I don't think so, sir.

TEMPLE: (*Pleasantly: smiling*) What do you mean? You
don't think so?

JOHN: Well, when I came out of the cottage – after
seeing Mr Baxter – I thought I heard someone
whistling.

TEMPLE: Perhaps you did hear someone whistling.

JOHN: I couldn't see anyone, sir.

TEMPLE: That doesn't matter, you still might have heard
someone. What did the whistling sound like?

JOHN: Oh, I don't know, sir.

25

TEMPLE: Was it a tune or was it a sort of – you know – a
         sort of call? (*He whistles: a definite call as if
         attracting attention*)
JOHN: (*Laughing*) Oh, it wasn't anything like that, sir.
TEMPLE: Well, what was it like?
JOHN: (*Doubtful: inclined to treat the matter as a joke*)
         Oh, I don't know. I suppose it was more like a
         tune than anything else.
TEMPLE: Well, there you are. (*Simply*) When you came out
         of the cottage you walked straight back home but
         on the way home you thought you heard
         someone whistling a tune. Is that right?
JOHN: Well – yes, sir.
TEMPLE: Did you tell the Inspector about this?
JOHN: No, sir.
TEMPLE: Why not?
JOHN: Well, I just didn't think it was important.
TEMPLE: But it might be, John. It might be very important.
         Now what kind of a tune was it you thought you
         heard someone whistling?
JOHN: Oh, I couldn't say, sir.
TEMPLE: Was it a jazzy tune – a modern sort of thing or …
JOHN: (*Highly amused*) Oh no, sir!
TEMPLE: (*Picking him up*) Then you recognised it?
JOHN: (*Faintly embarrassed*) Oh, no, I didn't recognise
         it, sir.
TEMPLE: But you must have done, otherwise how do you
         know that it wasn't a modern tune? (*Very
         pleasant: friendly*) You either recognised the
         tune itself, or you thought you recognised the
         person who was whistling it.
JOHN: (*Taken aback*) Why do you say that, sir?
TEMPLE: Well, it's obvious, isn't it, John? When I
         suggested just now that it might be a jazz tune,

you thought it was a silly suggestion – a joke. Obviously therefore, you recognised the tune – or you thought you recognised the person who was whistling it – who most certainly wasn't the sort of person you'd expect to whistle a modern tune.

JOHN: (*A moment: quietly*) I think the tune was Loch Lomond, sir.

TEMPLE: Loch Lomond? (*He whistles the tune*)

Tiny pause.

JOHN: Yes, sir.

TEMPLE: And who do you think was whistling it?

JOHN: (*A moment*) I don't know, sir.

TEMPLE: Are you sure you don't know?

JOHN: Yes, sir.

A pause.

TEMPLE: (*Suddenly: a change of topic*) John, tell me: have you ever heard of anyone called Curzon?

JOHN: (*Shaking his head*) No, sir.

TEMPLE: Supposing I asked you to write the name down on a piece of paper – how would you spell it?

JOHN: Curzon?

TEMPLE: Yes.

JOHN: Why – C.U.R.Z.O.N. (*Puzzled*) That's right, isn't it, sir?

TEMPLE: (*Smiling*) Yes, that's right, John. That's quite right. (*Slowly: as if to himself*) C.U.R.Z.O.N. (*Suddenly: pleasantly*) Come along, let's do something about that cup of tea!

FADE scene.

FADE UP music.

Slow FADE DOWN of music.

STEVE: I think young Draper enjoyed his tea.

27

TEMPLE: He certainly waded in!

STEVE laughs.

TEMPLE: Pour me another cup of coffee, Steve.

STEVE: (*Pouring the coffee*) What time did you say the train was tomorrow?

TEMPLE: 12.45.

STEVE: Can we get lunch on it?

TEMPLE: I should imagine so.

STEVE: Whoa! Whoa! Go easy on the sugar. (*A moment*) What did you think of young Draper, Paul?

TEMPLE: Well, what did you think of him?

STEVE: I'm rather inclined to agree with the Inspector. He's a strange boy. I don't know that I'd trust him.

TEMPLE: (*Thoughtfully*) M'm.

STEVE: And what does that mean exactly?

TEMPLE: It means precisely what it sounds like.

The door is suddenly opened.

TEMPLE: What is it, Charlie?

CHARLIE: I beg your pardon, sir, but …

MORGAN: (*Tensely: excited*) May I come in?

STEVE: (*Astonished*) Inspector!

TEMPLE: (*Equally surprised*) Why hello, Inspector! I thought you'd gone back to Dulworth Bay?

MORGAN: I started out for Dulworth Bay, sir, but … (*Quietly*) There's been a new development, Mr Temple, I thought perhaps you ought to know about it. (*Hesitates*)

TEMPLE: (*To CHARLIE*) That's all right, Charlie.

CHARLIE: O.K.

The door closes.

A moment, then:

TEMPLE: (*Quickly: tensely*) What's happened?

28

STEVE: What is it, Inspector?

MORGAN: (*Tensely: faintly overwrought*) I took young Draper back to Dulworth Bay on the 6.15. We had dinner on the train …

TEMPLE: Well?

MORGAN: At about a quarter to eight we left the dining car and made our way down the corridor to our carriage. Suddenly, while we were still walking down the corridor, the train went into a tunnel. Draper was ahead of me, perhaps ten or fifteen yards. It was fairly dark in the corridor and I lost sight of him. (*Slowly, hesitant, almost frightened*) When the train came out of the tunnel …

STEVE: Yes …

TEMPLE: Go on …

MORGAN: When the train came out of the tunnel …

TEMPLE: (*Quickly: tensely*) What's happened to him?! My God, Morgan, what's happened to the boy?

MORGAN: He's disappeared!

TEMPLE: (*Amazed*) Disappeared!

STEVE: What do you mean?

MORGAN: (*Completely bewildered*) I mean just what I say, Mrs Temple! The boy's gone! Vanished! Disappeared!

Quick, dramatic FADE UP of music.

FADE DOWN of music.
FADE UP background noises of a large railway station.
FADE noises to the background.

PORTER: I've put your cases in the last carriage but one, sir – it's at the end of the coach.

TEMPLE: Oh, thank you, Porter.

PORTER: If you intend to 'ave lunch, sir, I should go into the diner straight away.

STEVE: Is the train full?

PORTER: No, ma'am – but there's only one service an' the diner gets a bit crowded.

TEMPLE: (*Tipping the Porter*) Here we are.

PORTER: Oh, thank you, sir! You're due in Dulworth Bay about 2.50.

STEVE: Oh, that's not too bad.

TEMPLE: You say the cases are in the last carriage but one?

PORTER: Yes, two corner seats near the window. With a bit o' luck you should have the carriage to yourselves.

TEMPLE: Good.

STEVE: (*Aside*) How's your arm, darling?

TEMPLE: Oh, it's not too bad, Steve.

FADE UP of station noises.

FADE scene.

FADE UP of Music and slow across fade music to the sound of the train which is travelling fairly fast. The sound of the train continues for some little time:

A carriage door opens:

STEVE: (*With a sigh of relief*) Ah! Here we are!

TEMPLE: By Timothy, I feel as if we've walked to Dulworth Bay.

STEVE: (*Laughing*) Anyway, we've got the carriage to ourselves!

TEMPLE: Is that your case?

STEVE: Yes, they're both here. That's yours on the other side of … (*She stops*)

TEMPLE: What's the matter?

A moment.

30

STEVE: (*Quietly*) Paul, my case has been opened!

TEMPLE: Opened? Don't be silly, darling.

STEVE: It has. I can tell by the fastener. And look! One of my dresses is showing!

TEMPLE: Wait a moment! I'll get the case down!

TEMPLE reaches for the case and places it on the seat.

TEMPLE: Didn't you lock it?

STEVE: No.

STEVE opens the case.

A moment.

TEMPLE: Well?

STEVE: It's been opened ...

TEMPLE: Are you sure? It looks all right.

STEVE: No. No, it isn't, darling! I put the face powder in the corner and ... (*Suddenly*) Of course it's been opened! Just look at that dress!

TEMPLE: Wait a moment!

STEVE: What are you doing?

TEMPLE: I'm just wondering if my case has been opened!

A pause.

STEVE: Has it?

TEMPLE: (*Standing on the seat*) No. No, it appears to be all right. (*He climbs down*)

STEVE: Well, why on earth should they search my case?

TEMPLE: Is there anything missing?

STEVE: (*Looking in the case*) No, I don't think so ...

TEMPLE: They probably intended to search both our cases but were disturbed.

STEVE: Yes. Yes, that's about it! (*A note of tenseness*) Paul, do you think that this ...

TEMPLE: What?

STEVE: (*Slowly*) Do you think that this has got anything to do with why we're going down to Dulworth Bay?

31

TEMPLE: Well, it's rather a strange coincidence, isn't it? But if it has got anything to do with it, then what the devil were they looking for?

The train suddenly gives a warning shriek and, with the impression of gathering speed, enters the tunnel.

STEVE: We're in the tunnel!

TEMPLE: Yes.

STEVE: Isn't there a light?

TEMPLE: I expect it'll come on in a moment.

A pause.

STEVE: I suppose this is the tunnel the Inspector meant. The tunnel where young Draper ... disappeared ...

TEMPLE: Yes.

STEVE: (*Softly*) I wonder what happened to him, Paul? I wonder what really happened?

TEMPLE: Well, if it comes to that, what really happened to the Baxters ... (*Suddenly: wincing slightly*) Mind my arm, darling.

STEVE: What?

TEMPLE: I said mind my arm, Steve – you bumped against it.

STEVE: (*A moment, then astonished*) Bumped against it!

TEMPLE: Yes.

STEVE: Don't be silly, darling!

TEMPLE: What do you mean?

STEVE: I'm over here, Paul! On the opposite side – on the other seat, darling!

TEMPLE: (*Very softly: astonished*) What!

A tense pause:

Suddenly the third, and unknown occupant of the carriage commences to whistle: he whistles softly, as if to himself. The tune is Loch Lomond. He finishes whistling the tune.

32

STEVE: (*Tensely*) Paul, there's someone else in the carriage!

FADE UP music.

END OF EPISODE ONE

EPISODE TWO

WELCOME TO
DULWORTH BAY

ANNOUNCER: Paul Temple is visited by Sir Graham Forbes of Scotland Yard and by Chief-Inspector Morgan who wish to consult Temple about an affair known as the Curzon Case. Two schoolboys – Roger and Michael Baxter – have mysteriously disappeared. The name Curzon was found scribbled on a cricket bat belonging to Michael Baxter, but Curzon is a name quite unknown to the inhabitants of Dulworth Bay where the Baxter boys live. Later, Temple interviews a friend of the Baxter's – a schoolboy called John Draper. Draper tells Temple that shortly after Roger and Michael disappeared, he heard someone whistling the tune Loch Lomond. That night the Inspector informs Temple that John Draper has also disappeared. The following morning, Temple and Steve take the train for Dulworth Bay. On returning to their carriage from the dining car, Steve discovers that her suitcase has been taken down from the rack and searched.

FADE Announcer and FADE UP the sound of the train.
The train continues for a moment before Steve speaks.

STEVE: (*Slowly*) Do you think that this has got anything to do with why we're going down to Dulworth Bay?

TEMPLE: Well, it's rather a strange coincidence, isn't it? But if it has got anything to do with it, then what the devil were they looking for?

The train suddenly gives a warning shriek and, with the impression of gathering speed, enters the tunnel.

STEVE: We're in the tunnel!

TEMPLE: Yes.

STEVE: Isn't there a light?

37

TEMPLE: I expect it'll come on in a moment.

A pause.

STEVE: I suppose this is the tunnel the Inspector meant. The tunnel where young Draper disappeared.

TEMPLE: Yes.

STEVE: (*Softly*) I wonder what happened to him, Paul?

TEMPLE: Well, if it comes to that, what really happened to the Baxters ... (*Suddenly: wincing slightly*) Mind my arm, darling.

STEVE: What?

TEMPLE: I said mind my arm, Steve – you bumped against it.

STEVE: Don't be silly, darling! I'm over here. On the opposite seat, darling!

TEMPLE: (*Very softly: astonished*) What!

A tense pause:

Suddenly the third, and unknown occupant of the carriage commences to whistle: he whistles softly, as if to himself. The tune is Loch Lomond. He finishes whistling the tune.

STEVE: (*Tensely*) Paul, there's someone else in the carriage!

The noise of the train suddenly fades down as it emerges from the tunnel. Immediately the train comes out of the tunnel DR STUART speaks. The doctor is a rather eccentric Scotsman of about sixty.

STUART: That's better! Now why didn't they put the lights on instead of leaving us in the dark? (*Suddenly*) I'm sorry, Lassie! Did I frighten you barging into the carriage like that?

TEMPLE: As a matter of fact, we didn't hear you until you started whistling.

STUART: I beg your pardon?

TEMPLE: I said we didn't hear you until you started whistling.

STUART: (*Interrupting TEMPLE*) Just a moment! If you'll excuse me, I'll get this contraption of mine working! (*He is manipulating his deaf aid appliance*) I can't hear a blessed thing until …. Ah, that's better! Now, what were you saying?

TEMPLE: I was saying, we didn't hear you until you started whistling.

STUART: (*Amused*) Oh! Oh, I see. What did you think I was, a ghost or something? The whistling ghost! I must have given you both quite a shock. My word, you do look pale, Mrs Temple. (*Politely*) It is Mr and Mrs Temple, isn't it?

TEMPLE: Yes, how did you know?

STUART: (*Continuing*) Let me introduce myself? Dr Lawrence Stuart – at your service. I'm in practice at Dulworth Bay. I recently had the pleasure of meeting a friend of yours.

TEMPLE: Oh – who was that?

STUART: Inspector Morgan. He wanted a few details about the Baxter boys.

TEMPLE: Do you know the Baxter boys?

STUART: Know them! Why God bless my soul – I brought them into the world. (*Pointing at TEMPLE and STEVE to emphasise his remarks*) He's a very capable man that Inspector Morgan. There's a lot of people in Dulworth Bay that don't think so, they think he's sleeping on the job – but I don't agree. He's got brains that man. He's shrewd too – as shrewd as a box of monkeys.

STEVE: How did you know that he was a – friend of ours?

STUART: (*Smiling*) How did I know that you were Mr and Mrs Temple? Because I've seen your pictures in the papers. As soon as I saw you on the train, I knew that you were going up to Dulworth Bay. And I'll bet a nice new penny that I know exactly why you're going up there, Mr Temple.

TEMPLE: Oh? Why exactly?

STUART: To investigate that Baxter case of course! I told the Inspector. This is an unusual case, Inspector, I said, and it required unusual methods to deal with it. You can't handle this sort of case with old fashioned ideas …

TEMPLE: What do you think happened to the Baxter boys, Dr Stuart?

STUART: Why man, we know what happened to them! They've disappeared!

TEMPLE: Yes, but how?

STUART: (*Surprised*) How? They were kidnapped!

TEMPLE: By whom?

STUART: (*Quickly*) Ah! Ah, now that's the question, Mr Temple. The all-important question! By whom? What's your opinion? Do you think that young Draper was kidnapped by the same person – or persons – that kidnapped the Baxter boys?

TEMPLE: Yes, I do. But you know oddly enough, doctor, I'm chiefly interested in the motive for all this. Why were the Baxter boys kidnapped?

STUART: Well, you see what The Post said this morning. They think there's a maniac at large: they don't think there is any real rhyme or reason behind it all. They just think that the person responsible is a psychopathic case.

TEMPLE: Do you subscribe to that opinion?

STUART: (*Slowly: thoughtfully*) No. No, I don't think I do. But then I'm rather a queer sort of bird. I've quite a few notions of my own.

The train begins to slow down as if approaching a station.

STEVE:	Is this Dulworth Bay?
STUART:	(*Peering out of the window*) Yes. Yes, we're just coming into the Station. You see that field over there? That's where that dreadful air disaster was. You probably remember reading about it – all the passengers were killed.
TEMPLE:	Yes, I remember.
STUART:	It happened just after six o'clock in the evening. I was called out of my surgery. It was a most distressing business.

A moment.

TEMPLE:	Dr Stuart, did the Inspector ask you if you'd heard of anyone called Curzon?
STUART:	He did. The name was quite unknown to me.
TEMPLE:	I see. (*A moment*) You've heard of Miss Maxwell, I take it?
STUART:	You mean Diana Maxwell – Lord Westerby's niece?
TEMPLE:	Yes.
STUART:	Why, of course!
TEMPLE:	Is she a patient of yours?
STUART:	No, she's not a patient of mine, but I know the young lady. As a matter of fact, I know everybody in Dulworth Bay. (*Amused*) And they all know me! If you've got any secrets, Mr and Mrs Temple, I warn you they won't be secrets long, not if you're staying in Dulworth Bay.
STEVE:	In other words, everybody knows everybody else's business!
STUART:	That's putting it mildly. I may as well tell you now, straight away, before anybody else

41

	does it, they don't speak very highly of me in Dulworth Bay. I'm not exactly popular, as you might say.
STEVE:	Oh, I'm sure that's not true!
STUART:	It is true, Mrs Temple. I know what I'm talking about. Oh, they think I'm a good doctor but – well – they're just a wee bit afraid of me.
STEVE:	(*Pleasantly: faintly amused*) Afraid of you? Why should they be afraid of you, Dr Stuart?
STUART:	(*Slowly: quite pleasantly*) Well, you see now … a long, long time ago … I murdered a man …

Quick, dramatic FADE UP of music together with the noise of the train.
FADE SCENE.

FADE UP background noises of the station: people leaving the platform: sound of carriage doors opening and closing. TEMPLE and STEVE are met by INSPECTOR MORGAN who is obviously depressed and worried.

STEVE:	(*Surprised*) Why, here's the Inspector!
TEMPLE:	Hello, Inspector! I didn't expect to see you here!
MORGAN:	I was passing the station, so thought I might as well meet the train and drive you into the village.
TEMPLE:	That's very nice of you!
MORGAN:	Let me take that case, Mrs Temple.

They are walking out of the station towards the car park.

TEMPLE:	You look tired, Inspector.
MORGAN:	I feel it. I didn't get to bed until four o'clock and I was up again at a quarter past seven.

STEVE:	No peace for the wicked!
MORGAN:	I'm afraid not, Mrs Temple.
TEMPLE:	(*Quietly; serious*) Any news of Draper?
MORGAN:	(*Obviously worried*) No. His people are in a frightful state. We've got to find that boy – otherwise I don't like to think what will happen!
TEMPLE:	I've been thinking about last night, Morgan. I don't understand why you didn't stop the train.
MORGAN:	You mean immediately the boy disappeared?
TEMPLE:	Yes.
MORGAN:	But it took me some time before I realised what had happened. I got the alarm out as soon as we got to Dulworth Bay.
STEVE:	Did you search the train, Inspector?
MORGAN:	Yes, of course I did! But – well – I was on my own, Mrs Temple, and quite frankly, I don't mind admitting it, I was in a flat spin. I just didn't know what to do.
TEMPLE:	(*Changing the subject*) We travelled down from Town with a friend of yours, Inspector. Dr Stuart.
MORGAN:	Dr Stuart!
TEMPLE:	Yes.
MORGAN:	(*Smiling*) He's not exactly a friend of mine – as a matter of fact I don't think he's a friend of anybody's. I interviewed him the day the Baxter boys disappeared.
TEMPLE:	Isn't he very popular?
MORGAN:	Far from it. He's a queer old bird. Quite eccentric. Didn't he strike you that way?
TEMPLE:	Well, I must confess he seemed just a little odd.

43

They laugh.

MORGAN: They say there's quite a story behind the old
            boy, whether it's true or not I don't know.

STEVE: What do you mean?

TEMPLE: What sort of a story?

MORGAN: Apparently about fourteen or fifteen years ago
            he was quite a big noise in Harley Street.
            Then suddenly – for some unaccountable
            reason – he started drinking. One night, so the
            story goes, he was called out to do an
            emergency operation. Unfortunately, he'd just
            been to a party and …

TEMPLE: Don't tell me the doctor was drunk and the
            patient died?

MORGAN: Yes.

TEMPLE: Good Lord, I wrote that story twenty years
            ago – and even then, I didn't sell it.

MORGAN: (*Laughing*) Well, I'm afraid that's the story,
            Mr Temple. If you stay down in Dulworth
            Bay for long, you'll probably hear it half a
            dozen times.

TEMPLE: And I still shan't believe it. Of all the corny
            old chestnuts! (*He laughs*)

STEVE: (*Amused*) Is this your car, Inspector?

MORGAN: Yes. (*To TEMPLE*) Let me have your case –
            I'll put it on the front seat.

FADE SCENE.

*FADE UP noise of a car: it is travelling at an average speed
along a country road. The INSPECTOR is driving.*

MORGAN: What are your plans while you're down
            here, Mr Temple? Do you want me to take
            you up to the School this afternoon so that
            you can meet the Headmaster and …?

TEMPLE:	No … Don't you worry about us, Inspector. Just you carry on with your ordinary routine. I daresay we'll stroll up to the Hall sometime this evening and introduce ourselves to Lord Westerby. In any case, I want to meet Miss Maxwell.
MORGAN:	I saw Miss Maxwell this morning – just for a few minutes. If you ask me, she's in a pretty bad way.
TEMPLE:	What do you mean?
MORGAN:	She's sort of jumpy and – well – nervous all the time. The first time I met her she was quite different, a little too self-possessed if anything.
TEMPLE:	I suppose she knows about Draper?
MORGAN:	(*Watching the road ahead*) M'm – she must do – it's in all the papers. She didn't make any reference to it.
STEVE:	What's her uncle like?
MORGAN:	Lord Westerby? (*Vaguely*) Well – he's all right I suppose, but he's a bit too patronising for my liking. (*Suddenly*) There's Westerby Hall, over there. We shall be passing the Baxter place in a few minutes.
TEMPLE:	Slow down when you get to the cottage.
MORGAN:	Yes, all right.
STEVE:	Do we pass the school on the way to the village?
MORGAN:	Yes, the village is about a mile and a half away – it's over on the other side.

Pause. The car slows down.

TEMPLE:	Nice country, darling.
STEVE:	Most attractive.

MORGAN:	Here's the Baxter place. It's on the corner of the drive.
TEMPLE:	Which is the boys' bedroom – the one where you found the cricket bat?
MORGAN:	The one on the corner overlooking the drive. You can see it better when we pass the … (*He stops*)

The sound of another car is heard.

TEMPLE:	(*Quickly*) There's a car coming!
STEVE:	(*Suddenly*) Look out! It's coming out of the drive!

Quick FADE UP of the second car travelling at a very fast speed.

MORGAN:	It's Miss Maxwell!

MORGAN sounds his horn.

TEMPLE:	She certainly believes in taking the corner at a dangerous …
STEVE:	(*Quickly: desperately*) Look out!
TEMPLE:	Put your brakes on!!!!

(*The INSPECTOR slams on his brakes*)

STEVE:	She is going to hit us!

The second car brakes and there is a terrific tearing noise as the second car skids.

TEMPLE:	(*Breathless*) No … No, she's not!
MORGAN:	She'll hit the tree!!!!!!
STEVE:	Oh, Paul!

The second car continues to skid and then finally hits a tree at the side of the road. There is a tiny pause after the accident and then TEMPLE throws open the door of the car.

TEMPLE:	Come on, Inspector!
MORGAN:	(*Excited*) I think she's all right! Look! She's climbing out of the car!
STEVE:	There's a flask of brandy in your case, darling – shall I bring it?

TEMPLE: (*Urgently*) Yes, bring it, Steve!
FADE SCENE.

FADE UP of DIANA MAXWELL drinking from the flask of
brandy. She finishes drinking and catches her breath.

STEVE: Do you feel better?

DIANA: Yes, I feel much better now, thanks. Here's
               your flask.

STEVE: Thanks.

TEMPLE: Do you always take corners like that, or was
               that just for our benefit?

DIANA: (*A little breathless*) I'm afraid it was
               awfully careless of me. I'm terribly sorry,
               Inspector.

MORGAN: You've made a pretty nasty mess of your
               car, Miss Maxwell. What are you going to
               do?

DIANA: I think I'll walk back to the Hall and get my
               uncle to send his chauffeur down. I doubt
               whether he'll be able to do anything though.
               It looks pretty hopeless, doesn't it?

TEMPLE: Is there a garage in the village?

DIANA: Yes, but it's not very good.

TEMPLE: Why don't you get your uncle to …
               (*Suddenly*) Oh, by the way, I don't think
               we've introduced ourselves – my name is
               Temple.

DIANA: (*With a start of surprise*) Oh! Oh, Mr
               Temple! I didn't recognise you. I'm glad
               you've come down to Dulworth Bay,
               because I … (*Hesitates*)

TEMPLE: Yes?

DIANA:	(*Faintly annoyed*) I was going to say because I wanted to talk you, but what I really want is an explanation!
TEMPLE:	An explanation?
DIANA:	Yes. The Inspector here seems to be under the impression that I telephoned you last week.
TEMPLE:	(*Politely: interrupting DIANA*) Didn't you telephone me, Miss Maxwell?
DIANA:	(*Annoyed*) Of course I didn't! (*A moment*) Don't you believe me?
TEMPLE:	(*Slowly: watching DIANA*) Your voice is very familiar. It's certainly not unlike the one that spoke to me on the telephone.
DIANA:	(*Indignantly*) I don't understand this! What am I supposed to have said to you on the phone?
TEMPLE:	(*Still watching DIANA*) You told me that you knew why the Baxter boys had been kidnapped, and that you knew the identity of Curzon. You asked me to meet you at a restaurant in Greek Street – The Tabriz.
DIANA:	Go on …
TEMPLE:	I kept the appointment, Miss Maxwell, but you didn't. Instead, another girl came to the restaurant – a girl claiming to be Diana Maxwell.
DIANA:	(*Bewildered*) You mean …
TEMPLE:	I mean that the girl who turned up at the restaurant was not the girl who spoke to me on the phone. It's my belief that you spoke to me on the telephone, that you made the appointment, and then at the very last minute you changed your mind.

DIANA: (*After a definite pause: quietly*) That's a lie!
                I never spoke to you! If I'd taken the trouble
                to have made an appointment, I should
                have kept it.
TEMPLE: It's a good job you didn't, Miss Maxwell.
                The girl who impersonated you was
                murdered. (*Changing the subject*) Now, if
                you'd like us to drive you back to your ...

*As TEMPLE speaks there is the sound of a tremendously
loud explosion. It is quite near.*

MORGAN: (*Suddenly: astonished*) Good Lord, what's
                that?
STEVE: The car!!!!
MORGAN: Temple, what is it?
DIANA: Inspector, look at your car!!!
TEMPLE: By Timothy, just look at it! Look at it!!!!

A moment.

STEVE: (*Bewildered*) But what's happened?
DIANA: What on earth's happened?
TEMPLE: Come along, Morgan – let's get over to the
                car!

FADE SCENE.

*Slow FADE UP the noise of a burning car. The fire
continues through the following scene.*

STEVE: Don't get too near, darling!
TEMPLE: It's all right ...
MORGAN: Be careful, Temple! Be careful or you'll get
                burnt!
DIANA: What do you think happened?
MORGAN: I think it's pretty obvious what happened!
                There must have been a time-bomb in the
                car ...
TEMPLE: ... (*Softly*) ... Yes ...

49

MORGAN:	And it's my bet it was planted there while I was at the station meeting your train, unless …
STEVE:	A time-bomb!
DIANA:	(*Shocked*) A time-bomb!
STEVE:	Then … if … it … hadn't been for Miss Maxwell we'd have …
MORGAN:	We'd have had it, Mrs Temple! We'd have had it good and proper!
TEMPLE:	Well, that's one way of saying – Welcome to Dulworth Bay!

FADE UP of music.

FADE DOWN of music.
TEMPLE and STEVE are having tea in the lounge of the local Inn.

STEVE:	Would you like some more tea, Paul?
TEMPLE:	No, thank you, darling.
STEVE:	What did Charlie have to say when you phoned him?
TEMPLE:	He seemed a little surprised. I told him to pack two or three shirts and an extra pair of socks; he's bringing them down first thing tomorrow morning. You were darn lucky your case was thrown out of the car like that, Steve!
STEVE:	I just don't know what I should have done if I'd lost all my belongings … (*She hesitates*) Is this someone for us, darling?
TEMPLE:	(*Looking up*) No, I don't think so.
STEVE:	(*Quietly*) I think it is, Paul.

PETER MALO arrives. He is a well-educated, if somewhat precious young man of about thirty.

| MALO: | Mr Temple? |

50

TEMPLE: Yes?

MALO: I'm Peter Malo, sir. Lord Westerby's secretary.

TEMPLE: Oh, good afternoon, Mr Malo!

MALO: His Lordship asked me to present his compliments, sir – would you and Mrs Temple care to dine with him tomorrow evening?

TEMPLE: (*A little taken aback*) That's extremely nice of his Lordship. Yes, we shall be delighted.

MALO: Shall we say eight o'clock?

TEMPLE: Eight o'clock would suit us admirably.

MALO: I'll arrange for the car to call for you here at about ten minutes to eight. Is that convenient?

TEMPLE: Quite convenient – thank you, Mr Malo.

MALO: Miss Maxwell told me about the accident. It must have been <u>most</u> unpleasant.

TEMPLE: Fortunately, thanks to Miss Maxwell, it wasn't so unpleasant as it might have been.

MALO: (*Faintly amused*) I imagine you must have rather a bad impression of our peaceful little community! How long are you staying down here?

TEMPLE: We haven't decided – not yet.

MALO: (*Seriously*) The police don't seem to be making much headway, do they? I'm afraid his Lordship's extremely worried about this Baxter affair – to say nothing of the Draper development.

STEVE: Why should Lord Westerby be worried – any more than anyone else I mean?

MALO: His Lordship takes a sort of fatherly interest in the community, Mrs Temple. He always has done. In a way he feels personally responsible for what goes on in Dulworth Bay.

TEMPLE: Is Lord Westerby associated with the school at all?

MALO: St Gilberts? Yes, he's on the board of Governors. (*Rather surprised by the question*) Why?

TEMPLE: I wondered, that's all. (*Suddenly*) You don't happen to be going back to the Hall now by any chance?

MALO: Yes.

TEMPLE: Well, I wonder if you'd give us a lift as far as the school?

MALO: Yes, of course, I shall be delighted.

TEMPLE: (*To STEVE*) Are you ready, darling?

STEVE: Yes, I'm quite ready.

TEMPLE: (*Aside*) Waiter, how much do I owe you?

WAITER: Three shillings, please, sir.

TEMPLE: Here we are – keep the change!

WAITER: Thank you, sir! (*Suddenly*) Oh, I beg your pardon, sir! This note arrived for you about ten minutes ago, sir.

TEMPLE: Ten minutes ago!

WAITER: Yes, sir. It was sent to your room. The chambermaid's just brought it down, sir.

TEMPLE: I see. (*Takes note*)

TEMPLE opens the note. A pause.

STEVE: What is it, Paul?

TEMPLE: (*Casually: looking up*) M'm? Oh, it's nothing, Steve. It's just from the Inspector. (*Pleasantly*) Ready, Mr Malo?

MALO: Yes. Shall we go this way? My car's at the back, through the courtyard. (*To STEVE: FADE on speech*) Is this your first visit to Dulworth Bay, Mrs Temple, or have you been in this part of the world before?

FADE SCENE.

FADE Up on the sound of a car which draws to a standstill: the engine continues to tick over.

MALO: If you walk across the quadrangle, Mr Temple, and through that wicket gate, you'll see a red brick house. Unless I'm mistaken that's where you'll find the Head. (*A sudden thought*) I presume it is Mr Clarke you're wanting?

TEMPLE: (*Casually*) Yes, I thought I'd rather like to have a chat with him. (*Suddenly*) Thanks for the lift, Mr Malo!

MALO: A pleasure!

Changing gear.

MALO: Goodbye, Mrs Temple!

STEVE: We shall see you tomorrow night, I hope.

MALO: (*After a moment*) I hope so.

TEMPLE: Through the wicket gate, you said?

MALO: Yes, through the wicket gate and turn left. The house is covered in ivy – positively dripping with it – you can't miss it.

STEVE laughs as the car drives away.
FADE.

FADE UP the opening and closing of a small wicket gate.
TEMPLE and STEVE are strolling towards the house.

TEMPLE: There's the house over on the left.

STEVE: Yes. He's certainly right about the ivy.

A moment.

TEMPLE: Are you tired, Steve?

STEVE: (*Surprised*) No. Why?

TEMPLE: Because when I've had a word with this Headmaster Johnnie, I want to go back down to the cottage and have a talk to Mr Baxter.

STEVE: Was the note from Mr Baxter?

TEMPLE: (*Taken aback*) Yes. How did you know?

STEVE: I had a feeling it was, somehow. Just the good old intuition, darling.

TEMPLE: Now don't you start that good old intuition nonsense!

STEVE: (*Interrupting him: laughing*) What did Baxter say?

TEMPLE: Simply that he'd love to see me.

STEVE: (*Puzzled: seriously*) Paul, what do you make of this business?

TEMPLE: (*Quietly*) I don't know what to make of it. You see, the Baxter boys were abducted, and I think we can safely assume that they were ... (*Stops speaking*)

STEVE: What is it?

TEMPLE: (*Quietly*) Look who's here!

STEVE: (*Surprised*) Dr Stuart!

FADE UP of DR STUART who is strolling along, whistling to himself.

STUART: (*Surprised*) Why God bless my soul, I didn't expect to see you two quite so soon. Now what are you doing at St Gilberts?

TEMPLE: What's more to the point, doctor, what are you doing?

STUART: I'm doing my best to perform a miracle, but I've got a shrewd idea I'm not going to get away with it! One of the lads has twisted his ankle – and I'm trying to get him better for next Saturday.

STEVE: Why next Saturday in particular?

STUART: It's the swimming sports and the poor lad's the red-hot favourite. At least he was until he twisted his ankle. But what are you two up to, there's an air of mystery about the pair of you! You look like a couple of first-class conspirators to me.

TEMPLE: Well, we don't feel like a couple of conspirators, do we, Steve?

STEVE: (*Laughing*) I certainly don't.

STUART: Well, I hope you're not expecting to see the Rev Dudley Clarke, because if you are you'll be disappointed.

TEMPLE: Why? Is he away?

STUART: Ach, he's away until Saturday morning. He's apparently at some conference or other. I've never known a man to spend so much of his time flitting from one place to another. You'd think he was a commercial traveller instead of the Headmaster of a Public School.

TEMPLE: You sound as if you don't like Mr Clarke.

STUART: I don't. He's a gas bag. He talks too much, and he says too little. (*A sigh*) Well, I suppose I'd better be making a move. (*Looks at his watch*) A quarter past five. T't. (*A note of exasperation*) Ah, in another hour they'll be lining up at the Surgery like a lot of lost sheep! Snivelling and coughing and grumbling their heads off! Well, I expect I shall be bumping into you again. Take care of yourselves. (*Suddenly*) Oh! Oh, I heard about your time-bomb! That must have been quite an experience!

TEMPLE: Quite an experience!

STEVE: And one we could very easily have done without!

STUART: Aye! Aye! That's I don't doubt. (*Leaving*) Well, I'll be seeing you!

TEMPLE: Goodbye, doctor!

STEVE: Goodbye. (*A pause*) There doesn't seem to be much point in going up to the school if the headmaster is away, darling.

TEMPLE: No, let's go down to the cottage.

STEVE: Yes, all right.

TEMPLE: (*Thoughtfully*) Steve, do you remember what the old boy said when we were in the train? I asked him if he knew the Baxter boys and he said, "God bless my soul, I brought them into the world!"

STEVE: Well?

TEMPLE: Well, I've been thinking. Michael Baxter's nearly seventeen and yet, according to Inspector Morgan, fourteen or fifteen years ago, Dr Stuart was quite a big noise in Harley Street.

STEVE: In other words, Dr Stuart must have known the Baxters before he came down to Dulworth Bay.

TEMPLE: Exactly.

STEVE: Well, what does that prove?

TEMPLE: It doesn't prove anything. (*Thoughtfully*) But it's an interesting point.

FADE UP of music.

FADE DOWN of music.

TEMPLE and STEVE are strolling along the country lane.

Background noises of a quiet country lane can be heard.

STEVE: Have we much further to go, Paul?

TEMPLE: No, about another quarter of a mile, that's all. You can see the cottage.

STEVE: Is that it with the thatched roof?

TEMPLE: Yes.

STEVE: I suppose this is the lane the Baxter boys walked along.

TEMPLE: Yes, of course.

STEVE: Well, it seems very peaceful anyway. I can't imagine anything very dreadful happening down here.

TEMPLE: Let's hope you're right. (*A pause: then suddenly, intrigued*) Hello, what's this place?

STEVE: It's only a cottage.

TEMPLE: No, it isn't, it's a little shop. I never knew there was a shop down here. Morgan never mentioned it.

STEVE: Well, they're not open anyway.

TEMPLE: (*Quietly*) I wasn't thinking of that.

STEVE: You mean Roger and Michael must have passed here?

TEMPLE: Yes.

STEVE: I shouldn't think it's a hundred to one the Inspector's been in the shop. He wouldn't overlook a thing like that.

TEMPLE: You wouldn't think so. Are you sure it's closed?

STEVE: (*Trying the door*) Yes. Yes, it's closed all right.

TEMPLE: (*Rather amused*) I like the way they've got the window set out.

STEVE: They seem to stock almost everything.

TEMPLE: Yes.

STEVE: (*Amused*) Look at those garters!

TEMPLE: Where?

STEVE: Next to the liquorice-all-sorts!

TEMPLE: (*Laughing*) Yes …

Pause.

TEMPLE and STEVE are staring at the window.

STEVE: Apparently if you've got anything to sell you can advertise it for sixpence a week.

TEMPLE: Yes, I was just looking. Listen to this: (*Reading*) "£5 reward. Lost. Parrot. Red and green plumage. Answers to the name of Cheets. Apply within".

TEMPLE and STEVE laugh.

TEMPLE: Come on, let's walk up to the cottage!

FADE scene.

FADE UP on the opening and closing of a garden gate.

STEVE: What a sweet little cottage! Paul, isn't it nice!

TEMPLE: Yes, but it's not so little, darling! Look there are two or three rooms on the ground floor!

STEVE: I adore these thatched roofs.

TEMPLE: (*Quietly*) It looks as if Mr Baxter's expecting us, the door's open.

STEVE: (*Surprised*) Oh! (*A moment*) Isn't there a bell?

TEMPLE: Yes, here we are.

TEMPLE presses the bell push. We hear the sound of chimes in the hall of the cottage.

STEVE: I suppose this was the lodge at some time or other?

TEMPLE: Yes.

STEVE: Does it still belong to Lord Westerby?

TEMPLE: I should imagine so, it's part of the estate.

Pause.

STEVE: I should ring again, darling.

TEMPLE presses the bell push again. Another sound of chimes is heard.

A pause.

TEMPLE: There doesn't seem to be anyone in?

STEVE: I wonder if he's gone for a stroll?

TEMPLE: (*Thoughtfully*) Yes, that's probably why he left the door ajar.

STEVE: What are we going to do?

TEMPLE: Wait a minute!

TEMPLE pushes open the door.

STEVE: Darling, you can't go inside without first …

TEMPLE: Shsh! *Calling though the open door*) Hello, there! Anybody at home? (*Pause*) Hello, there!

58

From inside the cottage, we hear a strange and rather mysterious, screeching noise.

STEVE: (*Suddenly*) What's that?

TEMPLE: What?

STEVE: Didn't you hear it?

TEMPLE: No. What was it?

STEVE: It sounded to me like someone calling to you!

TEMPLE: Nonsense, Steve, I didn't hear it. (*A moment*) I'll try again. (*Calling*) Hello, there! Anybody in! Hello, there!

The screeching starts again.

STEVE: Now do you hear it?

TEMPLE: Yes. (*Amused*) That's darn funny! (*Casually*) Come on, Steve – let's have a look!

STEVE: Paul, we can't just walk into a person's home like this.

TEMPLE: It's all right, darling. Don't be silly!

They enter the hall of the cottage.

STEVE: (*Nervously*) Shall I close the door?

TEMPLE: No, leave it open …

A moment.

STEVE: I like the staircase, Paul!

TEMPLE: I was just admiring it.

STEVE: He's obviously spent a lot of money on this place!

TEMPLE: Yes, it only goes to show what you can do with some of these old places if only you take the trouble to … (*Suddenly*) What was that?

From an adjoining room we hear the screeching again.

STEVE: That's what I heard before!

TEMPLE: (*Puzzled, yet rather amused*) It's a peculiar noise! It sounds like a cat to me.

STEVE: I don't think it is.

TEMPLE: Well, what is it?

STEVE: Listen!

Pause.

TEMPLE: (*Across the hall: away from STEVE*) It's over here, Steve – in this room.

STEVE joins TEMPLE. After a moment's silence the screeching starts again.

STEVE: (*Bewildered*) What is it?

TEMPLE: We'll soon find out!

TEMPLE throws open the door of the room.

STEVE: (*Surprised*) Why, it's a parrot!

TEMPLE: (*Laughing*) Well, I'll be darned!

The parrot is very excited: screeching: moving restlessly about the cage.

STEVE: (*Amused*) Hello, Polly! Pretty Polly!

TEMPLE: By Timothy, you do seem to be in a temper old chap!

STEVE: Don't put your finger in the cage, darling. (*To the parrot*) That's a good bird! That's – a – good – bird! *(She makes a soft, gentle noise, trying to get on friendly terms with the parrot).*

TEMPLE: You know it's all a lot of nonsense about parrots being able to talk! Really talk I mean.

STEVE: Well, that's nonsense if you like! An aunt of mine had a parrot that used to talk its head off!

TEMPLE: Well, you don't seem to be getting a lot out of this fellow!

STEVE: Give us a chance! (*Cooing*) Pretty Polly! Pretty – Polly … Polly … Come along, Polly! Come along!

The parrot screeches.

TEMPLE: Well, what's that supposed to be?

STEVE: (*Laughing*) Be patient, Paul! The poor thing doesn't know us! (*To the parrot*) Hello, Polly! Hello, Polly! Come along, Polly.

The parrot screeches back at STEVE.

STEVE: (*Delighted*) There you are! Did you hear that?

TEMPLE: (*Pulling STEVE's leg*) Marvellous! Astounding! I wouldn't have believed it!!!! What did he say?

STEVE: (*Amused*) You know, you've got no faith in human nature, that's your trouble!

TEMPLE: I've got no faith in parrots!

STEVE: (*To the parrot*) Don't you take any notice of him, Polly! He's just a silly old man! … That's a good Polly …

The parrot screeches.

TEMPLE: Well, if he's got such a snappy line in conversation why shouldn't he open up a bit?

STEVE: He's shy.

TEMPLE: He doesn't look shy. (*To the parrot*) What's your name? Come on, Polly, what's your name? What do they call you? Come on, Polly, talk to Uncle? What's your name?

PARROT: (*Quite clearly*) Cheeta – Cheeta – Cheeta.

STEVE: (*Excitedly*) There you are! Did you hear that?

TEMPLE: (*Quietly: taken aback*) Yes … (*Suddenly*) Just a minute! (*To the parrot*) Say it again, Polly! (*A moment*) What's your name?

PARROT: (*Repeats*) Cheeta – Cheeta – Cheeta.

STEVE: (*Excited and delighted*) I told you, didn't I?

TEMPLE: (*Seriously: silencing STEVE*) Wait a minute, Steve! (*A moment, then quietly to the parrot*) What's your name, Polly? Say it again, Polly … (*Softly*) Go on, Polly! That's a good bird! Say it again!

PARROT: Cheeta – Cheeta – Cheeta.

STEVE: Now, Mr Clever, perhaps you'll believe me when I tell you that –

TEMPLE: (*Interrupting her*) Steve, don't you realise what he's saying?

STEVE: Yes, he's saying his name – Cheeta. (*Suddenly: a quick realisation*) Cheeta! That was the name on the card. The name on the card in the shop window!

TEMPLE: Yes.

STEVE: (*Bewildered*) Then this is the parrot! This must be the parrot that's missing!

TEMPLE: Yes.

STEVE: (*Confused, yet excited*) But I don't understand. If it's supposed to be missing, then what on earth is it doing here?

TEMPLE: (*Grimly*) Your guess it as good as mine, darling!

STEVE: But surely Mr Baxter wouldn't keep …

STEVE is interrupted by the voice of PHILIP BAXTER. He is outside, in the hall, and at the top of the staircase. He is obviously in very great pain. He is crying with anguish.

TEMPLE: (*Quickly*) Do you hear that?

STEVE: Yes!

TEMPLE: Come on, Steve!

TEMPLE and STEVE dash back into the hall.

STEVE: (*A gasp*) Oh!

TEMPLE: (*Softly*) Good Lord!

STEVE: (*Horrified*) Paul, look! There's a man at the top of the stairs …

TEMPLE: (*Very softly*) I've seen him …

STEVE: … But look! Look at him, Paul!

PHILIP BAXTER is moaning: dazed, bewildered, and in great pain.

TEMPLE: (*Tensely*) He must have been beaten up! Look at his face … just look at it!

STEVE: Oh, how horrible! Paul, how horrible!

62

TEMPLE:	(*Shouting to BAXTER*) Stay where you are! Don't move! Stay at the top of the stairs!
BAXTER:	Who are you? What do you want? What ... do ...
STEVE:	(*A frightened gasp*) Paul!
TEMPLE:	(*Quickly, desperately*) Stay where you are!
STEVE:	(*Screaming*) He's falling! He's falling!!!!

PHILIP BAXTER falls down the staircase and crashes into the hall below. STEVE starts to cry.

STEVE:	(*After a long pause: quietly*) Is he dead?
TEMPLE:	Yes.
STEVE:	(*A moment*) Is it Mr Baxter?
TEMPLE:	I think so. I noticed a photograph of him with the two boys. We'd better ...

The telephone interrupts him.

Pause.

The telephone continues. It rings for some considerable time.

STEVE:	What are you going to do?
TEMPLE:	I'm going to answer it. Now keep quiet! (*He picks up the receiver. A pause*) Hello?

The sound of coins dropping, and the pressing of button A is heard.

MICHAEL:	Hello – is that Dulworth 9862?
TEMPLE:	Er- yes. Who is that?
MICHAEL:	(*Quickly*) Is that you, Father?
TEMPLE:	(*Quickly; tensely*) Who is that? Who is that speaking?
MICHAEL:	(*Rather surprised*) This is Michael ...
TEMPLE:	(*Softy: staggered*) Michael!
MICHAEL:	Yes ... (*A note of excitement in his voice*) Tom's seen the card about Cheeta, Father. The card you put in the window ...

FADE UP music.

63

END OF EPISODE TWO

EPISODE THREE

TOM DOYLE

OPEN TO: *FADE UP of Steve crying.*

STEVE: (*After a long pause: quietly*) Is he dead?

TEMPLE: Yes.

STEVE: (*A moment*) Is it Mr Baxter?

TEMPLE: I think so. I noticed a photograph of him with the two boys. We'd better …

The telephone interrupts him. Pause. The telephone continues. It rings for some considerable time.

STEVE: What are you going to do?

TEMPLE: I'm going to answer it. Now keep quiet! (*He picks up the receiver. A pause*) Hello?

The sound of coins dropping, and the pressing of button A is heard.

MICHAEL: Hello – is that Dulworth 9862?

TEMPLE: Er- yes. Who is that?

MICHAEL: (*Quickly*) Is that you, Father?

TEMPLE: (*Quickly; tensely*) Who is that? Who is that speaking?

MICHAEL: (*Rather surprised*) This is Michael …

TEMPLE: (*Softy: staggered*) Michael!

MICHAEL: Yes … (*A note of excitement in his voice*) Tom's seen the card about Cheeta, Father. The card you put in the window …

TEMPLE: When did he see it?

MICHAEL: This afternoon on the way back from work, he told me to … (*He hesitates: a note of suspicion in his voice*) Your voice sounds different. Is anything the matter?

TEMPLE: No. No, nothing. Where are you speaking from?

MICHAEL: (*Surprised*) Why I'm speaking from the box near Tom's place! Remember you told me to telephone you the moment the card appeared in … (*He hesitates again*) Wait a

moment, Father! Here's Tom, he wants to
have a word with you.

*TOM DOYLE comes to the phone. He is a fisherman of
about forty-five. He has a very slight Irish accent.*

DOYLE: Mr Baxter?

TEMPLE: (*A moment*) Yes, this is Baxter. How are the
            boys, Tom?

DOYLE: (*Slowly: suspicious*) Why, they're fine! I
            noticed the card in the window, Mr Baxter,
            so I thought I'd better ... tell ... Michael ...
            to ... phone ... you ...

A moment.

TEMPLE: (*Suddenly: with authority*) Now listen!
            Don't ring off. Do you hear me? Whatever
            you do, don't ring off!

DOYLE: (*Quickly: tensely*) Who are you? Who is
            that?

TEMPLE: (*Quickly: urgently*) My name's Temple.
            Now listen, I don't know what this is all
            about, but you've got to believe what I'm
            telling you. Baxter's dead. He's been
            murdered.

DOYLE: (*Shocked*) Murdered! (*A little frightened*)
            No! No, I don't believe it! It's a trap! It's a
            trap to get the boys ...

TEMPLE: (*Urgently: almost a note of anger in his
            voice*) Listen to what I'm telling you!
            Baxter's dead. He's here, now, at the
            cottage. If you don't believe me, you can
            come and see for yourself.

DOYLE: (*Shaking his head: frightened*) No. No, it's a
            trap to get the boys! I'm not coming down
            to the cottage unless ...

TEMPLE: (*Quickly: frightened that DOYLE is going to ring off*) All right! All right, if you don't want to come down to the cottage, I'll tell you what to do. Wait a quarter of an hour and then get someone to ring through to the police station – tell them to ask for Inspector Morgan. If Morgan confirms that Baxter's dead, then will you bring the boys down to the cottage?

DOYLE: (*Slowly: cautiously*) If the Inspector says that Mr Baxter's dead, I'll – I'll take the boys down to the police station.

TEMPLE: (*Quickly*) When?

DOYLE: (*After a pause: obviously perturbed*) If Mr Baxter is dead, they'll be there in half an hour.

TEMPLE: (*A moment: then:*) All right.

TEMPLE replaces the receiver.

STEVE: (*Quickly: puzzled*) Paul, what is it? What's happened?

TEMPLE: (*Thoughtfully*) I think we've found the Baxter boys.

FADE UP music.

FADE DOWN music.

A door opens.

SERGEANT: (*Announcing*) Dr Stuart, sir!

MORGAN: (*Crisply*) Well, doctor?

STUART: There's nothing the matter with either of the Baxter boys. They're as fit as a fiddle.

TEMPLE: Did they ask anything about their Father?

STUART: No. I gather Doyle broke the news to them on the way down to the station.

MORGAN: Yes.

STUART:	Well, I must say they've taken it pretty well. I've given the young one a sedative. Don't badger the poor lad too much, Inspector.
MORGAN:	We've finished with him. All we want now is a chat with Michael and a statement from Doyle.
TEMPLE:	Is Tom Doyle a patient of yours?
STUART:	Aye, he's one of my panel patients.
TEMPLE:	How long have you known him?
STUART:	Oh – a year or so.
MORGAN:	What's your opinion of him?
STUART:	He's a pleasant, amiable sort of chap. Hard working. Bit of a donkey.
MORGAN:	M'm. (*Suddenly dismissing STUART*) All right, doctor. Thanks for coming along.
STUART:	(*Turning away*) Any time … any time, laddie. (*Turns back*) I was sorry to hear about Philip Baxter. I had a chat to the police surgeon. He tells me the poor wee man was in a terrible state.
MORGAN:	Yes, he was. He was beaten up. Whoever did it certainly made a pretty thorough job of it.
STUART:	Now why should anyone want to murder Philip Baxter of all people? (*A sigh*) T't, it's a funny world! I don't know whether you've noticed it or not, Mr Temple, but it's always the nice friendly sort of people that seem to come to an unfortunate end. I knew Philip Baxter. Known him for years. A nicer man you'd never wish to meet.
TEMPLE:	When did you first meet him?
STUART:	Oh, a long time ago. Longer than I care to remember. He was a stockbroker. Had one

or two lucky breaks and retired early in life. How old was he, Inspector? I suppose he couldn't have been more than fifty-two or three?

MORGAN: He was fifty-four.

STUART: I know he was quite young. Well, I'll be making a move. Goodbye, Mr Temple!

TEMPLE: Goodbye, doctor!

Door opens.

MORGAN: Sergeant!

SERGEANT: Yes, sir?

MORGAN: Bring Doyle in.

SERGEANT: Very good, sir.

The door closes.

TEMPLE: Does Sir Graham know about the Baxter boys?

MORGAN: Yes. I spoke to him on the phone about half an hour ago. He's relieved that they've turned up, of course, but he's still worried about Draper. You know, Temple, the thing that puzzles me about this case is the fact that nothing seems to fit together as it were. For instance, judging from your telephone conversation with Doyle, it rather looks as if Baxter himself was responsible for the disappearance of the two boys. In which case, was Baxter also responsible for the disappearance of John Draper? And there's another point – how does the name Curzon fit into all this?

TEMPLE: I'm not so sure that it fits into it at all.

MORGAN: I think it does. It's my bet that sooner or later we shall ... (*He stops speaking as the door opens*) Ah, come in, Doyle!

71

DOYLE: (*Nervous and apprehensive*) Thank you, sir.

MORGAN: Don't go, Sergeant! Sit down, Doyle – over there!

DOYLE: Thank you, sir.

MORGAN: I've had a word with the Baxter boys, and they've told me their version of what actually happened. Now I want to hear your side of the story.

DOYLE: Well, I don't suppose it's any different from what they've told you, sir.

MORGAN: Never the less I want to hear it.

DOYLE: Yes, sir.

MORGAN: The Sergeant here will take a note of anything you say, and I must warn you of course that your statement may – at a later date – be used in evidence. You understand that?

DOYLE: Yes, sir.

MORGAN: Your name is Thomas Edgar Doyle? You reside at Fernback Cottage, Dulworth Bay, in the county of Essex. You are in business on your own account as a fisherman and you are forty-four years of age. Is that correct?

DOYLE: Yes, sir.

MORGAN: Now, tell me, Doyle, how long had you known the late Mr Baxter?

DOYLE: I met him the first day I came to Dulworth Bay, sir. That was in 1946. I did one or two odd jobs for him, and – well, I've been doing them ever since.

MORGAN: You got on well with Mr Baxter, I take it?

DOYLE: Extremely well, sir – but then everybody did.

MORGAN: M'm – unfortunately not everybody.

DOYLE: (*Puzzled*) What do you mean, sir?

TEMPLE: The Inspector means that someone
                murdered him.

A pause. Then:

MORGAN: Tell us about the Baxter boys. Why have
                they been in hiding?

TEMPLE: And most important of all what have they
                been hiding from?

DOYLE: (*Quickly: a note of desperation*) I don't
                know, and that's the truth. I swear I don't
                know!

A moment.

MORGAN: (*Quietly*) O.K., Doyle. Let's have it. Let's
                have your side of the story.

DOYLE: Well, so far as I'm concerned, it all started
                about three weeks ago. One night when I
                got back from work there was a message for
                me asking me to call round and see Mr
                Baxter. I'd been expecting this because I
                knew that he had one or two odd jobs for me
                to do.

MORGAN: How did you know?

DOYLE: He'd spoken to me about them – and
                besides he'd just bought a lot of plants from
                one of the local nurseries and I knew that
                he'd want me to sort them out for him.
                Market gardening's by way of being a
                hobby of mine.

MORGAN: Go on …

DOYLE: I had a wash an' brush up, a cup of tea, and
                then I went along to the cottage. When I
                reached the cottage, Mr Baxter was stood in
                the doorway talking to Lord Westerby.
                There was another gentleman with them, a

rather good-looking man with an American accent. I'd never seen him before; he was a stranger to Dulworth Bay. Mr Baxter looked very worried. When I reached the gate, I hesitated a moment. I didn't know whether to go through into the garden or not. Suddenly, Mr Baxter looked up and saw me standing there. I called out to him ...

FADE SCENE.

FADE UP on the opening of a garden gate.

DOYLE: (*Calling*) I got your message, Mr Baxter!

BAXTER: Oh, yes, Tom! Come along inside, I've been expecting you.

TOM closes the gate and walks down the path.

WESTERBY: Well, we'll be making a move, Baxter. I think we've made the position quite clear.

BAXTER: (*Simply*) Quite clear, thank you, Lord Westerby.

WALTERS: I trust there's no bad feeling over this business. You understand that, so far as I'm concerned, there's nothing personal.

BAXTER: (*A little weary*) The position is quite clear and there's nothing personal.

WALTERS: You're not crazy, you know as well as I do that there's an awful lot of dough tied up in this deal. Naturally, we've got to be careful.

BAXTER: (*A note of sarcasm*) Naturally.

WESTERBY: I think we can safely assume, Walters, that Baxter sees our point of view – even if he doesn't appreciate it.

WALTERS: But he must appreciate it! That's the whole point. It isn't sufficient just to see our point

74

of view. I'm going to give you until Friday of next week, if by Friday you haven't …

WESTERBY: (*Stopping WALTERS*) Wait a moment!

DOYLE arrives at the door of the cottage.

BAXTER: Go inside, Tom. I'll be with you in a few minutes.

DOYLE: Very good, sir. Good evening, m'Lord.

WESTERBY: (*Very affable*) 'Evening, Tom! And how's the world treating you?

DOYLE: Can't grumble, sir.

WESTERBY: Can't you, by Jupiter! Well, that's something these days!

DOYLE: (*Passing WESTERBY and entering the cottage*) Excuse me, sir.

BAXTER, LORD WESTERBY and WALTERS continue their conversation. FADE on this conversation as TOM DOYLE enters the cottage and passes into the main room.

WALTERS: I shall telephone Westerby on Friday morning. If there is no news, then I'm afraid you'll just have to come up to Town – there's nothing else for it.

WESTERBY: (*Heart: trying to cover up*) Now don't be impatient, my dear fellow. Whatever happens we musn't be stupid about this business. We know it's serious but on the other hand …

WALTERS: (*Interrupting WESTERBY*) I'm extremely serious, brother. You know that as well as I do. I'll telephone you on Friday morning.

COMPLETE FADE: A pause:

FADE UP:
A door opens.

BAXTER: (*Quietly: rather tired*) Now, Tom …

DOYLE: (*Turning*) Oh, hello, Mr Baxter. I've just
                been looking at the bookshelves, sir. They
                look all right to me, sir. The top one's a bit
                loose but we can soon put that right.
BAXTER: (*Absent-minded*) The bookshelves? Oh, yes!
                Yes, the bookshelves! (*Quietly*) There's
                nothing the matter with the bookshelves.
DOYLE: (*Puzzled*) But I thought you said …
BAXTER: Sit down, Tom. I want to talk to you. (*A
                moment*) Would you like a drink?
DOYLE: Well, if there's a glass of beer going, Mr
                Baxter. I never say no to a glass of beer.
BAXTER: Yes, I think we can manage a glass of beer.
BAXTER crosses to the cupboard.
DOYLE: Did you get the plants, Mr Baxter?
BAXTER: Yes, they were delivered this morning. They
                want sorting out a bit, Tom – but we can
                leave that for the time being.
DOYLE: I thought perhaps that's what you wanted to
                see me about.
BAXTER: No. (*Returns to DOYLE with a drink*) No, I
                want to talk to you about something quite
                different. (*Handing over the drink*) Here
                you are.
DOYLE: Oh, thank you, sir! Your very good health,
                sir! (*Drinks*)
Pause.
BAXTER: (*Slowly: seriously*) Tom, I want to ask you a
                favour, and I don't quite know how to go
                about it.
DOYLE: Well, anything I can do to help, Mr Baxter, I
                shall be only too happy – you know that, sir.
Pause.

76

BAXTER:	You're very fond of the boys, aren't you, Tom?
DOYLE:	What – Roger and Michael?
BAXTER:	Yes.
DOYLE:	Why, sure! They're a couple of fine boys, Mr Baxter.
BAXTER:	Do you think they could stay with you for a little while, perhaps, for three or four weeks?
DOYLE:	Why of course! (*Laughing*) They'll 'ave to rough it a bit you know. I'm a bit slap-dash. But they'll be more than welcome. Are you going away, Mr Baxter?
BAXTER:	(*Hesitating*) No, I'm not going away. At least, not yet ...
DOYLE:	(*Puzzled*) Well – when would you like the boys to move in with me?

A pause.

BAXTER:	Tom, I don't think you quite realise what I'm asking.
DOYLE:	(*Puzzled*) No, sir?
BAXTER:	(*Drawing closer to DOYLE: slowly*) I want the boys to disappear. I don't want them to go to school, I don't want them to be seen about the village, I don't want anyone to know even that they're staying with you.
DOYLE:	(*Bewildered*) You mean you want me to hide them?
BAXTER:	Yes.
DOYLE:	You want me to hide them in my cottage for three or four weeks without anyone seeing them, without anyone ...
BAXTER:	Yes.
DOYLE:	But why? Why, for Pete's sake?

BAXTER: I can't tell you why. Even if I did tell you, I doubt whether you'd believe me.

DOYLE: But, Mr Baxter, the lads can't just disappear like that! There'll be all sorts of questions asked! What's the School going to say? Why even the police might get to hear of it and ask you a whole lot of darned awkward questions.

BAXTER: But the police will get to hear of it, Tom. I intend to report the matter to the police.

DOYLE: What d'you mean? I don't understand.

BAXTER: I want to give the impression – I've got to give the impression! – that the boys have either been abducted or that they've run away from home.

DOYLE: (*Hesitating: worried*) You mean you'll kick up quite a fuss about it? You'll actually talk to the police, have newspaper interviews and all that sort of thing?

BAXTER: Yes.

DOYLE: And all the time this is going on the boys'll be here in Dulworth Bay – in my cottage?

BAXTER: Yes.

DOYLE: I don't like it, Mr Baxter! (*Shaking his head*) I don't like it!

BAXTER: (*Slowly*) Tom, you said just now that you were fond of the boys.

DOYLE: I am! I am indeed!

BAXTER: Then you wouldn't like anything to happen to them, would you?

DOYLE: Of course I wouldn't! Why, what's likely to happen to them?

BAXTER: They're in danger, Tom. In terrible danger. However, if you feel that you can't do what I ask, then there's nothing more to be said.

78

DOYLE: But, Mr Baxter, if you know that the lads are in danger from something – or someone – why don't you go to the police about it?

BAXTER: (*A note of desperation*) That's impossible! Don't ask me why, it's … just … impossible … that's all.

A moment.

DOYLE: (*Slowly*) Supposing I did what you wanted. Supposing I take the boys in and hide them for three or four weeks …

BAXTER: Well?

DOYLE: Well, how do you know that by that time things will have changed? How do you know that this so-called danger you talk about will have blown over?

BAXTER: I don't. It may not have blown over, but in three or four weeks I should be able to cope with the situation.

DOYLE: What would you tell the boys?

BAXTER: The truth. That I simply wanted them to lie low for a little while. I don't think I'd have any difficulty with them. They're pretty good kids.

A tiny pause.

DOYLE: I don't like it. I don't like it at all, but you've been a good friend to me, Mr Baxter, one way and another and – well, all right … all right, I'll do it.

BAXTER: (*Softly: relieved*) Thank you, Tom. (*A moment: quietly*) Now look, I want to pay you for this. It's a hundred pounds. That'll pay for all the expenses and what's left over is yours.

DOYLE: Why, man, I wouldn't dream of …

BAXTER: Tom, please! Now listen to what I'm telling you. I shall try and arrange for Roger and Michael to turn up at your place sometime tomorrow. Once the boys arrive, I don't want you to get in touch with me. I don't want you to call here or to write or telephone or do anything – do you understand?

DOYLE: Yes, but supposing something happens – an emergency. One of them might be taken ill or …

BAXTER: In that case I'll tell you what to do. You know the little shop, the huckster's shop in the lane?

DOYLE: Mrs Vernon's? Yes.

BAXTER: Well, there's always a lot of postcards in the window – articles for sale, things lost, adverts for servants and …

DOYLE: Sure, I know the sort of thing.

BAXTER: Well, if you want me just put a card in the window. (*Thoughtfully*) Put on the card … "Three-wheeler bike for sale. Suitable for boy of ten. Two spare tyres."

DOYLE: (*Amused*) Yes, all right. And if you want me at all …

BAXTER: I shan't want you, Tom. Still, look in the shop every day. If you see a card which says – er – which says … "£5 reward. Lost. Parrot. Red and green plumage. Answers to the name of Cheeta" … you'll know everything's O.K. and the coast is clear.

DOYLE: And then what do I do?

BAXTER: In that case you throw your hat in the air and get Michael to telephone me. I'll tell him what to do over the phone.

DOYLE: Yes, all right. You'll send the boys along tomorrow afternoon?

BAXTER: Yes. What time do you get home tomorrow?

DOYLE: I shall be fairly early. I start at just after six tomorrow morning.

BAXTER: Good. You'll take care of them, Tom – won't you?

DOYLE: Yes, of course I will, you know that, Mr Baxter. Don't worry, they'll be all right.

BAXTER: (*FADE on this speech*) Now remember what I've told you, Tom. Don't write to me, don't telephone me, and certainly don't think of calling here. If I want you at all I shall put the card in Mrs Vernon's …

Complete FADE.

FADE UP of TOM DOYLE.

DOYLE: … The boys turned up the following afternoon and they stayed with me until – well, until this afternoon – until I saw the card in the shop window. When I saw the card, I dashed back to my place and told Michael about it. Naturally, the boy was excited. We both went out to the telephone box and – well the rest of the story you know.

MORGAN: M'm – thank you, Doyle.

DOYLE: Inspector, have you any idea who murdered Mr Baxter? Because if you have, I'd just like to get my hands on the swine.

TEMPLE: What's your theory? Have you any idea who murdered him?

DOYLE: (*Surprised by the question*) Not the slightest! I've told you – Mr Baxter was a most likeable chap, I just can't imagine anybody wanting to harm the poor fellow.

MORGAN:	I suppose you read about the disappearance of this other boy – John Draper?
DOYLE:	I did, and that frightened the life out of me! But Mr Baxter hadn't anything to do with that, sir.
TEMPLE:	How do you know?
DOYLE:	(*Puzzled*) Well, he can't have had, sir.
TEMPLE:	Did Mr Baxter mention John Draper to you during your conversation about Roger and Michael?
DOYLE:	Why no!
TEMPLE:	Did he mention anyone by the name of Curzon?
DOYLE:	No, sir.
TEMPLE:	Have you ever heard the name Curzon before?
DOYLE:	No, sir.
TEMPLE:	You say that when you turned up at the cottage to see Mr Baxter there were two men on the doorstep talking to him – Lord Westerby and another man?
DOYLE:	Yes, sir.
TEMPLE:	You described the other man as being rather good-looking with an American accent?
DOYLE:	Yes, sir. I heard his Lordship call him Mr Walters.
TEMPLE:	How old would you say Mr Walters was?
DOYLE:	It's difficult to say, sir. Thirty-three or four – perhaps a bit older.
TEMPLE:	I see.
A moment.	
MORGAN:	(*Dismissing DOYLE*) Thank you, Doyle. That's all for the time being. (*To*

SERGEANT*) I want to see Michael Baxter, Sergeant.

SERGEANT: Very good, sir.

The door opens and closes.

MORGAN: Well, that seems to tie up all right. It confirms what the two boys have already told me. I don't think there's any doubt that Doyle was telling the truth, in which case, what exactly was Philip Baxter frightened of?

TEMPLE: It might be quite an idea to ask Lord Westerby.

MORGAN: (*Thoughtfully*) Yes. Didn't you tell me you'd got a date with his Lordship?

TEMPLE: Tomorrow night – he's invited us to dinner. But I think it might be quite an idea if Steve and I short circuited the invitation and dropped in on the old boy this evening.

The door opens.

MORGAN: Yes. (*Suddenly: quite friendly*) Ah, come in, Michael!

MICHAEL: (*Quietly: a little frightened*) The Sergeant said that you wanted to see me, sir.

MORGAN: Yes. Yes, just for a moment or two. Sit down, Michael. Sit down over there.

MICHAEL: Thank you, sir.

MORGAN: Oh, this is Mr Paul Temple. I expect you've heard of Mr Temple – he writes all those detective novels and things.

TEMPLE: (*Smiling*) Chiefly detective novels, Inspector. (*To MICHAEL: friendly and rather charming*) Now, Michael, I know that this is pretty rotten for you, but you must understand that the police are doing

83

their duty and are trying to find out who murdered your father. You understand that?

MICHAEL: Yes, sir.

TEMPLE: I'm quite sure that both you and Roger will want to do everything you possibly can to help us.

MICHAEL: Yes, of course, sir.

TEMPLE: Now you've told the Inspector exactly what happened. You've told him why you and your brother went to stay with Tom Doyle but there's still one little point, Michael, which you haven't explained.

MICHAEL: What, sir?

TEMPLE: Why did you write the name Curzon on your cricket bat?

MICHAEL: What do you mean, sir?

TEMPLE: About two or three weeks ago, the Inspector searched your room and found a cricket bat. There was a list of names – signatures – on it. The last was the name Curzon. Did you write the name Curzon on your bat?

MICHAEL: Yes, sir.

TEMPLE: Why?

MICHAEL: So that I wouldn't forget it, sir.

TEMPLE: (*Faintly surprised*) So that you wouldn't forget it?

MICHAEL: Yes, sir. The bat was the only thing that was handy, sir, so – I wrote it on the bat.

MORGAN: When? When did you do that?

MICHAEL: (*Nervously*) One night, sir.

TEMPLE: Tell us what happened, Michael. (*Smiling*) It's all right, there's nothing to worry about, just take your time.

MICHAEL:	Well − there's nothing much to tell, sir. Late one night, when I was in bed, I suddenly heard voices. Loud angry voices. I was both frightened and curious, so I got out of bed and crept on to the landing.
MORGAN:	Go on …
MICHAEL:	My father was downstairs in the living room and there was another man with him; a man whose voice I didn't recognise. They seemed very angry with each other. My father kept shouting: "I don't care what Curzon says! I don't care what Curzon says and I am not obeying these instructions!"
TEMPLE:	And what did the other man say?
MICHAEL:	As far as I can remember the other man said: "It's no good being stupid, Baxter. Curzon calls the tune, and we have to dance and that's all there is to it."
TEMPLE:	I see. Did you hear anything else?
MICHAEL:	No, sir. I wrote the name Curzon down on the bat so that I shouldn't forget it and the next morning at breakfast I asked my father who Curzon was.
TEMPLE:	What did he say?
MICHAEL:	At first he was extremely angry and told me to mind my own business, then when I was leaving for school, he said − "Forget all about it, Michael. That was just an old friend of mine last night. He dropped in for a drink and we had a friendly argument."
TEMPLE:	Did you ever hear the name Curzon again?
MICHAEL:	No, sir.
TEMPLE:	Did you ever mention it again to your father?

MICHAEL:	No, sir.
TEMPLE:	You say you didn't recognise the voice of the man your father had the row with?
MICHAEL:	No, sir.
TEMPLE:	Well, what sort of a voice was it, Michael? Had it an accent for instance, or was it just an ordinary English voice?
MICHAEL:	It was just an ordinary well-educated voice, sir.
TEMPLE:	Well-educated?
MICHAEL:	Yes, sir.
MORGAN:	Tell me, Michael, did you father ever speak of a friend of his called Walters – Mr Walters?
MICHAEL:	Walters? No, sir.
MORGAN:	(*Dismissing the matter*) All right, Michael – thanks very much. Would you like a cup of tea?
MICHAEL:	No thank you, sir.
MORGAN:	Are you sure?
MICHAEL:	Quite sure, sir.
MORGAN:	Well, just go back to your brother for a few moments, Michael – we shan't keep you long.
MICHAEL:	(*After a moment*) Excuse me, sir …
MORGAN:	Yes?
MICHAEL:	I hope you aren't going to do anything to Tom, sir. He's been awfully good to us. I shouldn't like to think that just because he helped …
MORGAN:	Don't worry, Michael. Just take care of that young brother of yours, he needs all the help he can get.
MICHAEL:	Yes, sir.

MICHAEL goes out. The door opens and closes.

A pause.

MORGAN: Well, what do you think, Temple? Who do you think that was with Baxter? Do you think it was Lord Westerby?

TEMPLE: (*Slowly: thoughtfully*) It might have been. I'll ask him.

FADE UP music.

FADE DOWN music.

FADE UP the sound of the wind: it is quite strong, almost a gale.

FADE through the sound of the wind the noise of a motor car:

The car draws to a standstill. The car door opens and closes.

FADE outside noises as TEMPLE enters the Inn.

PORTER: Good evening, sir.

TEMPLE: Good evening. Any messages for me?

PORTER: No, sir. Mrs Temple is in the lounge, sir.

TEMPLE: Oh, thank you.

TEMPLE passes into the lounge.

STEVE: Hello, darling!

TEMPLE: Oh, hello, Steve. Are you ready?

STEVE: (*Laughing*) I was in the bath when you telephoned. The porter came upstairs and shouted something about meeting you in half an hour! What's all the excitement about anyway?

TEMPLE: We're going up to the Hall. I want to see Lord Westerby.

STEVE: I thought we were dining with him tomorrow night?

TEMPLE: We are – but I want to have a talk with him tonight.

STEVE: Why? (*Curious*) Is he mixed up in the Baxter affair?

TEMPLE: It's beginning to look like it. I'll tell you all about it on the way there.

STEVE: Well, how on earth are we going to get there? It's a terrible night.

TEMPLE: I've borrowed a car from the local garage.

STEVE: (*Apprehensive*) What sort of a car?

TEMPLE: You'll need your fur coat.

STEVE: What do you mean I'll need … Heavens above, it's not a tourer!

TEMPLE: (*Laughing*) I'm afraid so. Not only that, but part of the windscreen is missing so you'll need a scarf or something to wrap round …

STEVE: Which part?

TEMPLE: What do you mean?

STEVE: Which-part-of-the-window-is-missing, my sweet?

TEMPLE: (*Off-hand*) Oh, it's all right for the driver.

STEVE: Meet your new chauffeur, Mr Temple!

TEMPLE laughs.

PORTER: I beg your pardon, sir!

TEMPLE: Yes?

PORTER: You're wanted on the telephone, sir.

TEMPLE: Oh. (*To STEVE*) I shan't be a moment, Steve – it's probably Morgan.

PORTER: It's a personal call from London, sir.

TEMPLE: (*Faintly surprised*) Oh. Where's the box?

PORTER: This way, sir.

FADE scene.

FADE UP opening of the telephone booth door.

TEMPLE lifts the receiver.

TEMPLE: (*On the phone*) Hello?

FORBES: (*On the phone*) Is that you, Temple?

TEMPLE: Oh, hello, Sir Graham! How are you?

FORBES: (*Seriously*) I've just been having a talk with Morgan, Temple. I thought perhaps I'd better get in touch with you. There's been a new development.

TEMPLE: What do you mean?

FORBES: We've picked a girl out of the Thames this afternoon. Her name was Lita Ronson: she lives in Dean Street.

TEMPLE: Well?

FORBES: It looked like suicide, but we searched her flat. I don't want to say too much over the phone, Temple, but – we came across a letter. It was written by a man called Carl Walters.

TEMPLE: Walters? That's the name that Doyle mentioned. The man that was with Baxter and Lord Westerby.

FORBES: Yes, I know. I want you to check on Westerby, Temple. Find out if Doyle was telling the truth. Personally, I'm pretty sure he was but nevertheless, I'd like you to check.

TEMPLE: I'm doing that tonight. What about this man Walters? Do you know him?

FORBES: Yes. He runs one or two amusement arcades.

TEMPLE: Has he a record?

FORBES: No, I don't think so. You've got my private number. Give me a ring when you've seen Westerby.

TEMPLE: Yes, all right, I'll do that.

FORBES: And, Temple …

TEMPLE: Yes?

FORBES: You know what happened to Baxter. Watch your
step!

TEMPLE: (*Quietly*) Don't worry, Sir Graham. I'm watching
it.

FADE UP music.

FADE DOWN music and FADE UP the sound of the car.
The car is travelling at an average speed.
The wind is still fairly strong.

STEVE: (*Driving the car*) We're nearly there, aren't we?

TEMPLE: About another two or three hundred yards and
then you turn to the left. You'll see Baxter's
cottage on the corner. I should slow down,
Steve.

STEVE: Don't squash me, darling!

TEMPLE: I'm trying to keep behind the windscreen – what
there is of it!

STEVE laughs.

STEVE: Paul, do you think the Inspector was telling the
truth about your Draper?

TEMPLE: What do you mean?

STEVE: Well – it seems rather extraordinary that he
should have disappeared like that.

TEMPLE: Perhaps there's a perfectly simple explanation –
like the Baxter boys for instance.

STEVE: It's beginning to look as if Draper's
disappearance has got nothing whatever to do
with the Baxter boys.

TEMPLE: It's rather a remarkable coincidence if it hasn't.

STEVE: Well, supposing Draper was kidnapped, I still
don't see how anyone could have got him off the
train without the Inspector noticing it.

TEMPLE: The Inspector lost his head and dashed around
like a scalded cat. In that state of mind I doubt

whether he'd have noticed a Sunday School treat. Here we are, Steve – here's the cottage. Slow down and turn into the drive.

The car slows down and turns off the main road into the private drive. It proceeds along the drive up to the house.

TEMPLE: Take it steady …

STEVE: It's pretty dark …

TEMPLE: It's the trees …

STEVE: Yes.

Pause.

TEMPLE: I don't think much of these lights.

STEVE: No. (*Pause*) It's a very long drive.

TEMPLE: We've got a good way to go yet – the house is round the bend. (*Quickly*) Slow down, Steve!

STEVE: (*Alarmed*) What is it?

TEMPLE: There's something stretching across the drive …

STEVE: Where?

TEMPLE: Look!

STEVE: (*Peering*) I don't see anything!

TEMPLE: Look, it's stretching from that tree, it's about three or four feet off the ground … (*Suddenly*) It's a rope, Steve, it's a rope!!!!

STEVE: Darling, I can't see anything!

TEMPLE: Pull up or you'll hit it! Brake, darling!!!! Brake!!!!

STEVE slams on the brakes and the car comes to a standstill. The engine stalls.

TEMPLE: (*With relief*) Good girl!

STEVE: Good brakes!

TEMPLE: You've just caught it, Steve! It's across the front of the radiator. If you'd have gone another two yards, you'd have pushed the rope … (*He stops*)

STEVE: (*Suddenly*) What's that? (*Alarmed*) Paul, what is it?

A moment.

The tree on the side of the drive is slowly breaking and preparing to fall.

TEMPLE: It's the tree! It looks as if it's going to fall!

STEVE: Paul, then the rope must have been tied to the tree so that when the car hit it ...

TEMPLE: Yes! (*Tensely*) Watch it! Watch the tree! Steve, get ready to jump if it falls ... Watch it, darling, you can't always tell which way it's falling!

The tree breaks away and starts to fall.

STEVE: (*Tensely*) It's falling!!!!

TEMPLE: (*Slowly*) Watch .... it .... Steve!!!!

The free falls and crashes amongst the trees at the side of the drive.

STEVE: (*A tremendous sigh of relief*) Oh!

TEMPLE: (*Quietly*) Right! Now let's have a look at that rope! You stay in the car, dear.

The car door opens. A pause.

There is distant background noise: the sound of an approaching car.

TEMPLE returns:

STEVE: Well?

TEMPLE: (*A little breathless*) The tree was cut away, if you'd hit the rope full on, you'd have brought it down on top of us.

STEVE: Oh, Paul!

TEMPLE: (*Thoughtfully*) Yes, but it isn't to say it was intended for us, Steve. So far as I know no one knows that we were coming here except Sir Graham and the Inspector.

STEVE: Well, in that case ... (*She hesitates*) Is that a car?

A pause.

The sound of an approaching car is heard.

TEMPLE: Yes. (*A moment*) It's coming up the drive.

STEVE: I wonder who it is?

The car approaches and on reaching TEMPLE's car slows down to a standstill.

STEVE: It's Miss Maxwell …

TEMPLE: She's with that secretary fellow – Peter Malo.

DIANA: (*Calling surprised*) Why, hello, Mr Temple!

TEMPLE: (*Pleasantly*) Good evening, Miss Maxwell.

DIANA stops the engine and together with PETER MALO climbs out of her car.

MALO: Hello!

TEMPLE: Hello, Malo.

MALO: Good evening, Mrs Temple.

STEVE: Good evening.

DIANA: Have you had an accident or something?

MALO: I say, what on earth is that rope doing over there?

TEMPLE: Don't you know, Mr Malo?

MALO: What do you mean?

DIANA: (*Tensely*) What's happened?

TEMPLE: You see that tree?

MALO: You mean that one that's blown down?

TEMPLE: Yes, but it wasn't exactly blown down.

MALO: What?

TEMPLE: That rope was attached to it, it was tied to another tree on the other side of the drive. If we'd hit the rope full on, we'd have had the tree on top of us.

MALO: (*Astonished*) You mean that the rope was deliberately tied so that … (*Frightened*) I say, Di – I don't like the sound of this! It sounds to me as if we've …

DIANA: (*Sharply*) Be quiet, Peter! (*To TEMPLE: tensely*) Where were you going? Up to the house?

TEMPLE: But of course. I wanted to see Lord Westerby.

93

DIANA: (*Coldly*) It's a pity you didn't telephone, Mr Temple, you'd have saved yourself a journey. I'm afraid my uncle's out and won't be back until late this evening.

TEMPLE: What do you call late?

DIANA: I mean very late – it might even be one or two o'clock in the morning.

TEMPLE: I see.

DIANA: Was it important?

TEMPLE: Yes, I particularly wanted to see him.

DIANA: But surely you're dining with him tomorrow night – can't it wait?

TEMPLE: It looks as if it will have to. I'll turn my car round so that you can get by.

DIANA: Thank you.

TEMPLE: (*Suddenly*) Oh – how do you account for this business with the rope? It was quite obviously tied to the tree. Do you think your uncle was responsible?

MALO: We can't account for it unless…

DIANA: (*Silencing MALO*) Be quiet, Peter! My uncle's having certain repairs done and I believe one or two of the trees are being removed. I should imagine the work people must have left the rope … like … that. It was very careless of them.

TEMPLE: Very. What time did you leave the house this evening?

MALO: (*Without thinking*) We left about half an hour ago, we've only been down to … (*He stops*)

TEMPLE: Half an hour ago? Did you? That's interesting. I take it the rope wasn't across the drive half an hour ago?

DIANA: No, it wasn't.

TEMPLE: His Lordship must have an excellent staff.

DIANA: What do you mean?

TEMPLE: They obviously believe in working very late,
           Miss Maxwell. (*Turning*) Come along, Steve –
           we'll turn the car round.

FADE UP music.

*FADE DOWN music and FADE UP the sound of the car.
The car slows down almost to a standstill.*

STEVE: Darling, this is the Baxter place – what are you
           stopping here for?

TEMPLE: I'm going to have a look round. There are one or
           two things I want to check up on.

The car stops and the door opens.

STEVE: You mean things that Doyle told you?

TEMPLE: No, not exactly. Come along, Steve!

STEVE: (*Climbing out of the car*) Well, what sort of
           things?

TEMPLE: (*Thoughtfully*) I'm just wondering if our friend
           Miss Maxwell came here tonight.

STEVE: (*Surprised*) Miss Maxwell?

TEMPLE: Yes. Mind the gate, Steve.

STEVE opens the gate.

STEVE: What makes you think that Miss Maxwell came
           here?

TEMPLE: I'll show you. Wait till I get the torch and then
           … Ah, here we are! Now look at your shoes.

STEVE: What's the matter with them?

TEMPLE: They're like Miss Maxwell's: they're covered in
           red dust. It's off the path leading up to the gate. I
           noticed this afternoon that the path was
           covered with red chippings.

STEVE: (*Emphatically*) Then she must have been here!

TEMPLE: (*Amused*) Oh, no! Not necessarily! I don't
           suppose for one moment that this is the only

95

path in the district like that. Still, let's have a
look round.

STEVE: How are we going to get in?

TEMPLE: I've got a key. I borrowed it from the Inspector.

TEMPLE inserts the key and opens the door.

TEMPLE: Stand behind me, darling.

STEVE: Shall I close the door?

TEMPLE: Yes, but don't latch it.

STEVE: Where do you want to go first?

TEMPLE: Upstairs – I want to have a look round the
bedroom.

STEVE: You mean the one the boys occupied?

TEMPLE: Yes.

STEVE: We shall probably get half-way upstairs,
suddenly hear the parrot, and die of heart failure!

TEMPLE: (*Laughing*) The parrot isn't here. The Police let
the boys take it down to the Station.

STEVE: I'm delighted to hear it!

TEMPLE: Mind your step, that stair rod's a bit loose!

TEMPLE and STEVE ascend the staircase.

TEMPLE: I thought you liked parrots? I thought you were
the gal that went in for them in quite a big way!

STEVE: I do like them. But not in strange houses and at
this time of night.

TEMPLE: I ought to have put the light on.

STEVE: There should be a switch on the landing at the
top.

TEMPLE: (*Flicking the torch*) I'm afraid this torch isn't as
good as I thought it was! (*Suddenly stopping
STEVE*) Wait a moment!

STEVE: What is it?

TEMPLE: There's something near your foot. You're
treading on it, darling!

STEVE: Oh! It's a cigarette end.

TEMPLE: Let me have a look at it. (*He takes the cigarette end*)

A pause.

STEVE: It's got some lipstick on it.

TEMPLE: Yes – rather a lot.

STEVE: That's just what I was thinking. (*Opening her handbag*) Do you want to keep it? I've got an envelope in my bag.

TEMPLE: Yes, put it in the envelope. I'll have a look at it later when we get back to the Inn.

TEMPLE and STEVE climb the stairs until they reach the landing.

STEVE: Where's the light switch?

TEMPLE: It's near your head! (*Suddenly*) Wait a minute!

STEVE: (*Quickly: softly*) There's someone coming!

TEMPLE: Don't put the light on!

A long pause: outside we hear the sound of approaching footsteps.

STEVE: They're coming up the drive!

TEMPLE: (*A whisper*) Don't move, darling!

STEVE: What are you going to do?

TEMPLE: Wait until they push the door open …

STEVE: (*Tense whisper*) Then what are you going to do?

TEMPLE: I'll switch the torch on, and as soon as you see … (*Softly*) Sh! Quietly, darling.

The door opens: the visitor slowly enters the hall.

Pause.

STEVE: Who is it?

TEMPLE: I don't know! (*Pause*) Sh!

Pause.

STEVE: (*Tense whisper*) He's in the hall …

TEMPLE: Yes …

Pause.

STEVE: (*Suddenly*) Switch the torch on, Paul!

97

TEMPLE switches on the torch.

JOHN: (*Slowly*) Is that you, Mr Baxter?

STEVE: (*Stunned*) Paul! Paul, look – who – it – is!

TEMPLE: It's John Draper!!!!

Quick FADE UP of music.

END OF EPISODE THREE

EPISODE FOUR

MISS MAXWELL
KEEPS AN APPOINTMENT

OPEN TO:

STEVE: (*Quickly: softly*) There's someone coming!

TEMPLE: Don't put the light on!

A long pause: outside we hear the sound of approaching footsteps.

STEVE: They're coming up the drive!

TEMPLE: (*A whisper*) Don't move, darling!

STEVE: What are you going to do?

TEMPLE: Wait until they push the door open …

STEVE: (*Tense whisper*) Then what are you going to do?

TEMPLE: I'll switch the torch on, and as soon as you see … (*Softly*) Sh! Quietly, darling.

The door opens: the visitor slowly enters the hall.

Pause.

STEVE: Who is it?

TEMPLE: I don't know! (*Pause*) Sh!

Pause.

STEVE: (*Tense whisper*) He's in the hall …

TEMPLE: Yes …

Pause.

STEVE: (*Suddenly*) Switch the torch on, Paul!

TEMPLE switches on the torch.

JOHN: (*Slowly*) Is that you, Mr Baxter?

STEVE: (*Stunned*) Paul! Paul, look – who – it – is!

TEMPLE: It's John Draper!!!!

JOHN: (*Slowly dazed*) Is that you, Mr Baxter? This is John …

TEMPLE: Put the light on, Steve!

STEVE switches on the light.

JOHN: (*Surprised*) Oh! (*Slowly*) You're … not … Mr Baxter!

TEMPLE: (*Returning to the hall*) You remember me, John! Temple. You came to my house yesterday afternoon.

JOHN DRAPER is obviously suffering from loss of memory.
His manner is a little confused. He speaks rather slowly.

JOHN: Yesterday?

TEMPLE: (*By JOHN's side*) Yes, the Inspector brought you
          – don't you remember?

JOHN: No.

STEVE: But surely you remember, John! You had tea
          with us. Inspector Morgan – Sir Graham Forbes
          – and yourself.

JOHN: Yesterday?

STEVE: Yes. (*Watching JOHN: to TEMPLE*) Darling,
          what's the matter with him?

JOHN: I remember something about a train. I was in the
          corridor and a man came out of a carriage and ...
          (*He breaks off. Suddenly, staring about him*)
          This is the cottage! This is Mr Baxter's cottage,
          isn't it?

TEMPLE: Yes. (*Quietly*) Come along, John! Come and sit
          on the couch over there.

A pause.

STEVE: Shall I switch the fire on?

TEMPLE: (*To JOHN*) Are you cold?

JOHN: Yes. (*Shivering*) Yes, I am. (*Shaking his head*) I
          can't remember anything. It's funny but every
          time I try to think I get a headache and then ... I
          ... just ... can't ... remember.

TEMPLE: (*Friendly*) There's no need to worry. Take it
          easy. Your memory'll come back all right. How
          do you feel, apart from the headache?

JOHN: I feel all right. (*Shivering*) I'm a bit cold, but I
          feel better than I did last night.

TEMPLE: (*Very casually*) Where were you last night?

JOHN: In the train. (*Looking up at TEMPLE*) That's
          right, isn't it? I was in the train and then ...

102

(*Faintly distressed*) You see, I've got the headache. I can't remember. Every time I try to remember anything I get the headache and then … it's … no use. (*Shaking his head*) It's just no use.

TEMPLE: You'll feel better in a minute. Would you like a cigarette? (*Suddenly, smiling*) Oh! Oh, I suppose I mustn't offer you a cigarette?

JOHN: No, sir.

STEVE: Don't you smoke?

JOHN: No.

STEVE: Never?

JOHN: No, at least – (*A little laugh*) I once smoked a pipe. It … made me very sick.

TEMPLE: (*Lighting his cigarette. Casually*) When was that? A long time ago?

JOHN: Oh, yes, sir. I don't think I was thirteen.

TEMPLE: (*Smiling pleasantly*) Well, there you are, you see. You can remember about the pipe all right although it was a very long time ago.

JOHN: (*Slowly*) Yes. Yes, that's funny.

TEMPLE: (*Quietly*) John, why did you come here instead of going home?

JOHN: (*Listlessly*) I don't know. I suddenly found myself walking along and when I saw the cottage, I thought I'd like to call and see if Michael was … (*Suddenly shaking his head*) You see, I don't remember! I don't even remember how I got into the lane.

STEVE: I should imagine someone must have dropped you there in a car.

JOHN: Yes. Yes, I seem to remember a car! (*Suddenly, quickly*) Someone took me there in a motor car,

103

they told me to get out and … (*Lost again*) … walk down the lane …

TEMPLE: Who was it, John? Now try and think …

A pause.

JOHN: I don't know …

TEMPLE: Come along, old man. (*A moment*) Was it Miss Maxwell? Was it Miss Maxwell and Mr Malo?

JOHN: (*Tensely*) I just don't know. Please leave me alone …

TEMPLE: (*Quietly to STEVE*) Steve, go out into the hall and ring up Dr Stuart – I think it's Dulworth 92 – and tell him I want to see him – here – straight away.

STEVE: But oughtn't we to take the boy home?

TEMPLE: Yes, dear, we'll do that later, but first do as I tell you.

STEVE: All right.

STEVE passes into the hall, picks up the telephone and dials.

JOHN: (*In the background*) I don't know what my father will say. He'll want to know what's happened to me. He'll want to know where I've been and … (*Distressed*) He'll want to know all sorts of things that … I … can't … explain.

TEMPLE: (*In the background*) Don't worry, John. We'll talk to your father; everything'll be all right.

STEVE: (*On the phone*) Hello? Is that Dulworth 92?

MRS DUNCAN: (*An elderly, dour and very broad Scotswoman*) It is.

STEVE: I want to speak to Dr Stuart, please.

MRS DUNCAN: You can'na speak to the doctor, he's engaged.

STEVE: Who is that speaking?

104

MRS DUNCAN: This is the Housekeeper speaking – Mrs Duncan.

STEVE: Well, listen, Mrs Duncan. My name is Temple and I want to speak to Dr Stuart. It's extremely urgent.

MRS DUNCAN: You can'na speak to the doctor. He's having his supper and he won't be interrupted.

STEVE: Mrs Duncan, will you kindly tell Dr Stuart that I wish to speak to him – it's extremely urgent.

MRS DUNCAN: It's no use. I've told you, the doctor won't be interrupted. If you'd like me to deliver a message, then …

STEVE: (*Annoyed*) All right, deliver a message! Tell Dr Stuart that my husband and I are at Mr Baxter's and we want to see him immediately.

MRS DUNCAN: Immediately! But I've told you …

STEVE: (*Cutting MRS DUNCAN short*) Immediately! Straight away!! Now!!!

MRS DUNCAN: (*Forcefully, very dour*) I'll deliver the message!

STEVE: (*Forcefully, equally dour*) I'm greatly obliged to you, I'm sure!

FADE UP of music.

Quick FADE DOWN of music.

STUART: You can put your coat on again, laddie.

JOHN: Thank you, sir.

STUART: Here – let me give you a hand. (*He helps JOHN on with his jacket*) Now I'll tell you what we're going to do with you. Mrs Temple's going to drive you home and there's no need to worry my lad, absolutely no need at all. Mr T's already spoken to your father and the poor man's wildly

105

delighted to hear that you're safe and sound. That's true, isn't it, Mr Temple?

TEMPLE: Perfectly.

STUART: So just you take it nice and easy my boy and don't worry about anything. I'll be able to see you first thing tomorrow morning.

JOHN: (*Distressed*) But I can't remember anything, sir. Every time I try to remember anything ... I ... get ... this ... headache.

STUART: (*Sympathetically*) Yes, I know.

JOHN: (*Worried: perplexed*) I don't know what I shall say to my father. You see, he'll want to know what happened to me. He'll ask me all sorts of questions about what happened on the train and I shan't be able to answer him.

STUART: He won't ask you anything of the sort, laddie! Now you've no need to worry! Just run along with Mrs Temple.

STEVE: Come along, John! (*Quietly, aside to TEMPLE*) I'll see you later, Paul.

A pause.

Sound of the front door opening and closing.

During the following dialogue the sound of a departing car can be heard.

TEMPLE: (*Seriously, straight to the point*) Well, doctor – what's the matter with that boy?

STUART: Do you want half a guinea's worth of medical claptrap or ...

TEMPLE: I want it short and straight.

STUART: Physically – there's nothing the matter with him. Certainly nothing that a good night's rest and a hot meal won't cure. (*Ominously*) But, unfortunately, he'll never be able to remember anything.

106

TEMPLE: (*Faintly aggressive*) What do you mean – he'll never be able to remember anything?

STUART: You know what I mean without making me repeat myself! The laddie can't – and won't – remember anything. It's quite simple, his mind's a blank, and if you want my professional opinion it's going to remain a blank.

TEMPLE: I don't agree with you. For one thing, before you got here, he remembered quite a lot.

STUART: Did he now? Then why did you send for me? (*A moment*) The only reason you sent for me, Mr Temple, was because you thought I'd pull the laddie round and make him talk! Well, I don't think the laddie will talk for the simple reason that I don't think he'll ever remember what really happened to him.

A moment.

TEMPLE: (*Quietly*) We shall see.

STUART: Aye, we shall see. (*He picks up his case*) Well, there's no need for me to stay here any longer. I'll get back to my supper.

TEMPLE: One moment, doctor! Have you ever had a case like this before?

STUART: You mean – loss of memory?

TEMPLE: Yes.

STUART: Aye, I've had one or two. Not identically the same of course.

TEMPLE: What's the cause of it?

STUART: In this particular instance?

TEMPLE: Yes.

STUART: It's difficult to say. If I were forced to give an opinion, I should say the laddie's been drugged.

TEMPLE: (*Watching STUART*) Not hypnotised?

107

STUART: (*Slowly, thoughtfully*) No. No, I don't think so. When I was a young man – that's going back many years mark you! – I came across a poison known as Datura. It's a Malay poison, it's taken from the pods of the Datura tree. A large dose of this poison would unquestionably prove fatal – especially with a youngster like Draper – but a minute dose, carefully administered as it were, would … (*Hesitates*)

TEMPLE: Would what?

STUART: (*A moment*) Would destroy the memory.

TEMPLE: How would this poison be given? Is it a vaccine?

STUART: No. No, it's quite simple. They'd probably give it to the laddie in a cup of tea or coffee.

TEMPLE: I see. (*Suddenly*) Dr Stuart, when we met on the train you made one or two unusual observations. You told us, for instance, that everybody in Dulworth Bay knew everybody else's business.

STUART: Well?

TEMPLE: Well, you live in Dulworth Bay. You've been here for a great many years.

STUART: (*A sigh*) What are you getting at?

TEMPLE: I'm getting at the fact that you must know quite a lot of what goes on in this village.

STUART: (*A note of petulance*) You still haven't told me what you're getting at!

A moment.

TEMPLE: (*Bluntly*) Who murdered Philip Baxter?

STUART: (*Evading the question*) My dear Mr Temple, Philip Baxter was a patient of mine, but that doesn't mean to say that I'm acquainted with …

TEMPLE: (*Interrupting, facing STUART*) Who murdered Philip Baxter?

A pause.

STUART: You're supposed to be the detective, Mr Temple. Supposing you tell me ...?

TEMPLE: (*Slowly, still watching STUART*) I will, Dr Stuart. All in good time.

FADE UP music.

FADE DOWN music.

The door of the cottage opens and closes.

STEVE enters the hall.

STEVE: (*Calling*) Paul! (*A moment*) Paul!

TEMPLE appears on the landing.

TEMPLE: (*Calling down to STEVE*) I'm upstairs. Come along up. I'm in the bedroom.

FADE.

FADE UP of STEVE.

STEVE: (*A little out of breath*) What are you doing in here?

TEMPLE: I've been taking a good look round. Come along in!

STEVE enters, closing the door behind her.

STEVE: It's rather nice. This isn't the boys' room surely?

TEMPLE: No, it was Baxter's. I've made rather an interesting discovery, Steve.

STEVE: Oh? What?

TEMPLE: Take a look over here. You see this bookshelf?

STEVE: Yes.

TEMPLE: Watch it!

TEMPLE presses a button, and the shelf automatically reverses itself.

STEVE: Good heavens! The books must be dummies!

TEMPLE: Yes.

STEVE: (*Puzzled*) Well, what is it?

TEMPLE: It's a safe. Wait a moment.

TEMPLE slides back a concealed panel.

TEMPLE: There you are!

STEVE: Good heavens, how on earth did you manage to find that?

TEMPLE: (*Laughing*) I tried to pick up one of the books and found I couldn't lift it. It's rather ingenious, isn't it?

STEVE: Have you opened it?

TEMPLE: No, it's a combination safe. (*At the safe*) And goodness only knows what the combination is! I've been fiddling about with it for the last five minutes.

STEVE: Surely, it's rather odd that Baxter should have a concealed safe, especially in a bedroom.

TEMPLE: Yes. I shall be rather intrigued to know what's in it. (*Suddenly*) Oh, by the way, did you see Draper?

STEVE: Yes, and I can understand why the boy was nervous of him. I should imagine he's pretty strict.

TEMPLE: Well, I only hope he won't pester the poor chap with a lot of questions. If he does I very much doubt whether the boy will stand up to it.

STEVE: Paul, has anyone called here since I left?

TEMPLE: No. (*Looking up*) Why?

STEVE: Well, when I drove up to the cottage just now, I thought I saw someone near the front door. When they heard the car pull up, they ran across the lane and up the drive towards the hall.

TEMPLE: Was it a man?

STEVE: Oh, yes.

TEMPLE: Did you recognise him?

STEVE: No, not exactly, but …

TEMPLE: But you've got a pretty shrewd idea who it was?

STEVE: Yes. It was Peter Malo.

TEMPLE: Malo? (*Thoughtfully*) M'm.

STEVE: Have you been in touch with the Inspector?

TEMPLE: Yes, I phoned him soon after you left. As a matter of fact, he should be on his way here.

TEMPLE is still trying to open the safe.

TEMPLE: By Timothy, I wish I could do something about this safe before he gets here.

STEVE: (*A moment*) What did the doctor say?

TEMPLE: About Draper? He's under the impression he was drugged.

STEVE: Do you think he was drugged?

TEMPLE: (*Still at the safe*) I don't know.

STEVE: (*Thoughtfully*) You know, Paul, I don't quite see how Dr Stuart fits into all this? If John Draper saw the doctor – or rather heard him – the day that the Baxter boys were kidnapped, then surely …

TEMPLE: But the Baxters weren't kidnapped, not if we accept Tom Doyle's story.

STEVE: Do you accept it?

TEMPLE: Well, the Baxter boys confirm it, don't they?

STEVE: Then you don't think Dr Stuart's got anything to do with this business?

TEMPLE: I wouldn't say that. But you know, Steve, this affair has taken on a different aspect, hasn't it? First of all, the Baxter boys disappeared and then they turned up, then John Draper disappeared, and he turned up. So, in actual fact, so far as Scotland Yard's concerned, the only problem at the moment is …

STEVE: Who killed Philip Baxter and why?

TEMPLE: Exactly. (*Rising from the safe*) It's no good, I can't do anything with this safe.

111

STEVE: But when we find out why Philip Baxter was murdered then don't you think we shall … (*She stops*) Paul!

TEMPLE: What is it?

STEVE: Darling, do you smell something burning?

TEMPLE: (*Quickly*) Yes, I do! (*Suddenly*) Steve, open the door!

The door is thrown open.

Quick FADE UP the sound of a fire.

STEVE: (*Frightened*) Paul!

TEMPLE: Good Lord, there's a fire! Stand back, Steve!

STEVE: We'll have to get downstairs, darling! We can't stay up here.

TEMPLE: Wait a minute, Steve! Stay here!

FADE UP the noise of the fire.

In the background we hear TEMPLE coughing. He is leaning over the staircase peering into the hall below.

STEVE: Be careful, Paul!

TEMPLE returns to STEVE.

TEMPLE: (*Coughing slightly*) It looks pretty grim! The whole side of the staircase is ablaze!

STEVE: What are we going to do?

TEMPLE: We'll have to make a dash for it.

STEVE: (*Suddenly*) Listen! – What's that?

FADE UP the noise of the fire coupled with the collapsing of part of the thatched roof.

TEMPLE: It's the roof! It's the thatched roof.

STEVE: Someone must have thrown something on to the roof so that the fire would spread!

TEMPLE: (*Quickly, pulling STEVE aside*) Look out!!!!

With a tremendous crackling noise part of the thatched roof collapses.

TEMPLE: Give me your hand!

STEVE: (*Coughing*) Have you got a handkerchief?

112

TEMPLE: Yes, take this. Now stick close to me, Steve, and for goodness sake watch the roof!

FADE UP the noise of the fire as TEMPLE and STEVE descend the stairs. STEVE is coughing and gasping for breath. Part of the roof commences to fall.

STEVE: Look, Paul!

TEMPLE: Keep over!

The roof falls and crashes down the staircase.

STEVE: (*Frightened*) Paul!

TEMPLE: It's all right, darling – don't worry – we'll get down!

STEVE: (*Coughing, gasping*) Paul, I … don't … think … I … can … do … it!

TEMPE: (*Coughing*) Yes, of course you can do it! Now hold on, darling!

Pause.

FADE UP the sound of the fire.

STEVE: We'll never get across the hall, Paul! It's impossible!

TEMPLE: We're not going to try! We'll have to try for the room on the left. Now hold my hand and when I say "right" make a dash for it.

STEVE: (*Coughing*) Wait a minute! (*Stops coughing and tries to catch her breath*)

TEMPLE: Right!

FADE UP sound of the fire as TEMPLE and STEVE dash down the burning staircase and into the hall.

TEMPLE kicks open a door.

TEMPLE: In here, quick!

STEVE: (*Excited, relieved*) There's a French window, Paul.

TEMPLE: (*Quickly*) Stand back, I'm going to smash it!

TEMPLE picks up a chair and crashes it through the window.

TEMPLE: Come on, darling! Mind the glass!
FADE UP the sound of the fire.
FADE scene completely.

FADE UP background of the burning cottage.
TEMPLE: How are you feeling now, Steve?
STEVE: (*Still out of breath*) I feel much better. Gosh, doesn't my hair look a mess. I don't know what on earth I shall do with it.
TEMPLE: Well, you can always have a singe!
STEVE laughs.
TEMPLE: By Timothy, you women certainly take the cake! Fancy worrying about your hair at a time like this!
STEVE: There's someone coming.
TEMPLE: (*A little surprised*) It's Diana Maxwell!
STEVE: (*Quietly*) She's with Peter Malo.
DIANA: Hello, Mr Temple! (*Astounded*) What on earth's happening?
TEMPLE: I'm afraid there's been a fire.
DIANA: There still is by the look of things! (*Surprised*) You both look exhausted! (*Suddenly realising what has happened*) I say, you two weren't in the cottage by any chance?
TEMPLE: I'm afraid we were.
DIANA: You might have been burnt to death! (*Turning*) Peter, did you hear? Mr and Mrs Temple were in the cottage!
MALO: (*Apparently shocked*) No? In the cottage? How frightful for you! We saw the fire from the Hall and wondered what happened.
TEMPLE: I suppose you didn't think of sending for the fire brigade?

MALO: Good Lord, yes! We gave them a tinkle as soon
           as we saw the smoke rising, didn't we, Di?

DIANA: (*Her thoughts elsewhere, watching TEMPLE*)
           Yes, they should be here any minute now. You
           seem to be having rather an exciting time in
           Dulworth Bay, Mr Temple. What with the car
           incident, the tree falling and now the fire ...

TEMPLE: (*A note of sarcasm*) Yes, I shall be quite glad
           when the season's over and things get a little
           quieter.

*The sound of an approaching car is heard during the
following dialogue. The car eventually draws to a standstill.*

MALO: (*Smiling*) Mr Temple, please don't think me
           curious but what exactly were you doing in Mr
           Baxter's cottage?

TEMPLE: (*Bluntly*) Why do you ask?

MALO: (*Shaken*) Well, I wondered how the fire started.
           After all, if you were in the cottage, you must
           have some idea what started it.

TEMPLE: Are you asking me to express an opinion?

MALO: Well – yes.

TEMPLE: I think the cottage was quite deliberately set on
           fire.

DIANA: (*Apparently shocked*) Deliberately – set – on –
           fire?

TEMPLE: Yes.

DIANA: But that's absurd! Surely.

TEMPLE: Do you think it's absurd, Mr Malo?

MALO: (*Nervous, almost hurt*) I think it's a ridiculous
           suggestion. Perfectly ridiculous.

*As MALO finishes speaking, we hear the sound of the local
fire brigade, fire bells, etc. The fire engine comes to a
standstill. There is a sudden background of voices, a great
deal of general excitement.*

FIREMAN:	Stand back, please! Clear the way there! Stand back everybody!
TEMPLE:	Look out, Steve! Stand on one side, darling!
FIREMAN:	(*Calling*) Bring it through here, Turner! That's it, straight through! Join no 8, Wilson.
MORGAN:	Temple! Good Lord, what's going on here?
TEMPLE:	Hello, Inspector!
MORGAN:	But when did this happen?
TEMPLE:	About a quarter of an hour ago. Steve and I were in the cottage, we only just got out in time.
MORGAN:	Good Lord! Are you all right, Mrs Temple?
STEVE:	Yes, I'm all right now, thanks.
TEMPLE:	Have you seen young Draper?
MORGAN:	Yes, I've only just left him.
TEMPLE:	How is he?
MORGAN:	He's all right, but you were dead right. He can't remember a thing.
TEMPLE:	I hope you didn't worry the boy.
MORGAN:	No, as a matter of fact I had very little to say to him. I could see it was no use. Where the Dickens did the boy come from? Did you get anything out of him?
TEMPLE:	No. I tried – so did the doctor – but it was hopeless. By the way, what have you done with the Baxter boys?
MORGAN:	We discovered Mrs Baxter had a niece near Harwich, so we've sent them over there. I spoke to the girl on the phone – she sounded quite decent.
TEMPLE:	Good.

116

MORGAN:	Of course, we shall keep an eye on them. (*Suddenly*) By the way, did you find anything in the cottage?
TEMPLE:	(*Confidentially*) Yes, I found a safe. It was in the bedroom concealed behind a bookshelf. If I were you, I should keep a sharp look out for it.
MORGAN:	If it isn't fire-proof I'm afraid we've had it.

FADE UP the sound of fire.

FIREMAN:	(*Shouting*) Stand clear over there! Please do as you are told and stand clear!
2nd FIREMAN:	(*Calling*) We shall have to do something about these trees, sir, otherwise it'll spread!

FADE UP background noises of firemen, noise of water spraying etc.

FIREMAN:	Tell Harper to spray them – he ought to have done that already! Stand clear, please!
MORGAN:	(*Suddenly*) Oh, good evening, Miss Maxwell. Evening, Mr Malo.
DIANA:	Oh, hello, Inspector! I was just saying to Peter I hope the fire doesn't catch those trees.
MALO:	It's going to be a pretty bad show if it does!
MORGAN:	I don't think it will. I think they'll stop it all right.
TEMPLE:	Are you cold, Steve?
STEVE:	Yes, I am rather.
TEMPLE:	We're going back to the Inn, Inspector. Drop in on us later if you feel like it.
MORGAN:	Yes, all right, Mr Temple.
DIANA:	Good night, Mrs Temple.
STEVE:	Good night!
MALO:	Good night!
STEVE:	Good night!

117

TEMPLE: The car's over here.

FADE noises and sounds of the fire to the background.

The car door opens.

STEVE: (*Shivering*) I suppose it isn't really very cold, but I started to get the shivers. I just couldn't stop.

TEMPLE: (*Starting the car*) What you need is a good stiff whisky and a couple of aspirins.

STEVE: (*Suddenly*) Wait a minute, Paul! Here's Miss Maxwell.

TEMPLE: <u>Now</u> what does she want?

A pause.

DIANA MAXWELL arrives, she is faintly out of breath.

DIANA: Mrs Temple, is this your glove? I found it on the grass near where you were standing.

STEVE: Why, no!

DIANA: (*Quietly*) Listen, Peter Malo's watching us – take the glove and pretend it's yours.

STEVE: (*Bewildered*) But …

TEMPLE: (*Quickly*) Do as she says, Steve.

STEVE: (*With a little laugh, taking the glove*) Oh, thank you, Miss Maxwell!

DIANA: Mr Temple, I can't talk now but there's an awful lot I want to explain. Can we meet tomorrow sometime?

TEMPLE: Yes, I don't see why not. When would you like to meet?

DIANA: We've got to be careful. I don't want Peter Malo or … (*Suddenly*) Listen! I've got a yacht; it's out in the bay. I usually go out in it at about half past ten in the morning and stay there till about four. Get someone to bring you out tomorrow morning – I'll expect you any time after half past ten.

TEMPLE: Yes, all right. What do they call this yacht of yours?

118

DIANA: It's called the Windswept. You can't mistake it. Ask any of the fishermen, they'll row you out to it.

TEMPLE: All right, Miss Maxwell. I'll see you tomorrow morning – half past ten.

STEVE: (*Softly*) Malo's watching.

DIANA: (*Raising her voice pleasantly*) Good night, Mrs Temple!

STEVE: (*Raising her voice*) Good night! Thanks for the glove!

FADE UP on the car driving away.

FADE scene.

FADE UP the car ticking over.

The car door opens.

TEMPLE: I shan't be a second, Steve.

STEVE: It's all right, darling. I don't feel so bad now.

TEMPLE walks down a short path, reaches the door of a cottage and – using the door knocker – knocks on the door. A pause.

TEMPLE knocks again and then the door is slowly unbolted and opened.

DOYLE: (*Surprised*) Why, Mr Temple! Come in, sir! Come inside, sir!

TEMPLE: No, I won't come in, Tom. I just wanted to have a word with you.

DOYLE: If there's anything I can do to help, sir – anything at all – you've only got to ask.

TEMPLE: Oh, this isn't a professional call, Tom. It hasn't got anything to do with the Baxter affair. I was merely wondering if you could take me out tomorrow morning.

DOYLE: (*Puzzled*) Take you out, sir? Do you mean in one of the boats?

119

TEMPLE: Yes, I want to go out to a yacht. I believe it's anchored in the bay. The Windswept.

DOYLE: Lord Westerby's old tub, sir?

TEMPLE: Lord Westerby's?

DOYLE: Yes, it used to belong to Lord Westerby though I believe Miss Maxwell runs it now. They do say the old boy gave it to her as a Christmas present.

TEMPLE: Is Miss Maxwell fond of sailing?

DOYLE: No, she uses the boat as a retreat more than anything else. She's a funny soul – writes poetry and plays and that sort of stuff. (*Smiling*) Have you met the secretary?

TEMPLE: Mr Malo?

DOYLE: Yes. (*Amused*) Now he's a character if you like. He spent two hours with me one morning out on the bay. Why the devil he came with me I don't know. Mind you the boy's clever. He's a bit of a ninny but by golly he's no fool.

TEMPLE: (*Curious*) When was this – when did Mr Malo go out with you?

DOYLE: Oh, it's about six or seven weeks ago now.

TEMPLE: Did he help you at all – with the fishing, I mean?

DOYLE: Help me! Be'dad he nearly fell overboard! The only time I had any peace of mind was when he was peering through his binoculars.

TEMPLE: Did Mr Malo spend most of his time peering through his binoculars?

DOYLE: He did that, an' it was a godsend! (*Suddenly*) Well, will ten o'clock be all right? We can meet outside The Feathers.

TEMPLE: Yes, that'll do nicely. Ten o'clock.

DOYLE: Ten o'clock it is!

FADE UP of music.

Slow FADE DOWN of music.

*FADE UP the sound of TOM DOYLE rowing TEMPLE and
STEVE out to the Windswept.*

DOYLE: There she is! She's not a bad looking yacht. Looks a great deal better since she had a coat of paint.

STEVE: You say it used to belong to Lord Westerby?

DOYLE: Yes, Ma'am.

STEVE: Does he still use it?

DOYLE: I couldn't say, I'm sure.

Pause.

TEMPLE: There doesn't appear to be any sign of Miss Maxwell.

STEVE: No.

DOYLE: Would you like me to wait for you, sir?

TEMPLE: No. Can you call back for us in about an hour?

DOYLE: Sure …

A moment.

STEVE: It all seems very quiet. No sign of life anywhere.

TEMPLE: What size crew would they have on a boat like this?

DOYLE: Well, when his Lordship had it there used to be two men and a boy. Whether they're still there or not I don't know.

TEMPLE: Were they local people?

DOYLE: No, sir. The boy was a foreigner. I don't know what he was, I'm sure. The men came from Jersey. They were a queer crowd. Kept very much to themselves. It used to be quite a bone of contention amongst the local people.

STEVE: What do you mean?

DOYLE: Well, they felt that his Lordship ought to have employed locals. I know if it was my boat, I'd want to do what his Lordship did and please myself. (*Suddenly*) Don't put your hand over the side, Ma'am.

The boat slows down. DOYLE takes one of the oars out of the water.

STEVE: Have we got to climb up that ladder, Paul?

TEMPLE: Yes. (*Laughing*) Well, you would come! I told you to stay at the Inn!

DOYLE: (*Moving about in the boat*) Now it's all right, there's nothing to worry about!

DOYLE is taking in the oars.

DOYLE: All you've got to do is to take it nice and easy.

TEMPLE: Shall I go up first?

They are moving about in the boat.

DOYLE: Now just a minute, let's get sorted out a bit.

DOYLE moves in the boat.

DOYLE: Yes, you go up first and then I'll help Mrs Temple.

TEMPLE climbs out of the boat and on to the rope ladder.

DOYLE: That's it ... can you manage?

TEMPLE: (*On the ladder*) Yes, I'm all right.

TEMPLE climbs the ladder.

STEVE: Be careful, Paul!

TEMPLE: (*Very sure of himself*) It's all right. I could do this with my eyes closed. (*He suddenly slips*) Whoa!!!!

DOYLE: (*Quickly*) Watch it!

The boat rocks.

STEVE: You look much better with your eyes open, darling!

TEMPLE: You're telling me!

TEMPLE continues to climb and eventually reaches the deck.

DOYLE: (*Calling up to TEMPLE*) Are you all right?

TEMPLE: Yes. Take it easy, Steve!

DOYLE: Now just grip the sides and keep your head well up, Mrs Temple.

STEVE: (*Climbing on to the ladder*) Give me your hand when I get to the top, Paul!

The boat sways slightly.

DOYLE: That's it … Steady! (*Pleased*) Ah, that's beautiful.

TEMPLE: (*Helping STEVE over the side*) By Timothy, you're better at this than I am!!!

STEVE: Wait a minute! Wait a minute, don't rush me! (*Carefully, swinging her legs over the side*) I'm wearing nylons, darling, and … I … don't … want … to … ladder … them.

TEMPLE: I should think you don't, not at the price you pay for them.

STEVE lands on the deck.

DOYLE: (*Shouting from below*) All aboard?

TEMPLE: (*Leaning over the side and shouting down*) Yes, all serene!

DOYLE: (*Shouting*) I'll be back in about an hour.

TEMPLE: All right, Tom!

In the background we hear the sound of TOM replacing the oars in the water. The boat departs during the following dialogue.

STEVE: (*Looking about her*) Still no sign of Miss Maxwell.

TEMPLE: She's probably in the cabin.

TEMPLE and STEVE stroll across the deck.

STEVE: You'd have thought she'd have heard us by now.

TEMPLE: Well, here's the cabin … (*Opening the door*) And it doesn't look as if she's in here!

STEVE: No.

A moment.

TEMPLE: It's rather attractive, isn't it?

123

STEVE: Yes, it is rather. I adore those cushions.

TEMPLE: Let's have a look round the other side.

TEMPLE and STEVE leave the cabin, closing the door. They stroll across the deck.

STEVE: (*Suddenly*) Paul! Listen!

TEMPLE: What is it?

DIANA MAXWELL is calling to them from the other side of the yacht. She is in the sea – having been for a swim.

DIANA: (*From a distance, in the water*) Hello! Hello, Mr Temple!

TEMPLE: That's Miss Maxwell!

STEVE: (*Away from TEMPLE*) She's over here, Paul! She's in the sea!

TEMPLE and STEVE cross the deck.

DIANA: (*Much nearer, calling up to the TEMPLES*) Hello!

TEMPLE: (*Calling down to DIANA*) We wondered where you'd got to!

DIANA: (*Brightly, calling up to the TEMPLES*) I've been for a swim. Sorry to have kept you waiting!

TEMPLE: (*Calling down*) That's all right. We've only just arrived.

DIANA: (*Gasping for breath*) I very nearly got lost. I went for miles. I'll be with you in a minute!

DIANA swims to the rope ladder.

STEVE: (*Quietly*) She seems rather bright this morning.

TEMPLE: That's what I thought.

STEVE: She's certainly different from what she was last night.

DIANA is dragging herself out of the water and on to the rope ladder.

TEMPLE: She's coming up.

STEVE: Yes.

TEMPLE: (*Calling down to DIANA*) I hope you're better on that thing than I am.

DIANA: (*Laughing*) Why – did you slip?

TEMPLE: Very nearly.

DIANA: (*Climbing the ladder*) I'm used to it!

TEMPLE: Give me your hand when you get to the top.

DIANA: (*Still climbing*) I'm all right.

As soon as DIANA speaks there is from the distant background, the sound of a shot.

DIANA: (*Crying out with pain*) Oh!

STEVE: (*Astonished*) Paul! Paul, what was that?

TEMPLE: (*Quickly, tensely*) Good Lord, she's been shot!

STEVE: Shot!!!!

TEMPLE: (*Shouting down to DIANA*) Hang on, Miss Maxwell! Whatever you do don't let go of the ladder.

DIANA: (*Gasping in obvious pain*) Oh! Oh …

TEMPLE: (*Climbing over the side*) Don't let go!

STEVE: (*A cry of alarm*) She's falling!!!! Paul, she's falling!!!!

DIANA falls from the ladder back into the sea.

TEMPLE: (*Quickly, desperately*) Hold my coat!

STEVE: (*Alarmed*) Paul, what are you going to do?

TEMPLE: Don't argue, darling – get hold of it!

STEVE: Paul, be careful!!!!

TEMPLE climbs over the side and jumps into the sea.

FADE UP the sound of the sea and of DIANA struggling in the water. She is in great pain and during the scene with TEMPLE completely loses consciousness. TEMPLE swims to her side.

TEMPLE: Turn over on your back! Try and turn over on your back!

DIANA: I can't … It's no use … I can't … I can't move my legs.

TEMPLE: Now it's all right. Don't panic … Just relax …
It's all right, I've got you.

DIANA: (*Desperately*) I can't … I can't move my legs.
There's something the matter with them.

TEMPLE: (*Rather frightened*) Now look, do as I tell you.
Don't try and swim!

DIANA: (*Desperately fighting against the water*) I've got
to! If I don't swim, I'll go under!

TEMPLE: Miss Maxwell, turn over on your back! You'll
never make it! You'll never get back to the boat
like that!

DIANA: (*In a panic, near hysteria*) You've got hold of
my arm! Let me go! Leave me alone!

TEMPLE: Miss Maxwell, please! If I don't hold you, you'll
sink! Now get over on your back!

DIANA: (*Fighting wildly*) No! No! I've got to get back to
the ladder. If I don't get hold of the ladder, I'll
… (*Desperately frightened*) I can't move my
legs! I can't move my legs!!!! What's happened?
Oh … Oh …

STEVE: (*Shouting from the yacht*) Paul, here's the
lifebelt. Watch out!

STEVE throws the lifebelt, and we hear it hitting the water.

TEMPLE: Now give me your arm! (*Sharply*) Miss
Maxwell, do as I tell you!

*DIANA is fighting for breath, struggling and obviously in
pain.*

DIANA: What was that? What … was ... that … that …
hit … the … water just now?

TEMPLE: It's a lifebelt! (*Stretching*) Hold on … Hold on,
I've … nearly … got ... it …

DIANA: (*Dazed*) A lifebelt?

TEMPLE: (*Suddenly*) I've got it! Now turn over … That's
it!

DIANA:	(*Slowly*) I felt something hit the water ... What was it?
TEMPLE:	It's all right ... Don't talk!
DIANA:	(*Frightened*) I can't see ... I just can't see anything. It's dark! Why is it dark? I can't see any more ... (*Desperately*) I can't see anything! I can't see ... (*She loses consciousness*)

TEMPLE makes a desperate attempt to swim with DIANA towards the yacht. The sound of an approaching motor launch is heard.

STEVE:	(*Calling from the yacht*) There's a boat coming along, Paul! Hold on! Hold on, darling!

FADE UP the noise of TEMPLE struggling in the water.

Quick FADE UP the sound of the approaching motor launch.

FADE UP of music.

FADE DOWN of music.

A door opens and closes.

MORGAN:	Is she still unconscious?
TEMPLE:	Yes, and it looks as if she's going to be – for some time.
MORGAN:	What does the doctor think?
TEMPLE:	He hasn't said a great deal, but I think he's fairly hopeful. I gather Lord Westerby wants to move her?
MORGAN:	Yes, but the doctor won't hear of it. He insists that she stays here at the hospital. (*A note of surprise*) I thought the old boy was pretty cut up, Temple.
TEMPLE:	You mean Westerby? Yes, I thought so too.

MORGAN: As a matter of fact, it affected him more than I expected.

TEMPLE: He's obviously very fond of his niece – unless he's putting on an act for our benefit. By the way, he doesn't know that we had an appointment with her. He simply thinks that Steve and I went on a fishing trip and heard the shot.

MORGAN: That's all right, I shan't mention it. Where do you think that shot was fired from, Temple? From the shore?

TEMPLE: It could have been fired from the shore. On the other hand, it might easily have been fired from one of the boats. The bay was pretty full. I gather it always is at that time of the morning. (*Suddenly*) By the way, have you had a word with Westerby?

MORGAN: You mean about what Doyle told us – about Westerby's visit to Baxter?

TEMPLE: Yes.

MORGAN: No, I'm afraid I haven't. I did ask him, quite casually, whether he knew a man called Walters. He said that he didn't.

TEMPLE: M'm. It rather looks as if he's going to deny the story.

MORGAN: Looks like it.

TEMPLE: He's offered to drive me back to the village. I'll have a word with him if you like.

MORGAN: It might be quite a good idea; then I can check back on him later.

TEMPLE: Yes.

A door opens.

MORGAN: Here he is …

128

TEMPLE: (*Aside*) Let me know as soon as Miss
               Maxwell comes round …

MORGAN: Yes, of course. (*Departing*) I'll contact you
               later.

TEMPLE: Right!

WESTERBY: (*In the background*) Thank you, Doctor. I'm
               sure you'll do everything you possibly can.
               (*He joins TEMPLE*) Ah, so here you are,
               Temple! I've sent for the car. It'll be along
               in a few moments.

TEMPLE: Good.

WESTERBY: At the risk of sounding the most
               unmitigated bore, I want to thank you again
               for what you've done. I'm most terribly
               grateful to you.

TEMPLE: Nonsense!

WESTERBY: No, but I am! Diana means a great deal to
               me, Temple. (*Suddenly*) I'd just like to get
               my hands on the swine who was responsible
               for that!

TEMPLE: (*Quietly*) Lord Westerby, there's something
               I want to ask you. Do you mind if we sit
               down for a moment?

WESTERBY: No. No, of course not.

TEMPLE and WESTERBY sit.

TEMPLE: (*Taking out his cigarette case*) Will you
               have a cigarette?

WESTERBY: Er – no, I won't, not just at the moment,
               thank you.

TEMPLE lights his cigarette.

TEMPLE: I believe the Inspector spoke to you about a
               man called Walters?

WESTERBY: Yes, as a matter of fact, he did! He asked
               me if I knew the fellow. I told him I didn't.

TEMPLE:	Was that the truth?
WESTERBY:	(*Taken aback*) What do you mean?
TEMPLE:	Lord Westerby, we have reason to believe that the day before the Baxter boys disappeared you visited Mr Baxter with a man called Carl Walters.
WESTERBY:	(*Pleasantly*) Obviously you've been misinformed. In the first place I don't know anyone called Walters and in the second place I was not in the habit of visiting Mr Baxter.
TEMPLE:	(*A moment*) I see.
WESTERBY:	(*Smiling*) Is that all you wanted to speak to me about?
TEMPLE:	Yes.
WESTERBY:	Well, I'm sorry not to have been more helpful. (*Suddenly*) Ah, here's the doctor!

DR STUART arrives. He is faintly excited.

STUART:	Excuse me, but I thought you might like to know that Miss Maxwell has regained consciousness.
WESTERBY:	(*Delighted*) Oh, good! Splendid!

A moment.

STUART:	(*Slowly*) She's asking for Mr Temple ...

FADE UP of music.

END OF EPISODE FOUR

EPISODE FIVE

PRESENTING CARL
WALTERS

FADE IN of TEMPLE.

TEMPLE: I believe the Inspector spoke to you about a man called Walters?

WESTERBY: Yes, as a matter of fact, he did! He asked me if I knew the fellow. I told him I didn't.

TEMPLE: Was that the truth?

WESTERBY: (*Taken aback*) What do you mean?

TEMPLE: Lord Westerby, we have reason to believe that the day before the Baxter boys disappeared you visited Mr Baxter with a man called Carl Walters.

WESTERBY: (*Pleasantly*) Obviously you've been misinformed. In the first place I don't know anyone called Walters and in the second place I was not in the habit of visiting Mr Baxter.

TEMPLE: (*A moment*) I see.

WESTERBY: (Smiling) Is that all you wanted to speak to me about?

TEMPLE: Yes.

WESTERBY: Well, I'm sorry not to have been more helpful. (*Suddenly*) Ah, here's the doctor!

DR STUART arrives. He is faintly excited.

STUART: Excuse me, but I thought you might like to know that Miss Maxwell has regained consciousness.

WESTERBY: (*Delighted*) Oh, good! Splendid!

A moment.

STUART: (*Slowly*) She's asking for Mr Temple ...

WESTERBY: (*Surprised*) Mr Temple?

STUART: Yes. (*To TEMPLE*) Will you come this way?

TEMPLE: Thank you.

WESTERBY: (*Stopping STUART*) Oh, Dr Stuart! (*Anxiously*) Is she going to be all right?

STUART: Aye, but she had a narrow squeak and no mistake. If the bullet had been just a wee bit … Ah, well it wasn't, so there's no point in looking on the black side. Just at the moment she's suffering from shock more than anything else.

WESTERBY: Well – perhaps you'll be kind enough to tell my niece that I'm still here, Temple. Just in case she'd like to see me.

TEMPLE: Yes, of course.

TEMPLE and DR STUART walk down the corridor.

A door opens.

STUART: Now don't excite the lassie. You understand? She's in no condition to be excited.

TEMPLE: (*Smiling*) I understand, Doctor.

Door closes.

Pause.

DIANA: (*Softly; from her bed*) Is … that … Mr Temple?

TEMPLE crosses to the bed.

TEMPLE: (*Quietly*) Yes. Are you feeling any better?

DIANA: (*Obviously still under an emotional strain*) Yes, I feel much better now, thank you.

TEMPLE: Well, just you rest. Take it easy for a few days. There's nothing for you to worry about.

DIANA: Is my uncle still here?

TEMPLE: Yes, as a matter of fact he's just outside. He's going to run me back into the village.

DIANA: He knows of course … about … what … happened?

TEMPLE: He knows that you were swimming and that you were shot. He doesn't know that I had an appointment to see you – unless of course you've told him.

DIANA: No. No, I ... haven't.

A moment.

TEMPLE: Miss Maxwell, have you any idea who fired that shot?

DIANA: (*Tensely*) No.

TEMPLE: (*A little surprised*) But you must have some idea?

DIANA: (*Still tense*) No. No, I don't know. I don't know who fired the shot!

TEMPLE: Was it Peter Malo?

DIANA: I told you – I don't know!

A tiny pause.

TEMPLE: Why did you make that appointment to see me?

DIANA: Mr Temple, please don't ask me that! Please!

TEMPLE: I'm afraid I've got to ask you, Miss Maxwell. Why did you want to see me?

DIANA: (*Nervous: hesitant*) There was something I wanted to explain to you. Something that I thought perhaps you ought to know ...

TEMPLE: Well?

DIANA: (*Tensely*) It's no use. It's too late now. Mr Temple, please don't think me rude but – would you leave me alone. I ... can't bear to talk about things. I'm too upset ... too distressed ...

TEMPLE: (*Gently: friendly manner*) Miss Maxwell, I don't want to upset you, but I've got a feeling that you've had a pretty rotten time just lately and that what happened this morning wasn't entirely a surprise to you. But do, please, listen to what I'm saying. Several days ago, when you

135

telephoned my flat – Oh, I know that you did telephone me – you'd made up your mind to tell me the truth about this affair. Suddenly, and I rather suspect at the last moment, you were persuaded to change your mind. Exactly the same thing happened this morning.

DIANA: (*Quickly*) No. No, it didn't! It didn't! I changed my mind last night after I'd spoken to you. I knew then that I'd … (*Desperately*) Oh, what's the use! You don't understand! You just don't understand!

A pause.

TEMPLE: Well, if you've changed your mind, why did you tell the Doctor that you wanted to see me?

DIANA: I just wanted you to know … I'm terribly grateful.

TEMPLE: Because I fished you out of the water?

DIANA: Yes.

TEMPLE: That was nothing. (*Turning: resigned*) Well, if you change your mind again, I hope you'll get in touch with me.

DIANA starts to cry; she is obviously both distressed and overwrought.

The door opens.

STUART: Hello? Hello, what's all this? (*To TEMPLE*) Now I told you not to excite the patient, Mr Temple.

DIANA: It's all right, Doctor! It's nothing, I'll try and pull … myself … together. Please forgive me, Mr Temple, I didn't mean to give way like this.

DIANA stops crying.

TEMPLE: Goodbye, Miss Maxwell. Remember what I've told you.

136

STUART:	You can tell Lord Westerby he can come back this afternoon and see Miss Maxwell – late this afternoon. Not before four o'clock.
TEMPLE:	All right, Doctor.

The door opens and closes.

A pause.

WESTERBY:	(*Anxiously*) How is she?
TEMPLE:	She's a little upset at the moment, but she'll be all right. The Doctor says you can see her this afternoon but not before four o'clock.
WESTERBY:	Oh, good. (*Pleasantly*) Why did she want to see you, Temple – was it anything important?
TEMPLE:	Apparently, she's under the impression that I saved her life.
WESTERBY:	But you did!
TEMPLE:	She wanted to thank me.
WESTERBY:	Oh, I see.
TEMPLE:	You thought perhaps she might have told me something?
WESTERBY:	Yes, I was hoping she'd give you some idea who fired the shot.
TEMPLE:	Unfortunately, she didn't. (*A moment*) Lord Westerby, I've been meaning to ask you, did the Inspector ever ask you anything about a person called Curzon?
WESTERBY:	Yes, he did as a matter of fact. He asked me if I know anyone called Curzon. I told him I didn't.
TEMPLE:	I see.

WESTERBY:	When I asked him why he seemed rather mysterious. Had it anything to do with the Baxter affair?
TEMPLE:	Yes, it has. (*Suddenly*) Hello, here's your secretary!
WESTERBY:	Ah, that means the car's arrived!
MALO:	Good morning, sir. Good morning, Mr Temple.
TEMPLE:	Good morning.
MALO:	How is Miss Maxwell, sir?
WESTERBY:	She seems a little better, Peter – but unfortunately, I haven't seen her. However, Mr Temple has, and I gather there's every reason to be hopeful.

A moment.

MALO:	(*Quietly*) That's good news, sir.
WESTERBY:	Is the car ready?
MALO:	Yes, sir. But I thought perhaps you'd like to see this letter, in view of your engagement this evening.
WESTERBY:	Oh! (*He takes the envelope and extracts a letter*) When did this arrive?
MALO:	By the second post.
WESTERBY:	Excuse me, Temple. (*He reads the letter: thoughtfully*) M'm. Have you replied?
MALO:	Yes. I said you'd be there.
WESTERBY:	(*A sigh*) I suppose there's no alternative. (*To TEMPLE: pleasantly*) Temple, I'm most terribly sorry but it looks as if I shall have to cancel our engagement for this evening, unfortunately I've got to go up to Town. I've a board meeting first thing tomorrow morning.

TEMPLE: That's all right. (*Smiling*) Business before pleasure …

WESTERBY: Unfortunately. (*Suddenly*) Well – shall we go? I'll drop you at the Inn.

FADE UP of music.

FADE DOWN of music.

TEMPLE enters the Inn: there's background noise of the Hall of the Inn.

1st MAN: Can I have my key, please?

PORTER: What number?

1st MAN: Room 9.

PORTER: (*After a moment*) The key doesn't appear to be here. It's probably in the door – if it isn't the chambermaid'll let you in. (*Brightly*) Good morning, sir!

TEMPLE: Good morning. Is my wife upstairs?

PORTER: No, Mr Temple, she's in the dining-room.

TEMPLE: Thank you.

TEMPLE passes into the dining-room.

There is a slight background of chatter.

TEMPLE: Good morning, Mrs Temple!

STEVE: Oh, hello, darling!

TEMPLE: What's that you're eating?

STEVE: If only I knew! Ah, sweet mystery of life!

TEMPLE laughs.

STEVE: (*Seriously*) How's Miss Maxwell?

TEMPLE: Well, she's certainly much better than she was. I think she'll get over it all right.

STEVE: Did you see her?

TEMPLE: Yes, as a matter of fact I had a talk with her.

STEVE: (*Anxiously*) What did she say?

TEMPLE: (*After a moment*) She's changed her mind.

STEVE: (*Surprised*) What do you mean – changed her mind?

TEMPLE: She won't talk.

STEVE: You mean she's frightened – because of what happened this morning?

TEMPLE: (*Faintly depressed: studying the menu*) It looks like it. (*Suddenly*) When you've had lunch, darling, I want you to pack. We're going back to Town on the 3.40.

STEVE: (*Curious*) Has anything happened?

TEMPLE: Yes. I want to have a talk with Sir Graham: telephone him and ask him to meet me at the flat any time after seven.

STEVE: Yes, all right. (*A sudden thought*) But I thought we had a date tonight with Lord Westerby?

TEMPLE: He's cancelled it, he's apparently got a business appointment.

STEVE: In Town?

TEMPLE: Yes.

STEVE: Is he going up on the 3.40?

TEMPLE: I don't know. As soon as I've had lunch I'm going to the harbour. I want to see Doyle. Telephone Sir Graham and then get in touch with Morgan.

STEVE: What do you want me to tell Morgan?

TEMPLE: Tell him we're going back to Town. Oh, and tell him about Westerby.

STEVE: (*Watching TEMPLE*) Yes, all right, darling. You look rather depressed, Paul!

TEMPLE: I feel it.

STEVE: Why? What's happened?

TEMPLE: Oh – I had a hunch, and it just hasn't turned out like I expected.

WAITRESS: Good morning, sir.

140

TEMPLE:	(*Looking up*) Oh – good morning!
WAITRESS:	What would you like, sir?
TEMPLE:	Well, I should like a steak and chips.
WAITRESS:	(*Droll*) Yes, I expect you would. What's it to be – Cod?

FADE UP music.

FADE DOWN music.
FADE UP background noises of the Harbour.

TEMPLE:	Excuse me. Have you any idea where I could find Tom Doyle?
OLD MAN:	Yes, he's at the end of the jetty. You'll have to be quick – he's just shoving off! (*Suddenly*) Wait a minute! (*He cups his hands and calls across to the jetty*) Tom! Tom Doyle!
DOYLE:	(*From the background; calling back*) What is it?
OLD MAN:	(*Calling again*) Hold on a bit! There's someone wants to see you!
TEMPLE:	Thanks very much!
OLD MAN:	That's all right, sir.

FADE UP of Harbour background.
Slight background of the sea.
TEMPLE reaches the end of the jetty and talks down to TOM DOYLE.

TEMPLE:	Hello, Tom!
DOYLE:	(*Surprised*) Oh, hello, Mr Temple! I wondered what old George was shouting about.
TEMPLE:	I'm going back to London this afternoon. I wanted to have a word with you before I left.
DOYLE:	Sure.

TEMPLE: (*Sitting on the end of the jetty*) Tom, you remember the night you went to Mr Baxter's – the night he asked you to take care of the boys?

DOYLE: (*After a moment; a shade worried*) Yes.

TEMPLE: You told the Inspector that when you arrived at the cottage you saw Lord Westerby and a man called Carl Walters. You said they were talking to Mr Baxter. Is that right?

DOYLE: Yes, sir. (*Hesitates*) That's – what – I – told the Inspector, sir.

TEMPLE: (*Faintly surprised*) Well, it's true, isn't it?

DOYLE: Yes, sir. (*A moment*) I think so, sir.

TEMPLE: What do you mean – you think so?

DOYLE: (*A little uncertain*) Well, I think it was Lord Westerby, sir.

TEMPLE: You think it was Lord Westerby! But when you made your statement, you seemed pretty sure it was Westerby. You said he spoke to you.

DOYLE: I ... might have been mistaken.

TEMPLE: How could you be mistaken? You know Lord Westerby ...

DOYLE: Yes, sir – but now I come to think – I believe it was the other man that spoke to me.

TEMPLE: Walters?

DOYLE: Yes.

TEMPLE: But you said Walters was a stranger: you said you'd never seen him before. Why should he speak to you?

DOYLE: (*A shade petulant*) Well, why shouldn't he? I nodded so he said – "Good evening!" – that's all.

TEMPLE: I see. So when you arrived at the cottage you saw Mr Baxter, this man called Walters and another man you think was Lord Westerby.

DOYLE: Yes, sir.

142

TEMPLE: But you're not really sure it was his Lordship?

DOYLE: (*Quietly*) No, sir.

TEMPLE: In fact, the more you think about it the more you realise that it might not have been Lord Westerby after all?

DOYLE: (*Very subdued*) Yes, sir.

A tiny pause.

TEMPLE: Tom, you've already made a statement in which you said you saw and spoke to Lord Westerby.

DOYLE: (*Suddenly: slightly surly and shame-faced*) Well, I can change my mind, can't I?

TEMPLE: You appear to have done so – rather suddenly too, if I may say so!

DOYLE: What do you mean? What are you getting at?

TEMPLE: Tell me, just as a matter of curiosity, have you seen Lord Westerby since you made that statement?

DOYLE: (*Quickly: an immediate denial*) No! No, I haven't!

TEMPLE: (*Watching Tom*) You seem pretty definite on that point anyway.

DOYLE: I know what you're thinking! You think I've been bribed, don't you? Well, I haven't! T'is the truth I haven't!

TEMPLE: (*Quietly*) Tom I don't think you've really considered the seriousness of the situation. Suppose the police decide that you didn't see Lord Westerby, that you were in fact mistaken.

DOYLE: Well?

TEMPLE: They might decide that you were mistaken about quite a lot of things. (*With authority*) They might decide for instance that the whole of your statement was pure fabrication, a tissue of lies from beginning to end!

143

DOYLE: (*Quietly; afraid*) What do you mean?

TEMPLE: (*Still with authority*) Supposing they believe you didn't see Lord Westerby for the simple reason that you didn't go to the cottage.

DOYLE: (*A note of desperation*) But I did go to the cottage! I saw Baxter! He told me about the boys!

TEMPLE: Yes, but supposing they don't believe that? Supposing they say, he lied about one thing so obviously he'll lie about another.

DOYLE: (*Shaken*) Mr Temple, you don't believe that, do you? You know I went to the cottage! You know I saw Baxter!

TEMPLE: (*Quietly: watching TOM*) I also know that you saw Lord Westerby, didn't you, Tom?

DOYLE: (*After a pause: frightened and a shade surly*) No. No, I didn't. It wasn't his Lordship. I was mistaken.

DOYLE puts the oars into the water, ready to leave the jetty.

DOYLE: I've got to go. I've got a lot to do this afternoon.

DOYLE starts to manipulate the oars into position.

DOYLE: I've got to shove off.

TEMPLE: All right. (*Quietly*) But just between friends, Tom – a word of warning.

DOYLE: (*Pausing*) Well?

TEMPLE: Don't get out of your depth.

FADE UP of music.

FADE DOWN of music.

PORTER: Your luggage is down, sir.

TEMPLE: Oh, thank you. (*Tipping him*) Here we are!

PORTER: Oh, thank you very much, sir!

STEVE: Has the car arrived, darling?

144

PORTER: (*Smiling*) Yes, I've just put your cases in –
               you're all ready for the station.
STEVE: Oh!
TEMPLE: Goodbye!

The PORTER opens the door.

PORTER: Goodbye, sir. Pleasant trip, sir. Goodbye,
               madam.
STEVE: Goodbye!

MORGAN arrives. He is out of breath.

MORGAN: Oh – just in time! I thought I'd missed you.
TEMPLE: (*Surprised*) Why, hello, Inspector!
STEVE: My word, you have been running!
MORGAN: Temple, I wonder if you'd be good enough
               to take this back to Town for me and hand it
               over to Sir Graham?
TEMPLE: Yes, certainly. (*A moment*) What is it – a
               diary?
MORGAN: Yes. Or rather the remains of one. It's been
               pretty badly burnt, I'm afraid. (*Quietly*) It
               was in the safe.
STEVE: You mean at the cottage?
TEMPLE: At Baxter's?
MORGAN: Yes.
TEMPLE: Was there anything else in the safe?
MORGAN: Not a thing.
TEMPLE: (*Quietly*) Have you been through this?
MORGAN: Yes. There's a lot of calculations and
               figures – it doesn't make sense. Not to me at
               any rate.
TEMPLE: (*Thoughtfully*) Do you mind if I have a look
               at it?
MORGAN: No, of course not. You can study it on the
               train. I hope you'll make more sense out of
               it than I did.

145

TEMPLE:	(*Thoughtfully*) It looks to me as if it's in code.
MORGAN:	That's what I thought. Anyway, that's not my department – thank the Lord! Let Browning have a crack at it, he's the expert! Goodbye, Mrs Temple!
STEVE:	Goodbye, Inspector!
MORGAN:	(*To TEMPLE*) I've got your number. I'll give you a ring if anything develops.
TEMPLE:	Yes. (*Suddenly*) Oh, Steve told you about Westerby?
MORGAN:	Yes. If he goes up to Town by train, I'll have a man on his tail the moment he arrives.
TEMPLE:	Good. Don't worry, I'll see Sir Graham gets this all right.
MORGAN:	Thank you. Au-revoir!
TEMPLE:	Au-revoir, Inspector!

FADE UP of music.

FADE DOWN of music.
FADE UP of a train steaming into a station.
The sound of carriage doors opening and closing is heard.
Background sounds of an extremely busy railway terminal.

TEMPLE:	By Timothy, I doubt very much whether we shall get a taxi, Steve.
STEVE:	Looks pretty hopeless, doesn't it? I think we'd better get the underground, darling.
TEMPLE:	Yes, I think so. Can you manage that case?
STEVE:	Yes, of course!

FADE UP station background noises.
FADE AWAY and FADE UP noises of the entrance hall of an Underground Station.
People are queuing for tickets: TEMPLE is in the queue.

146

We hear the voices of various people asking for tickets and the sound of the machine issuing tickets and delivering change.

TEMPLE: Two – Green Park, please.

The sound of tickets and change being delivered.

TEMPLE: Thank you.

KENZELL: Leicester Square.

KENZELL is a foreigner: about thirty-five.

2nd MAN: Where?

KENZELL: (*Impatiently*) Leicester Square!

The sound of the ticket machine.

WOMAN: Two – Oxford circus.

Ticket machine.

FADE SCENE.

FADE UP the sound of the electric train pulling into the station: doors open: crowds emerge on to the platform.
People crowd into the train.
Slight pause.

3rd MAN: (*Railway Official: shouting: slight cockney accent*) Hurry along there! Hurry along, please! Stand clear of the doors! Stand clear!

The sound of doors closing.
The train commences to move away from the platform and gathers speed.
FADE.

FADE UP the sound of the train.
TEMPLE and STEVE are standing in the crowded train.

STEVE: (*Faintly exhausted*) Gosh, what a crowd!

TEMPLE: Talk about the rush hour!

STEVE: This is it! (*Swaying slightly*) Whoa!

147

TEMPLE:	(*Laughing*) You'd better hang on to this strap, darling!
STEVE:	I'd better hang on to something!

A moment.

STEVE:	It's the next station, isn't it?
TEMPLE:	Yes.

A pause.

The train suddenly slows down and several people over-balance and bump into each other.

KENZELL falls against TEMPLE.

KENZELL:	Oh! I'm terribly sorry!
TEMPLE:	(*Pleasantly: amused*) That's quite all right.
KENZELL:	Did I hurt you?
TEMPLE:	No, not at all.
KENZELL:	You're quite sure?
TEMPLE:	Yes, of course! (*Trying to move*) But if you could just leave go of my arm for a moment so that ...
KENZELL:	Oh! I beg your pardon! I'm so sorry!
TEMPLE:	(*Laughing*) That's all right.

The train slows down.

STEVE:	Here we are, Paul. Get hold of the case.
TEMPLE:	You get to the door, Steve. I can manage the cases.
KENZELL:	Please – let me move this one for you.
TEMPLE:	(*Struggling to turn round*) Oh, thank you!

The train pulls up at the station.

Doors open: people crowd out of the train on to the platform.

TEMPLE:	(*Struggling through the door*) Are you all right?
STEVE:	(*Struggling*) Yes ... Yes, carry on!

TEMPLE and STEVE emerge on to the platform.

TEMPLE:	By Timothy!

STEVE: (*Laughing*) Look at your hat!

TEMPLE: Look at yours, darling!

STEVE: (*Hand to hat*) Oh, don't!

4th MAN: (*In the near background*) Hurry along, please! Hurry along, there!

STEVE: Where's the exit?

TEMPLE: It's at the other end of the platform. Come along, Steve! (*Suddenly: stopping*) Oh!

STEVE: What's the matter?

TEMPLE: (*Searching his pockets*) That's funny!

STEVE: What is it?

TEMPLE: (*Slowly: still searching*) That's funny! I've lost that diary …

STEVE: You had it on the train – you were looking at it in the dining car.

TEMPLE: Yes, I know. It was in this pocket. (*Slowly*) That's very odd. I know it was in this pocket because … (*Suddenly*) By Timothy, I've had my pocket picked! (*Quickly*) Steve, go on to the flat! (*Dashing back to the train*) I'll see you later.

STEVE: (*Bewildered: calling to TEMPLE*) Where are you going?

TEMPLE: (*Calling back to STEVE*) I'll see you later, darling!

STEVE: (*Alarmed*) Paul, you can't get on the train!!!! Paul!!!!

The doors of the train are closing.

4th MAN: (*Shouting to TEMPLE*) Stand clear, there! Stand clear!!!! Look out!!!

The doors bang.

TEMPLE is on the train: he is out of breath.

5th MAN: I say, by George, that's cutting it fine, old boy!

TEMPLE: (*Trying to regain his breath*) Yes …

FADE UP on the train.

FADE Scene.

FADE UP of the train arriving at the next station.
The door opens: people crowd out of the train.
A pause.
FADE UP the sound of an escalator.
TEMPLE races up the escalator.

TEMPLE: (*Climbing up the escalator*) Excuse me ... I
                beg your pardon ... Thank you ... Excuse
                me ... I beg your pardon ... (*He reaches the
                top of the staircase and catches KENZELL
                by the arm*) Ah, just a moment, my light-
                fingered friend!

KENZELL: (*Turning: surprised*) Oh! Hello. I ...
                thought you got off at the other station?

TEMPLE: I did. I changed my mind though and got
                back on the train again. Come over here, I
                want to have a talk to you.

People are filing past them.

KENZELL: Well – what is it? What do you want?

TEMPLE: Come over here!

KENZELL: (*Nervously*) I'm in a hurry, I can't stop!

TEMPLE: (*With authority*) Come over here!

*TEMPLE and KENZELL move away from the top of the
escalator.*

*FADE the noise of the escalator and people to near
background.*

KENZELL: Please leave go of my arm!

TEMPLE: (*Quietly*) I want that diary.

KENZELL: I ... don't know what you're talking about!

TEMPLE: You know what I'm talking about all right –
                I want that diary.

KENZELL: (*Indignantly*) Diary? What do you mean –
                diary?

TEMPLE:	Listen, my friend. When you bumped up against me in the train you went through my pocket and took the diary. Now don't let's waste any more time ...
KENZELL:	(*Frightened: tensely*) I haven't got the diary! I don't know what you're talking about! Now please leave me alone!
TEMPLE:	(*A note of anger*) You heard what I said – give me that diary!
KENZELL:	I haven't got it! (*Trying to release himself from TEMPLE's grasp*) If ... you ... don't ... leave ... me ... alone ... I ... shall ... call ... the police.
TEMPLE:	Nonsense – you won't send for the police and you know it! (*Extremely angry: tough*) Now I'm going to give you five seconds and if you don't produce the diary, I shall pick you up by the seat of the pants and throw you head-first down the escalator!
KENZELL:	You wouldn't have the impertinence to do a thing like that!
TEMPLE:	(*Interrupting KENZELL: determined*) Wouldn't I, my friend, you'd be surprised! (*Quietly*) Now give me that diary.
KENZELL:	I ... haven't ... got ... it.
TEMPLE:	All right. (*Taking a firm grip of KENZELL*) You've asked for it! One – two – three – four – fi ...
KENZELL:	No. No, don't! Leave me alone! (*Struggling*) All right, all right ... Here it is!
TEMPLE:	(*Taking the diary*) That's better. (*A moment*) Now why did you take this? (*Angry*) Why did you take it?

151

KENZELL: (*Frightened*) A friend of mine wanted it. He
              told me to pick you up at the station and …
              take … it … from … you.

TEMPLE: Do you know why he wanted it?

KENZELL: (*Quickly: with sincerity*) No. No, I haven't
              the slightest idea. That's the truth, Mr
              Temple. I swear to you it's the truth.

TEMPLE: What do they call this friend of yours? (*A
              pause*) Well?

KENZELL: His name's … Walters.

TEMPLE: Carl Walters?

KENZELL: (*After a moment*) Yes.

FADE UP of music.

FADE DOWN of music.
The sound of coffee being poured.

FORBES: (*Holding out his cup*) Temple, you say this
              fellow was a foreigner – about thirty-three
              or four?

TEMPLE: Yes. I should say he's probably a German –
              or Austrian.

FORBES: Was he good-looking?

STEVE: Quite.

TEMPLE: He was well-dressed: short, about five-foot
              six. He'd got rather a lot of hair.

STEVE: Yes, and quite a lot of obnoxious brilliantine
              to go with it.

FORBES: (*Thoughtfully*) I thought so. It sounds to me
              like Lou Kenzell. We'll pick him up
              tomorrow and have a talk to him.

STEVE: Don't you think it might be quite a good
              idea, Sir Graham, if you picked up Mr
              Walters instead?

152

FORBES: (*Amused*) On what charge, Steve? We've got to be careful with Walters, he's a pretty shrewd bird.

TEMPLE: Doyle said he has an American accent – is he an American?

FORBES: No, but he's lived in the States for many years and I think he rather fancies himself as a sort of Chicago Big Shot.

TEMPLE: Isn't that a little out of date?

FORBES: Not for Walters it isn't.

STEVE: Sugar?

FORBES: Oh, thank you. (*He helps himself to sugar*) You know, Temple, I think of all the cases we've worked on, this Curzon case is in many ways the most curious. First of all, it started with the disappearance of two boys – the Baxter boys – and then suddenly, quite out of the blue, the Baxter boys turned up. Now the point, so far as I see it, is this: we've either got to believe Doyle's story about the boys or disbelieve it. Personally, in spite of what Lord Westerby says, I believe Doyle. I think that Doyle went to the cottage – I think he saw Westerby and Carl Walters talking to Baxter and I think Baxter did, quite genuinely, arrange with Doyle for the boys to go into hiding.

TEMPLE: I agree. I don't think there's any doubt on that point.

FORBES: Well, now, Michael Baxter states that one night he heard his Father having a row with someone – a pretty first-class row too, according to all accounts. During this row the name of Curzon was repeatedly mentioned. Now, to my way of thinking, it's a pretty safe assumption that

153

whatever is going on at Dulworth Bay – or whatever is behind the murder of Philip Baxter and the kidnapping of the Draper boy – the person responsible is not Westerby or Carl Walters but this third and unknown personality – Curzon.

TEMPLE: But why are you so certain that Westerby isn't Curzon, or Carl Walters for that matter? You know from past experiences, Sir Graham, that more often than not the outsider romps home in a case of this kind.

FORBES: (*Bluntly*) Well, do you think Lord Westerby or Carl Walters is Curzon?

TEMPLE: I've never met Walters so until I do I shouldn't really express an opinion. But I'm quite certain that the person behind this affair – call them Curzon if you like – is either Lord Westerby, Carl Walters, Tom Doyle, Peter Malo, Miss Maxwell or Dr Stuart. And if I had to put my money on anybody, I should …

FORBES: Yes?

TEMPLE: (*Changing his mind: thoughtfully*) I should give the whole matter very careful consideration.

STEVE: Well, personally, I think the first thing we ought to do, darling, is meet Mr Walters.

FORBES: That shouldn't be difficult. You'll find him almost every night at the Canford Hall.

TEMPLE: Canford Hall?

STEVE: What's that?

FORBES: It's a roller-skating rink, not far from Shepherds Bush.

TEMPLE: Does Walters own it?

FORBES: I'm told he's got a very big share in it, but that's not the reason he frequents the place. He's a first-class skater.

TEMPLE: Oh, I see. Well, I'm afraid roller skating isn't exactly my cup of tea.

FORBES: (*Laughing*) Nor mine…

STEVE: No, but it's mine, darling. Don't you think it would be rather fun if I went along and picked up Mr Walters?

TEMPLE: I certainly don't! According to all accounts Walters is a pretty tough egg – we're taking no chances.

FORBES: (*Thoughtfully*) I don't know. I'm not so sure that it isn't a good idea. I shouldn't be surprised if Steve wouldn't get a great deal more out of Walters than you or I, Temple. For one thing there's no earthly reason why he should recognise her and secondly – well – he's more likely to talk to a woman.

TEMPLE: And what happens when he stops talking?

STEVE: Don't be silly, darling. I can take care of myself.

TEMPLE: Where have I heard that one before? (*Shaking his head*) It's too risky, Steve. (*Suddenly*) By the way, Sir Graham, what happened about that girl – the one that you picked out of the river?

FORBES: Lita Ronson? Well, it still looks like suicide, but – I don't know, Temple. When we searched her flat, we found a letter from Carl Walters …

TEMPLE: (*Nodding*) So you said …

FORBES: It was rather a friendly sort of letter – to say the least. We questioned him about it but I'm afraid we didn't get anywhere.

TEMPLE: What do you mean?

155

FORBES: He simply said that she used to be an old flame of his and he hadn't seen her for months. So far, we haven't been able to prove otherwise.

TEMPLE: M'm. What sort of a girl was this Lita Ronson?

FORBES: A very bad character – in every sense of the word.

TEMPLE: I see.

FORBES: (*Suddenly*) Well, I suppose I'd better be making a move. I want Browning to have a look at this diary.

TEMPLE: I hope he makes more out of it than I can.

FORBES: He's a very good man at this sort of thing.

TEMPLE: I'll run you back to the Yard, Sir Graham. I'd like to have a chat with Browning.

FORBES: Yes, all right, Temple.

TEMPLE: (*To STEVE*) I shan't be long, Steve – but don't bother to wait up.

STEVE: All right. (*Casually*) I may slip out to the flicks for an hour or so. (*Pleasantly*) Good night, Sir Graham!

FORBES: Good night, Steve!

FADE UP of music.

FADE DOWN of music.

FADE UP background noises of a large and popular roller-skating rink.

Canned music blares out over the rink.

FADE UP noise of skaters.

6th MAN: (*Racing round the rink*) Look out, ducks! Look out!

7th MAN: (*Racing past*) Mind yourself! Look out!

DAISY: (*Broad cockney: with sarcasm*) Look out yourself! I don't know what this place is coming to, I don't really!

156

STEVE:	(*Drawing level with DAISY*) Are you all right?
DAISY:	Yes, I'm all right, ducks! But what a crowd!
STEVE:	Is it always like this?
DAISY:	T'is on a Wednesday. (*Irritated*) I never know what to do with this scarf, if I leave it off, I'm perishin' and if I keep it on, I'm as hot as the devil.
8ᵗʰ MAN:	(*Racing past*) Look out! Watch yourself!
DAISY:	(*Nearly falling over*) Coo – here's another of 'em!
STEVE:	(*Laughing*) It's all right, I've got you!
DAISY:	I think I'll give it a rest for a bit.
STEVE:	Yes, I think I would if I were you. (*Suddenly*) Oh – you see that man over there, the one in the middle of the rink?
DAISY:	What 'im what's showing off?
STEVE:	(*Laughing*) Yes. Do you happen to know his name?
DAISY:	'Course I know it, ducks – it's Carl Walters.
STEVE:	Carl Walters.
DAISY:	Yes. So long!
STEVE:	(*Thoughtfully*) So … Goodbye!

FADE UP the noise of the rink.
FADE UP the sound of Carl Walters skating.
STEVE skates across to where WALTERs is skating and then suddenly bumps head-long into him. They both fall to the ground.

WALTERS:	(*Angrily*) Say, what's the idea? What's the big idea?
STEVE:	(*In an artificial debutante manner*) Oh, I'm so sorry. So terribly sorry! Did I hurt you?
WALTERS:	(*A moment: impressed*) No. No, I'm O.K. (*Smiling*) Let me give you a hand.

157

STEVE:	(*Getting to her feet*) I can manage all right. (*She slips*)
WALTERS:	(*Laughing*) That's what you think! Now get hold of my hand! That's it! Now … (*He pulls STEVE to her feet*) … There we are.
STEVE:	(*Laughing: girlish*) Oh, thanks awfully. It's very sweet of you.
WALTERS:	Not at all. (*Stopping STEVE: pleasantly*) No, don't go away! Don't go away! Say, you're new around here, aren't you?
STEVE:	I haven't been here before if that's what you mean.
WALTERS:	Yeah, that's what I mean all right. Do you dance?
STEVE:	You mean here – on these things?
WALTERS:	Sure.
STEVE:	I'm afraid I don't. It's all I can do to stand.
WALTERS:	Yeah, I can see that. Oh, did you hurt yourself just now?
STEVE:	No, I don't think so.
WALTERS:	(*Amused*) You don't think so?
STEVE:	Well, I've got so many bruises it's rather difficult to sort them out.
WALTERS:	What you need is a nice strong cup of coffee.
STEVE:	(*Playfully*) But where can I get a nice strong cup of coffee?
WALTERS:	Follow me, lady!
STEVE:	I think it might be safer if I took your arm.
WALTERS:	Sure! Safety first every time. I'm all for it. By the way, my name is Carl Walters. What's yours?

STEVE:	(*Girlish*) I'm not at all sure whether I ought to tell you my name, Mr Walters. I don't really think Daddy would approve.
WALTERS:	(*Dumb*) What's Daddy got to do with it?
STEVE:	(*Laughing*) Well, after all you did pick me up, didn't you?
WALTERS:	What did you expect me to do, leave you on the floor?
STEVE:	(*Playfully, flattering WALTERS*) Obviously you're a very determined individual. My name is Carlton. Pamela Carlton.
WALTERS:	O.K., Pam! Let's grab that coffee!

FADE UP the sound of the rink.
FADE DOWN.
FADE scene.

FADE UP of STEVE talking: background of the rink.

STEVE:	… And then, of course when Daddy retired from the Navy I simply had no alternative, I simply had to get a job. But I suppose that's life, isn't it, Mr Walters?
WALTERS:	Sure. Are you still at Berridges?
STEVE:	Yes, on the Perfumery. It's ghastly, but there you are!
WALTERS:	I know. The pay's terrible but the smell's terrific!

STEVE laughs.

WALTERS:	Do you live in Town?
STEVE:	Yes, I live with a friend of mine in Kensington. I usually manage to go home at weekends.
WALTERS:	Where's that?

159

STEVE: My home? Oh, I don't suppose you've ever even of the place. It's a little fishing village called Dulworth Bay.

WALTERS: (*Astounded*) Dulworth Bay? Why sure I know Dulworth Bay! I've got a whole heap of friends down there. Do you know Doc Stuart?

STEVE: Why yes, frightfully well. He actually brought me into the world.

WALTERS: (*Delighted*) No! Well, what d'you know? Good old Doc!

STEVE: Do you know the Baxters?

WALTERS: Baxters? (*Thoughtfully*) Now wait a minute … No. No, I can't place the Baxters. (*Grinning*) I expect you know the big noise though?

STEVE: Lord Westerby?

WALTERS: Yes.

STEVE: Oh, frightfully well. He's an old crony of Daddy's. Do you know him?

WALTERS: We're not exactly on visiting terms.

STEVE: They say he's frightfully rich.

WALTERS: Who – Westerby? (*Laughing*) Don't you believe it – he hasn't got a nickel he can call his own.

STEVE: I don't know whether you've been down to Dulworth Bay recently or not but they're making some very big changes.

WALTERS: Yeah – I was down there about a fortnight ago.

STEVE: You're not an old Gilterian by any chance?

WALTERS: An old what?

STEVE: (*Laughing*) Gilterian.

WALTERS: I don't know what that is, Lady, but whatever it is I'm strictly not one of 'em!

STEVE: No, somehow, I thought you weren't. It's the school St Gilberts. I was wondering if you went there.

WALTERS: My upbringing was strictly Bronx. No, when I go down to Dulworth it's purely pleasure. It's a pretty fascinating coast down there.

STEVE: Oh, it's really lovely!

WALTERS: (*Drawing closer to STEVE*) Say, you know, you and I have a great deal in common. We ought to see more of each other.

STEVE: (*Playfully*) You men are all alike! You really are the most frightful bounders.

WALTERS: No, I mean it. Seriously. (*Very friendly*) Tell me, are you interested in Art – drawings, etchings, that sort of thing?

STEVE: (*Laughing at him: girlishly*) But of course. I think culture's terrible important.

WALTERS: Well, I've got the most wonderful collection of etchings you've ever seen.

STEVE: Oh, Mr Walters, please! Now where have I heard that before?

WALTERS: No, seriously. I'm not kiddin'. They really are terrific. I'd like you to see them sometime.

STEVE: And where is this fascinating collection?

WALTERS: At my flat in Baker Street. Let me take you along there and show them to you. Besides, I've got some snapshots that may interest you. Pictures of Dulworth Bay and I daresay one or two people you know.

STEVE: That sounds interesting.

WALTERS:	(*Pleased*) O.K., it's a date!
STEVE:	(*Slightly taken aback*) You mean now – tonight?
WALTERS:	(*Laughing*) Well, I don't mean next Shrove Tuesday! (*Taking STEVE by the arm*) Come along, Sugar, get your things!
STEVE:	Really, I don't know what to say! You Americans! You positively sweep a girl off her feet! (*Laughing*) I'll see you at the main entrance near the cash desk. I'm going to powder my nose.
WALTERS:	(*Grinning: delighted*) O.K.

Bring up the noise of the rink: the noise is held and then suddenly the noise of a telephone box door opening and closing is heard. As the door closes the noise of the rink becomes more background again.

STEVE lifts the receiver, inserts coins, and dials. We hear the number ringing out and after a moment the receiver is lifted at the other end.

STEVE:	(*On phone*) Is that you, darling?
TEMPLE:	(*On phone*) Hello, Steve! Where are you?
STEVE:	Have you been in long?
TEMPLE:	Yes, about an hour. (*Curious*) Where are you? Where are you speaking from?
STEVE:	I'm at Canford Hall.
TEMPLE:	(*Puzzled*) Canford Hall? (*Suddenly, remembering*) What?!
STEVE:	(*Quickly: urgently*) Paul, listen! I've met Walters. I'm quite friendly with him. I think I'm on to something, darling.
TEMPLE:	(*A note of tenseness*) What do you mean?
STEVE:	He's been down to Dulworth Bay. I think he goes down there quite a lot. He seems to know everybody – he's quite frank about it.

162

TEMPLE: Where are you now? Where are you actually speaking from?

STEVE: (*Seriously*) I'm in a call box at the rink but I'm just leaving, darling. I'm going up to his flat, he's going to show me his etchings.

TEMPLE: (*Exploding*) He's what!!!!

STEVE: He's going to show me his etchings. Etchings, darling. You know, pictures, drawings …

TEMPLE: I know all right, but, Steve, are you out of your mind – are you crazy?

STEVE: (*Laughing*) Don't worry, I can take care of myself. (*Quickly*) Listen, the flat's in Baker Street. I don't know the number but I daresay you can get it from Sir Graham. If I'm not back in two hours storm the Bastille!

TEMPLE: (*Tensely: quickly*) Steve! Steve, this man may be dangerous! Terribly dangerous!

STEVE: (*Quickly*) Goodbye, darling! See you later!

STEVE rings off and opens the door of the telephone booth: FADE UP the noise of the rink.

FADE the noise of the rink to distant background.

STEVE: Oh, so here you are! I'm terribly sorry to have kept you waiting.

WALTERS: That's O.K. The car's outside. Ready?

STEVE: Yes, I'm quite ready, thank you.

FADE scene.

FADE UP the noise of the car. It is a very modern car and is travelling at an average speed.

STEVE: (*Apparently thrilled*) Isn't this an adorable car!

WALTERS: Do you like it?

STEVE: It's heavenly! It's just like floating on air.

WALTERS: It's the new Pan-American Roadstar.

163

STEVE:	But how do <u>you</u> manage to get a car like this?
WALTERS:	(*Amused*) What a question, Lady!
STEVE:	(*Staring at the inside of the car*) It's really most luxurious. How long have you had it, Mr Walters?
WALTERS:	About ten days, and not so much of the Mr Walters?
STEVE:	It wouldn't take you long to go down to Dulworth Bay in this.
WALTERS:	I should say not.
STEVE:	(*Suddenly*) By the way, do you know Diana Maxwell?
WALTERS:	Westerby's girlfriend?
STEVE:	Girlfriend! I thought she was his niece?
WALTERS:	Well, maybe she is, maybe she isn't. I wouldn't know. She's certainly a pain in the neck so far as I'm concerned.
STEVE:	I'll bet you say that about all the girls!

WALTERS laughs.

Pause.

WALTERS:	If you'd like a cigarette just help yourself. (*He touches a spring on the dashboard*).
STEVE:	Oh! I say, isn't that cute!
WALTERS:	There's a lighter by your elbow.
STEVE:	Oh, thank you.

A moment.

WALTERS:	Would you like the radio on?
STEVE:	No, I don't think so. I never like radios in cars. I don't quite know why but I find they're so distracting. (*Suddenly*) Oh! Oh, you should have turned left there and gone down Park Lane.
WALTERS:	Why?

164

STEVE:	(*A little laugh*) Well, if we're going to Baker Street …
WALTERS:	But we're not going to Baker Street.
STEVE:	(*Taken aback*) No?
WALTERS:	No.
STEVE:	(*Trying to be gay*) Well – where are we going?
WALTERS:	I'll give you three guesses … Mrs Temple.

FADE UP of music.

END OF EPISODE FIVE

EPISODE SIX

A MESSAGE FOR CHARLIE

FADE UP the noise of a motor car: it is traveling at an average speed.

WALTERS: Would you like the radio on?

STEVE: No, I don't think so. I never like radios in cars. I don't quite know why but I find they're so distracting. (*Suddenly*) Oh! Oh, you should have turned left there and gone down Park Lane.

WALTERS: Why?

STEVE: (*A little laugh*) Well, if we're going to Baker Street   ...

WALTERS: But we're not going to Baker Street.

STEVE: (*Taken aback*) No?

WALTERS: No.

STEVE: (*Trying to be gay*) Well – where are we going?

WALTERS: I'll give you three guesses ... Mrs Temple.

STEVE: (*Softly, in her normal voice*) Oh! ... So you know?

WALTERS: (*Quietly*) Yeah. That telephone call of yours was a mistake.

STEVE: (*Tensely*) You listened in! You heard what I said?

WALTERS: Sure ...

STEVE: (*Frightened*) Where are you taking me?

WALTERS doesn't reply.

STEVE: Where are you taking me?!

WALTERS: (*Softly; almost to himself*) Wouldn't you like to know, Sugar?

STEVE: Stop the car! Stop this car! Do you hear what I say, stop the car!

WALTERS: Don't get excited! Keep calm! You'll find out where I'm taking you – all in good time!

STEVE: (*Quietly*) Mr Walters ...

WALTERS:	Yeah?
STEVE:	You see this revolver?
WALTERS:	(*Quietly: driving*) Be kinda difficult not to see it, wouldn't it? You're sticking it right under my nose.
STEVE:	(*Determined*) I'm going to give you five seconds. If you don't stop the car, I shall pull the trigger.
WALTERS:	O.K. O.K., pull the trigger.

A moment.

STEVE:	I'm serious.
WALTERS:	Sure …
STEVE:	I'm dead serious, Mr Walters.
WALTERS:	You look it. You look serious. Gee, it's a long time since I saw a gal looking so serious.
STEVE:	(*Nervous*) You don't think I'll shoot, do you? You don't think I've got the nerve.
WALTERS:	You've got the nerve! (*Chuckling*) You've got plenty of nerve – but you won't shoot!
STEVE:	(*Indignantly*) No?!
WALTERS:	(*Shaking his head*) No. (*A pause*) Well, I'm still breathing! I'm still with you!
STEVE:	(*Suddenly angry, yet in spite of herself faintly amused*) You're the most conceited egotistical man I've ever met!
WALTERS:	Sure! Sure! You can't tell me anything about myself that I don't already know. I've got a flashy car and a phoney accent, but I've never double-crossed a pal yet and I've certainly never done a gal – a decent gal – a bad turn. You might remember that.
STEVE:	You sound as if you're in love with yourself.

WALTERS:	I'm nuts about myself!
STEVE:	Where are you taking me?
WALTERS:	Don't you want to see my etchings?
STEVE:	I do not want to see your etchings!
WALTERS:	(*Shaking his head*) T't. T't. You just don't know what you're missing!
STEVE:	Mr Walters, for the last time, will you please tell me where you're … (*She stops: surprised*) Why, this is Half Moon Street!

The car slows down.

WALTERS:	Yeah.
STEVE:	(*Astonished*) This is the flat – this is where I live!
WALTERS:	(*Amused*) Sure.
STEVE:	(*Amazed*) But you've brought me home!

The car comes to a standstill.

WALTERS:	Isn't this what you wanted?
STEVE:	(*Astonished*) Why, yes, but I thought …
WALTERS:	Yeah, I know what you thought, sugar, and you'd better get out of the car before I change my mind!

STEVE jumps out of the car and slams the door behind her.
WALTERS starts to laugh.
FADE UP of music.

FADE DOWN of music.

TEMPLE:	(*Eating a piece of toast*) You don't seem to be eating a very good breakfast, darling!
STEVE:	(*Faintly petulant*) I don't feel like eating.
TEMPLE:	I expected you to be full of beans this morning, simply brimming with vitality. Pass me the butter …
STEVE:	Well, I'm not!
TEMPLE:	Have you got a headache?

STEVE: No.

TEMPLE: Do you feel sick?

STEVE: No.

TEMPLE: Toothache?

STEVE: No.

TEMPLE: Well, what is the matter with you? Pass the marmalade …

STEVE: If you want to know, I feel annoyed with myself. If I hadn't made that slip and telephoned you I should probably have made a complete fool out of Walters and he'd have told me all we wanted to know.

TEMPLE: I doubt it. For one thing I'm not at all sure that he knows all that we want to know. (*Helping himself to toast and marmalade*) I'm pretty sure he doesn't know all that I want to know. Still, you didn't do so badly, darling!

STEVE: (*A little brighter*) Well, he was quite obviously taken in by me up to the time of the telephone call.

TEMPLE: Which means precisely what?

STEVE: Well, it means that until he found out who I was he was telling the truth.

TEMPLE: Always providing of course that Mr Walters makes a habit of telling strange young ladies the truth.

STEVE: Well, he didn't deny that he knew Lord Westerby and Dr Stuart, and he didn't deny that he was in the habit of going down to Dulworth Bay!

TEMPLE: Why should he? But he denied that he knew the Baxters, didn't he? And that seems to me to be the important point. I suppose you didn't see any

172

	sign of this other fellow – the man who tried to steal the diary off me.
STEVE:	No. He wasn't at the rink.
TEMPLE:	I was a fool to let him get away so easily. I ought to have brought him back to the flat with me.
STEVE:	Didn't Sir Graham say he was going to pick him up?
TEMPLE:	Yes, but I expect Walters'll make him lie low for a little while.
STEVE:	Why do you think Walters wanted that diary?
TEMPLE:	Presumably for the same reason that Baxter wanted it. I hope to know more about the diary this afternoon.
STEVE:	Are you seeing Sir Graham this afternoon?
TEMPLE:	Yes, we're lunching together and then going back to the Yard. By the way, Steve, I've booked a table at Marietta's for this evening. You'd better meet me there at about 8.15.
STEVE:	Yes, all right, darling.
TEMPLE:	I was rather interested to hear what Walters said about Westerby.
STEVE:	You mean about him not having any money?
TEMPLE:	Yes.
STEVE:	Do you think it's true?
TEMPLE:	I shouldn't be a bit surprised. (*Suddenly*) Steve, tell me: did Walters give you the impression that he frequently went down to Dulworth Bay and that he'd been going down there for some time?
STEVE:	What do you mean, Paul – for some time?
TEMPLE:	Well, did he speak of Dulworth Bay as if it was his home town – as if he knew the place when he was a boy?
STEVE:	(*Thoughtfully*) No. No, I rather got the impression that although he knew the place quite

173

well it was all rather new to him as it were –
something in the way of a novelty.

TEMPLE: I see. He didn't tell you when he first went down
there?

STEVE: No. (*A pause*) I told you what he said about
Diana Maxwell, didn't I?

TEMPLE: Yes.

STEVE: Do you think she is a girl friend of Westerby's?

TEMPLE: (*Thoughtfully*) Could be …

A moment.

STEVE: Paul, what do you think is behind all this? Do
you think that Baxter was running a blackmailing
racket and suddenly … (*She stops*)

TEMPLE: What is it?

STEVE: (*Slowly*) I've just thought, darling! Supposing
Baxter was a blackmailer. Supposing he found
out that Diana Maxwell wasn't Lord Westerby's
niece and suddenly started to blackmail him.
(*Faintly excited*) Don't you see, it all fits
together, Paul. Westerby murdered Baxter
because he realised that sooner or later Baxter
would squeeze him dry. Having murdered
Baxter, he then decided …

TEMPLE: … To set the cottage on fire, do away with his
girlfriend, kidnap John Draper and put an end to
our little adventure. It fits together beautifully,
doesn't it, Steve? Like heck it does! (*Rising
from the table*) I'm off, darling! I'll see you
tonight at Marietta's.

STEVE: Yes, all right.
TEMPLE: Oh – if you've nothing to do this
afternoon I'm told there's an awfully good
exhibition at Barchester House.

174

STEVE: (*Very interested*) Oh! An exhibition of what, darling?

TEMPLE: Etchings.

STEVE: (*Angry*) Pig!

TEMPLE laughs.

The door opens and Charlie enters.

CHARLIE:Can I clear now?

TEMPLE: (*Still laughing at STEVE*) Yes, we've finished, Charlie.

STEVE: No, we haven't! As a matter of fact, I haven't even started! Charlie, I think I'll have some bacon and eggs!

CHARLIE:(*Nodding*) Okedoke, Mrs Temple!

TEMPLE: (*Astonished*) Bacon and eggs! I didn't know we had any bacon and eggs!

STEVE: (*Apparently very sorry for TEMPLE*) Didn't you, my sweet?

FADE UP of music.

FADE DOWN of music.

A door opens and closes.

FORBES: Sit down, Temple!

TEMPLE: Oh, thank you, Sir Graham!

FORBES: (*At his desk*) Hello, what's this? I only have to be out of the office for five minutes and the work simply piles up on me. (*A moment: interested*) Oh! I think this report will interest you, Temple!

TEMPLE: What is it?

FORBES: Apparently the Special Branch people have identified that girl – the one that was killed in the café.

TEMPLE: You mean the girl that impersonated Diana Maxwell?

FORBES: Yes. (*A tiny pause*) Her name was Doris White. She used to be a small part actress and then became mixed up with the Bedford Gang. According to this she seems to have had quite a career. Here read it for yourself.

TEMPLE: (*Taking the document*) Thanks.

FORBES: I'll see if there's any news of our friend Lou Kenzell. I should imagine Vosper's picked him up by now. (*Presses button on the intercom system on his desk*) Vosper!

VOSPER: (*On speaker*) Yes, sir?

FORBES: Any news of Kenzell?

VOSPER: Yes, sir. He's here now, sir. I picked him up in Oxford Street about twenty minutes ago.

FORBES: Good. Bring them up to my office, I've got Mr Temple with me.

VOSPER: Very good, sir.

FORBES: (*Pressing the button again: to TEMPLE*) You heard what he said?

TEMPLE: Yes. What do you know about this man Kenzell, Sir Graham? Is he a notorious crook or simply one of the small fry?

FORBES: It's rather difficult to say. He's been through our hands once or twice and the Paris people seem to have quite a fair-sized dossier on him. At one time he used to play the boats.

TEMPLE: You mean a card-sharper?

FORBES: Yes. I should go easy with him, Temple, he's inclined to be a little temperamental.

TEMPLE: Yes, so I gathered when I threatened to throw the gentleman down the escalator! By the way, what happened with Lord Westerby?

176

FORBES: Westerby came up to Town last night. He's staying at the Ritz. He had a board meeting this morning and I gather he's got another one this afternoon. He's Chairman of a company known as Wyoming Consolidated.

TEMPLE: Is he alone?

FORBES: No, he's got his secretary with him. What do they call the fellow?

TEMPLE: Peter Malo.

FORBES: That's it, Malo!

A knock and then the door opens.

BROWNING: May I come in? (*MAJOR BROWNING is a well-spoken man of about 55*)

FORBES: Ah, yes! Come in, Major! Temple, I don't think you know Major Browning.

TEMPLE: No, I don't think I've had the pleasure. (*Shaking hands with BROWNING*) How do you do, Major?

BROWNING: How do you do, sir? (*To FORBES*) I'm sorry to disturb you, Sir Graham, but I've brought this diary back – the one you gave me last night.

FORBES: Oh, yes! Have you finished with it?

BROWNING: (*Thoughtfully*) Yes. Yes, I've finished with it but I'm afraid I haven't a very satisfactory report for you. When I first examined the diary, I thought the whole thing was in code: the old numerical device for concealing a particular word or series of words. You know the sort of thing I mean, Temple.

TEMPLE: Yes.

BROWNING:	In actual fact however it's nothing of the sort.
TEMPLE:	(*Interested*) Oh?
BROWNING:	(*Faintly amused*) No. I'm rather afraid that the figures are precisely what they appear to be: simply figures.
TEMPLE:	Yes, but to what do they refer?
BROWNING:	Well, so far as I can gather, they refer to a particular – how can I explain it? – a particular distance from a given object.
TEMPLE:	A measurement?
BROWNING:	Yes.
TEMPLE:	Have you been able to work it out?
BROWNING:	You mean the actual measurement? Yes, that wasn't difficult, not once I got the hang of it. I've jotted the details down on a piece of paper, you'll find it in the diary.
FORBES:	But you haven't the slightest idea to what it refers?
BROWNING:	(*A laugh*) Not the slightest, and you can take my word for it the diary doesn't give so much as a clue.
FORBES:	M'm. (*Suddenly, dismissing BROWNING*) All right, Major! Thanks very much.
BROWNING:	Sorry not to have been more helpful. (*To TEMPLE*) Goodbye, sir.
TEMPLE:	Goodbye, Major.

The door opens and closes.

TEMPLE:	Well, quite obviously Carl Walters knows what the figures mean otherwise he wouldn't have instructed Kenzell to steal the diary.

178

FORBES: (*Thoughtfully*) Yes. I wonder if Kenzell knows. I wonder if he was bluffing yesterday, Temple?

TEMPLE: (*Shaking his head*) Somehow, I don't think so.

A knock and the door opens.

FORBES: Ah, come in, Kenzell!

VOSPER: Shall I stay, sir?

FORBES: No, that's all right, Vosper – thank you.

The door closes.

KENZELL: (*Angry: indignant*) What is the meaning of this? Who are you, sir? Why have I been brought to Scotland Yard?

FORBES: You know perfectly well who I am, Mr Kenzell, and you know why you have been brought to Scotland Yard. Now please sit down!

TEMPLE: (*Smiling: quietly*) Good afternoon, Mr Kenzell.

KENZELL: (*Surprised: suddenly*) Oh! Oh, I didn't notice you. (*Nervously*) I thought it was someone else standing there, I … I … (*His words trail away*)

TEMPLE: (*Pleasantly*) Will you have a cigarette?

KENZELL: (*Tensely*) No. No, I won't have a cigarette. No, thank you. Now what is it you want? I'm a very busy man and I can't afford to waste time like this!

FORBES: Then we'll come straight to the point, shall we? Yesterday afternoon you attempted to steal a diary from Mr Temple. (*He taps the desk*) This diary. Why?

KENZELL: (*Nervous: a little frightened*) I don't know what you're talking about!

179

TEMPLE:	(*Moving closer to KENZELL*) Don't you? Well, supposing I refresh your memory. Yesterday afternoon you followed me from Liverpool Street to Green Park Station. During the course of the journey, you stole this diary. When I discovered that the diary was missing, I suddenly realised what had happened and got back on the train. I caught you just as you were leaving the station at Leicester Square. When I asked you about the diary you told me that you'd been instructed to steal it by a man called Carl Walters.
KENZELL:	(*Angry*) Well?
TEMPLE:	Well, we've since discovered, Kenzell, that you were not telling the truth, that Walters did not in fact ask you to steal the diary.
KENZELL:	(*Taken aback*) What the devil do you mean? Who says he didn't?
TEMPLE:	He says so himself!
KENZELL:	(*Intensely angry: losing control of himself*) Then he's lying! The filthy double-crossing devil!
TEMPLE:	Can you prove that he's lying? Can you prove that Walters did in fact ask you to steal the diary?
KENZELL:	Of course, he asked me to steal it! If Walters didn't ask me to take it then why do you think I took the trouble to follow you – why do you think I bothered to steal the damn thing?
TEMPLE:	Well, obviously because <u>you</u> wanted it!
KENZELL:	Because I wanted it?
TEMPLE:	Yes.

180

KENZELL:	But why should I want the diary?
TEMPLE:	Well, if it comes to that, why should Walters want it?
KENZELL:	(*A shrug*) I don't know. That's no concern of mine. He told me that he wanted the diary and that he would pay me two hundred pounds if I got it for him.
FORBES:	When did he tell you that?
KENZELL:	Yesterday afternoon. He telephoned me: as a matter of fact, I was in the bath at the time. (*A shrug*) Two hundred pounds. It's a lot of money. It seemed so easy. All I had to do was to follow you and Mrs Temple and keep close to you in the tube.
TEMPLE:	When Walters made this proposition to you, did you ask him why he wanted the diary?
KENZELL:	Of course.
TEMPLE:	What did he say?
KENZELL:	He told me to mind my own business. (*Smiling*) It was excellent advice.
TEMPLE:	Kenzell, have you ever heard of a person called Curzon?
KENZELL:	Curzon? (*Shaking his head*) No.
FORBES:	You're sure?
KENZELL:	But of course I'm sure! If I'd heard of the name I should say so!

A moment.

FORBES:	(*Quietly: dismissing KENZELL*) All right, Kenzell. You can go.
KENZELL:	(*Rising*) Thank you.
FORBES:	You'd better see Inspector Vosper on your way out.
KENZELL:	I shouldn't dream of leaving without saying goodbye to the Inspector. Goodbye, Mr

	Temple, I regret that we met under such unpleasant circumstances. However, perhaps we shall meet again sometime.
TEMPLE:	Perhaps.
KENZELL:	Do you play cards?
TEMPLE:	Occasionally – for very small stakes.
KENZELL:	(*A smile*) Oh, that's unfortunate – for me. Good afternoon, gentlemen.

The door opens and closes.

FORBES:	I think he was telling the truth about Walters.
TEMPLE:	I wonder?
FORBES:	Do you know I've a damn good mind to pull him in!
TEMPLE:	Walters, you mean?
FORBES:	(*Thoughtfully*) Yes. If I thought I could hold him I'd do it like a shot. Even now I'm tempted to tell Vosper to … (*Suddenly: determined, on the intercom system*) Vosper!
VOSPER:	(*On the speaker*) Yes, sir?
FORBES:	I want you to get a warrant out for the arrest of Carl Walters! Come up to my office and I'll give you the details!
VOSPER:	Yes, sir.

FORBES switches off the intercom.

TEMPLE:	(*Quietly: deep in thought*) Sir Graham, I wonder if you'd do something for me?
FORBES:	Yes, of course. What is it?
TEMPLE:	(*Slowly: thoughtfully*) You remember that air crash down at Dulworth Bay – about six weeks ago?
FORBES:	Yes?
TEMPLE:	I'd like to see the report on it.
FORBES:	You mean the official report?

TEMPLE: Yes. Can you get it for me?

FORBES: Yes, of course I can. But what the devil do you want to see that for?

TEMPLE: I'm rather curious about something, that's all.

FORBES: Well – is there anything else you'd like?

TEMPLE: Yes, if it isn't included in the official report, I want a copy of the passenger list. In other words, I want to know exactly who was on the plane.

FORBES: That shouldn't be difficult. (*Slowly, looking up*) You know of course that there were no survivors?

TEMPLE: (*Deep in thought*) Yes. Yes, I know that.

FORBES: Temple, you don't think that that air disaster had anything to do with this business – with the Curzon case?

TEMPLE: (*Slowly*) I don't know, Sir Graham. (*A moment*) I don't know …

FADE UP of music.

FADE DOWN of music.

FADE UP background of a crowded restaurant and a small dance orchestra.

PIERRE: Good evening, Mr Temple!

TEMPLE: Oh, hello, Pierre! You appear to be very crowded tonight!

PIERRE: Yes, we seem very busy this evening.

TEMPLE: Has my wife arrived?

PIERRE: Yes, sir. She's at the table in the corner. If you'll follow me, sir.

TEMPLE: Thank you. (*TEMPLE bumps into someone*) Oh, I beg your pardon!

MALO: That's quite all ri … (*Surprised*) Why, Mr Temple!

TEMPLE: Hello, Malo! What are you doing here?

183

MALO:	(*Faintly annoyed*) Well, I was supposed to meet His Lordship here at seven o'clock. It's now a quarter-past-eight.
TEMPLE:	He's not very punctual, is he? You'd better come over to our table and have a drink with us.
MALO:	(*Hesitating*) Well, actually I have one or two telephone calls to make so, perhaps, later if you don't mind?
TEMPLE:	No, of course not. Please yourself, old boy. We're sitting over in the corner.
MALO:	It's really very sweet of you. I'll probably see you later.
TEMPLE:	Yes, all right.
PIERRE:	This way, sir.

FADE UP of the dance orchestra slightly.

STEVE:	Oh, hello, darling!
TEMPLE:	(*Stunned: staring at STEVE*) Hello!
PIERRE:	Would you like a drink, sir?
TEMPLE:	What? (*Suddenly*) Oh, yes. Bring me a whisky and soda – a double.
STEVE:	Well, have you had a pleasant afternoon?
TEMPLE:	I don't know about pleasant. I suppose I've had … Steve, where <u>did</u> you get that hat?
STEVE:	(*Delighted with it*) Do you like it?
TEMPLE:	(*Aghast*) I think it's the most extraordinary hat I've ever seen! Whatever are you going to do with it?
STEVE:	What do you mean, what am I going to do with it? I'm going to wear it.
TEMPLE:	But, Steve, have you seen it? Have you looked in a mirror?

STEVE:	Of course I've looked in a mirror. You don't think I bought the hat without looking in a mirror! (*Angry*) It's always the same, every time I buy a hat you …
TEMPLE:	Now, darling, please!
STEVE:	(*Angry*) You just deliberately go out of your way to make me feel uncomfortable! Well, I think it's a jolly nice hat!
TEMPLE:	(*Calming STEVE*) Yes, all right, darling.
STEVE:	(*Still angry*) As a matter of fact, it's the smartest hat I've had for a very long time.
TEMPLE:	Yes, darling.
STEVE:	Here, hold this mirror and don't hold it cockeyed! (*A moment: definite*) It's very, very smart.
TEMPLE:	(*Nodding*) Yes, dear.
STEVE:	I'm delighted with it.
TEMPLE:	(*Nodding*) Yes, dear.
STEVE:	It's very, very … (*Suddenly*) I wish the blasted thing wouldn't slip to one side like that!
TEMPLE:	Never mind, Steve, it's very, very smart.
STEVE:	(*Laughing*) You really are a beast! No, seriously, Paul – don't you like it?
TEMPLE:	Enormously, darling. (*Suddenly*) Hello, here's Westerby!
STEVE:	Westerby! Was that his secretary I saw you talking to?
TEMPLE:	Yes.
STEVE:	I thought I recognised him.
WESTERBY:	(*Pleasantly*) Hello, Temple. Peter said you were over here, so I thought I'd drop along and pay my respects.

185

TEMPLE:	That's very nice of you. I don't think you've met my wife? Steve, this is Lord Westerby.
WESTERBY:	How do you do, Mrs Temple? I must apologise for putting you off last night. It was a great disappointment to me. I was looking forward to our little dinner party. However, I hope you'll very soon pay another visit to Dulworth Bay.
STEVE:	I hope so. It certainly seems a very exciting place.
WESTERBY:	(*Quietly: seeing the point*) Yes. Yes, I see what you mean.
TEMPLE:	How's Miss Maxwell, by the way – have you heard?
WESTERBY:	Yes, I was on the phone this morning. She seems much better.
TEMPLE:	Oh, good.
WESTERBY:	I'm hoping she'll be able to come home by the end of the week. I certainly intend to have a word with the doctor about it. Ah, here's Peter!
MALO:	I beg your pardon, sir, but ... (*Pleasantly*) Oh, good evening, Mrs Temple!
STEVE:	Good evening.
MALO:	Your guests have arrived, sir.
WESTERBY:	Oh, thank you, Peter. I shan't be a moment. Order some cocktails for them.
MALO:	Very good, sir. (*He departs*)
WESTERBY:	I'm frightfully glad I bumped into you this evening, Temple, because there was a point I rather wanted to talk to you about. When I arrived here in London, I mean, I had the curious feeling that someone was following me. I intended, quite frankly, to report the

matter to the police but when I mentioned it to my secretary, he made rather an extraordinary comment. He said that in his opinion I was probably being followed by the police.

TEMPLE: What made him say that?

WESTERBY: I don't know.

TEMPLE: Did you see the person that was following you?

WESTERBY: Yes. Yes, as a matter of fact, I did. I must confess he looked remarkably like a police officer.

TEMPLE: (*Smiling*) Well, in that case I think I should have a word with the Assistant Commissioner.

WESTERBY: But surely you know whether I'm being followed or not?

TEMPLE: (*Amused*) I'm not au-fait with everything they do at the Yard, Lord Westerby.

WESTERBY: Yes, but I thought …

TEMPLE: (*Interrupting*) Do you know of any particular reason why you should be followed by the police?

WESTERBY: (*Puzzled*) No. Not unless they consider that my life's in danger, and that I need some kind of protection. I think I shall do what you suggest and contact the Commissioner.

TEMPLE: (*Nodding*) Yes, I think I should.

WESTERBY: (*Suddenly*) Well, goodbye, Mrs Temple! I'm delighted to have met you. I hope we shall meet again very soon.

STEVE: I hope so.

WESTERBY: Goodbye, Temple!

TEMPLE: Goodbye!

LORD WESTERBY departs.

A moment.

STEVE: (*Quietly*) Is he being followed?

TEMPLE: Yes. Remind me to telephone Sir Graham when
         we get back to the flat. I don't want him to …
         (*He stops: amused*)

STEVE: What is it?

TEMPLE: (*Astounded*) Look who's here! Look who's just
         arrived!

STEVE: (*Staggered*) Charlie!

TEMPLE: Didn't you leave him at the flat?

STEVE: Of course!

TEMPLE: It's not his night out, is it?

STEVE: Not officially!

TEMPLE: He's spotted us – he's coming over here.

A pause.

STEVE: Hello, Charlie!

CHARLIE:(*A shade breathless*) Good evening. 'Evening,
         sir!

TEMPLE: Good evening, Charlie.

CHARLIE:I got here as quick as I could. Had a bit of a
         game getting a taxi.

STEVE: (*Politely*) Were you in a hurry?

TEMPLE: Just a minute, Steve! (*To CHARLIE*) What do
         you mean, Charlie – you got here as quickly as
         you could?

CHARLIE:What do you think I mean? As soon as I got your
         message …

TEMPLE: (*Quickly*) What message?

CHARLIE:(*Taken aback*) What message? Why, your
         blinkin' message!

TEMPLE: I never sent you a message!

CHARLIE:(*Amazed*) You didn't? Well, who the 'ell did?

TEMPLE: (*Quickly*) Listen, Charlie! Start at the beginning. What happened?

CHARLIE:(*Bewildered*) Why, I 'ad a telephone call from here about fifteen minutes ago. A foreign sort of chap said he was the head waiter and that you'd asked 'im to telephone me. He said that you and Mrs T. wanted to see me. Said it was urgent.

STEVE: But, Paul, why should anyone do that? Why should they telephone Charlie?

CHARLIE:(*Laughing*) Is it a joke?

TEMPLE: No, it isn't a joke! Someone knew that we were here, and they wanted to get you out of the flat! (*Suddenly: quickly*) Steve, get your coat! We're going back to the flat! Quickly, darling! Quickly!!!

FADE UP of music.

FADE DOWN on music.

FADE UP of TEMPLE attempting to open the door of the flat.

TEMPLE: (*Softly: quickly*) The door's locked. If anyone's been in here, they've used a skeleton key. I expect you closed the door behind you, Charlie?

CHARLIE:Yes, sir.

TEMPLE: Have you got your key, Steve?

STEVE: (*Searching her bag*) Well, I did have it! I must have it somewhere … I … oh, here we are!

TEMPLE: Thanks. Now wait a minute! Let me go in first, darling. Charlie, you stand behind me with Mrs Temple.

CHARLIE:Okedoke.

TEMPLE uses the key and opens the door.

TEMPLE: (*Shocked*) Good Lord!

STEVE: (*Entering the flat; amazed*) Paul!

CHARLIE:(*Staggered*) Cor' blimey!

TEMPLE: Just look at the drawers in that table!

STEVE: (*Aghast*) Paul, what's happened? What on earth's happened?

TEMPLE: (*Opening a room door*) The place has been searched: Steve, come over here! Look at that desk! Darling, just look at it.

CHARLIE:Blimey, what a mess! Coo, it'll take a month of Sundays to get the blinkin' place straight!

STEVE: (*Softly: dismayed*) Oh, Paul!

CHARLIE:They don't seem to have pinched much – in fact, there doesn't seem to be anything missing!

TEMPLE: (*Quietly*) No.

STEVE: (*Quickly: tensely*) Paul, they must have been after the diary. Whoever it was they must have thought ... (*Stops*)

TEMPLE: What is it?

STEVE: Listen!

Softly, in the background, we hear a low moan. It is the cry of a man in great pain.

CHARLIE:(*Tensely*) What is it?

TEMPLE: Ssh!

We hear the cry again: slightly louder.

STEVE: (*Suddenly*) Paul, there's someone in the bathroom!

CHARLIE:In the bathroom?

TEMPLE: Yes, I think you're right.

TEMPLE crosses to the bathroom and throws open the door.

As the door opens – FADE UP the sound of the man crying with pain.

STEVE screams with horror.

CHARLIE:(*Shocked*) God's strewth! Look at him! Just look at him – he's been beaten up!

STEVE:	Paul, it's Carl Walters!
TEMPLE:	Walters!
WALTERS:	(*Desperately ill and in great pain*) Don't touch me! Don't touch me, Temple, I … I … (*He gasps with pain*)
TEMPLE:	(*Kneeling beside WALTERS: tensely*) Walters, listen! Who was it that came here? Who did this?
WALTERS:	(*Trying to speak: in pain*) It's … my … heart. I've got a weak heart and they … Could I have some … brandy?
TEMPLE:	(*Turning: tensely*) Get some brandy, Charlie! Quickly!
STEVE:	It's all right, darling! I'll get it!
TEMPLE:	Now, Walters, listen! (*Quietly*) What were you looking for – the diary?
WALTERS:	Yes.
TEMPLE:	Did you search the flat – did you turn everything upside-down?
WALTERS:	(*In pain*) No. No, I didn't. I … was … interrupted … I … I … (*Suddenly: with an effort*) Temple, you've got to stop Curzon from getting the diamonds! Do you hear … what … I … say?
TEMPLE:	(*Tensely*) Yes. Yes, I can hear. Go on, Walters!
WALTERS:	Don't let the swine get them! Whatever happens, don't … let … Curzon … get … the … diamonds … (*Suddenly: in great pain*) Oh! Oh …
TEMPLE:	Walters!
STEVE arrives.	
STEVE:	(*Breathless*) Here's the brandy.
A moment.	

191

TEMPLE: (*Quietly*) It's too late. He's dead.

FADE UP of music.

FADE DOWN of music.

A door opens and closes.

FORBES: They won't be long, Temple. I think they've taken most of the photographs they want.

TEMPLE: Yes, all right, Sir Graham.

The door opens again.

VOSPER: Excuse me, sir. Can we go through into the bedroom again?

TEMPLE: Yes, of course. You'll find my wife in there, she's tidying up.

VOSPER: We shan't disturb her only I want the Sergeant to have another look at the wardrobe.

TEMPLE: Any luck?

VOSPER: Not so far, sir. By the way, I'm afraid we shall have to trouble you for your fingerprints – and Mrs Temple.

FORBES: That's all right, we've already got them Vosper. They're in a private file.

VOSPER: Oh, I see, sir.

TEMPLE: You'd better take Charlie's.

VOSPER: (*Smiling*) We've already done it – after a certain amount of persuasion.

TEMPLE crosses the room and opens a door.

TEMPLE: (*Calling*) The Inspector wants to examine the wardrobe again, Steve. He won't be a minute.

STEVE: (*Calling from the background*) That's all right, darling!

TEMPLE returns to FORBES.

FORBES: I suppose there's no doubt in your mind that they were after the diary?

TEMPLE: (*Shaking his head*) No doubt.

192

FORBES: (*Thoughtfully*) Temple, I've been thinking about what you told me. Do you think Walters was delirious or do you think the poor devil knew what he was saying?

TEMPLE: He was certainly in a pretty bad way, but he knew what he was saying all right.

FORBES: He said: "You've got to stop Curzon from getting the diamonds?"

TEMPLE: Yes.

FORBES: You're sure he said that?

TEMPLE: Quite sure.

FORBES: Is this the first time you've heard diamonds mentioned – in connection with this affair?

TEMPLE: Yes. Why do you ask?

FORBES: Because when we were at the Yard this afternoon, you asked me to get you details of the plane: the one that crashed at Dulworth Bay.

TEMPLE: Have you got them?

FORBES: (*Watching TEMPLE*) Yes, as a matter of fact, I have. The plane was a French plane, a Koroma. It was en route for New York from Amsterdam –

TEMPLE: Oh.

FORBES: (*Quietly*) Didn't you know that it was from Amsterdam?

TEMPLE: Yes, now that you come to mention it, I seem to remember reading something about it.

FORBES: I've got a list of the passengers – there were six of them.

TEMPLE: Were they all accounted for?

FORBES: They were all identified, if that's what you mean.

TEMPLE: No, I didn't mean that.

FORBES: Oh, you want a sort of "Who's Who?"

TEMPLE: Yes.

FORBES: Well, there was a North country businessman and his secretary, two Foreign Office officials, a Dutch schoolteacher and a Frenchman called René Duprez. No one seems to know anything about Duprez. The Airline people haven't been able to contact his relatives, and so far, we've had no inquiries about him.

TEMPLE: There's no doubt that he was killed?

FORBES: None whatsoever.

TEMPLE: Have you contacted the French authorities?

FORBES: Yes, but you see, unfortunately, we've very little to go on. His passport and all personal papers were destroyed.

TEMPLE: Was he booked through to New York?

FORBES: No, to London. One of the airport officials at Schipol remembers talking to him. He says he gave him the impression that he was something to do with the Motor car industry.

TEMPLE: M'm.

FORBES: Temple, why are you interested in his man, Duprez?

TEMPLE: I'm taking a lead out of my wife's book, Sir Graham. I've got a sort of intuition.

STEVE enters.

STEVE: What's all this about an intuition?

TEMPLE: Oh, hello, dear! Have you got the bedroom straight?

STEVE: It's not quite so chaotic. Oh, Paul, did you tell Sir Graham about Lord Westerby?

TEMPLE: Yes, darling.

FORBES: Yes, he did! I always thought Foster was a pretty good shadow, but he certainly seems to have bungled the Westerby assignment.

TEMPLE: I shouldn't be too sure about that. I've got the feeling that Westerby rather expected someone to shadow him.

The telephone rings.

TEMPLE: Now I wonder who that is?

STEVE: It's rather late, darling!

TEMPLE: Yes.

TEMPLE lifts the receiver on the phone.

TEMPLE: Hello?

We hear the sound of Button A being pressed and coins dropping.

DOYLE: (*On the other end of the phone: he is very nervous*) Hello? Who is that?

TEMPLE: This is Circle 1789.

DOYLE: Mr Temple?

TEMPLE: Yes, this is Paul Temple speaking.

DOYLE: This is Doyle, Mr Temple. Tom Doyle.

TEMPLE: (*Surprised*) Hello, Tom! Are you in London?

DOYLE: (*Nervously: urgent*) Yes, I've just arrived. I got in on the 10.15. I want to talk to you, Mr Temple. That's why I've come up to London. I've got to see you, Mr Temple, as soon as possible.

TEMPLE: What is it you want to see me about, Tom?

DOYLE: About … Curzon. I've thought about what you said, Mr Temple, and it's no use. I've got to tell you the truth.

TEMPLE: (*Calmly: pleasantly*) All right. Come along to the flat.

DOYLE: No. No, I don't want to do that. It's too risky. I might be followed.

TEMPLE: Followed? What do you mean?

DOYLE: (*Agitated*) Please don't ask me to explain, not over the phone. I'll tell you when I see you.

TEMPLE:	All right. Where do you want me to meet you?
DOYLE:	Well – where would you suggest? I don't care where it is! I'll meet you anywhere, Mr Temple.
TEMPLE:	Do you know London well?
DOYLE:	No. No, but you suggest a place. I'll find it.
TEMPLE:	Meet me in Trafalgar Square – near one of the fountains. All right?
DOYLE:	Yes. Yes, that's O.K. What time?
TEMPLE:	I'll be there in about a quarter of an hour.
DOYLE:	All right, Mr Temple. Thank you.

DOYLE rings off and TEMPLE replaces the receiver.

STEVE:	Paul, who was it?
TEMPLE:	(*Thoughtfully*) It was Tom Doyle. He's in London – he wants to see me.
FORBES:	Tonight?
TEMPLE:	Yes. I've promised to meet him in Trafalgar Square in about a quarter of an hour.
STEVE:	But what does Tom Doyle want – what's he doing in London?
TEMPLE:	(*Thoughtfully*) He wants to talk to me about Curzon.
FORBES:	Are you sure it was Doyle? Are you sure it isn't a trap?
TEMPLE:	(*Quietly*) I don't know. It sounded like Doyle. It sounded remarkably like Doyle, and yet he refused to come to the flat. (*Suddenly*) Steve, where's the Railway Guide?
STEVE:	(*Puzzled*) It's on the bookcase, darling.
FORBES:	What do you want a Railway Guide for?
TEMPLE:	(*At the bookcase examining the guide*) He said he'd just arrived here on the 10.15. I've

got a feeling that there isn't a 10.15 from Dulworth Bay. (*Flicking pages*) Darlington … Derby … Dewsbury … Dulworth Bay … Here we are! (*A moment*) Yes, he's right, there is! Dulworth Bay 8.21 – Liverpool Street, 10.15.

FORBES: M'm.

TEMPLE: (*Looking up*) Have you got a car here, Sir Graham?

FORBES: Yes, I've got a police car.

TEMPLE: (*Nodding*) We'll keep that appointment!

FADE UP of music.

FADE DOWN of music.

FADE UP of TEMPLE and FORBES walking along the pavement.

A car door opens.

FORBES: Here we are, Temple.

DAWSON: (*A police officer; about thirty-five*) 'Evening, sir!

TEMPLE: Good evening!

FORBES: I want you to take us to Trafalgar Square.

DAWSON: Very good, sir.

TEMPLE: He'd better drive round the square, Sir Graham, and then drop me near Admiralty Arch. If Doyle sees me get out of a Police car he might get frightened and take to his heels.

FORBES: (*With a little laugh*) Yes, I suppose there's something in that.

DAWSON: Are we in a hurry, sir?

TEMPLE: No, there's plenty of time.

FORBES: Jump in, Temple!

The car door closes.

DAWSON returns to his seat in the front of the car.
The sound of a second door closing.
The car starts.
FADE UP of the car cruising along at an average speed.

FORBES: It's perfectly obvious that Walters was after the diary, went to the flat and was disturbed by Curzon. The point is, Temple, who is Curzon? Quite frankly, I suspected Lord Westerby, but in view of this new development, I'm not so sure.

TEMPLE: Why aren't you so sure?

FORBES: Well, I just don't see how Westerby could be in two places at once? You said yourself he was at Marietta's.

TEMPLE: Oh, yes, he was at Marietta's all right. So was Peter Malo. But that doesn't mean that neither Westerby nor Malo is our mysterious Mr Curzon.

FORBES: You mean you don't think that Curzon did murder Walters?

TEMPLE: I'm sure he didn't. The person who searched the flat and murdered Walters was acting on instructions from Curzon, but it wasn't Curzon himself, I'm quite sure of that.

FORBES: Then who was it?

The sound of a high-powered motor bike can be heard, it is drawing level with the car.

TEMPLE: Sir Graham, I think we made rather a blunder this afternoon.

FORBES: What do you mean?

TEMPLE: I mean that our little German friend – Lou Kenzell – pulled the wool over our eyes. It's my bet that he wasn't working for Walters but was working for Curzon.

FORBES:	(*Surprised*) You mean that it was Kenzell that murdered Walters?
TEMPLE:	Yes.
FORBES:	But why should you think that? Why should … (*He stops: suddenly*) I say, what the devil's this fellow doing on the motor bike?
DAWSON:	He won't pass, sir. I've waved him on.
FORBES:	Well, wave him on again.
TEMPLE:	It's a Despatch rider.
DAWSON:	Yes, sir.
TEMPLE:	I never know why they dress them up like that! Surely there's no earthly reason to get them up to look like robots.
FORBES:	(*Irritated*) Wave the confounded fellow on!
DAWSON:	(*A little laugh*) I keep doing it, sir!
TEMPLE:	(*Suddenly*) Sir Graham!
FORBES:	What is it?
TEMPLE:	Look! Look, he's got a revolver!
FORBES:	A revolver! What on earth's he going to do with a revolver? Why should he want … (*Suddenly*) Good God!
TEMPLE:	(*Quickly: desperately*) Look out, Dawson, he's pointing it at you! Look out!!!!
FORBES:	(*Alarmed*) Temple!

There is a revolver shot.

The motorbike rider revs up during the following scene and departs.

TEMPLE:	(*Desperately*) He's hit him!
FORBES:	Dawson! Dawson, are you all right?
TEMPLE:	No, he's not! He's been hit! Grab the wheel! Grab the wheel, Sir Graham! Quickly!

The car swerves across the road and mounts the pavement.

FORBES:	I can't get hold of the wheel – he's slumped across it!

TEMPLE:	Grab the wheel! For God's sake, grab the wheel! Be quick!!!
FORBES:	We're going for the shop window! Look out!!!!

The car crashes into a shop window: there is a violent and tremendous smashing of glass, woodwork, etc., as the shop front collapses with the sudden impact.

The noise of the crash gradually dies down.

FORBES:	(*Struggling to get out of the car*) Temple, where are you?
TEMPLE:	(*Also struggling to free himself*) I'm over here ... I fell off the seat when the car hit the kerb. (*Still struggling*) It's lucky for me I did.
FORBES:	Are you all right?
TEMPLE:	Yes. (*He opens the car door*) What about you?
FORBES:	I caught my shoulder on the back of the seat, but it'll be all right. Can you get out?

FADE UP background noises of excited voices; the sound of a police bell ringing.

TEMPLE:	Yes. Yes, I can manage. (*Quietly*) Dawson's dead ...
FORBES:	Where did the bullet hit him?
TEMPLE:	(*Softly*) You can see for yourself.
FORBES:	(*A moment*) Poor devil! (*Quietly*) We'd better get him out of here.
TEMPLE:	Yes. I'll push the front seat back.
FORBES:	That's made it much easier.

TEMPLE starts to move the front seat.

Suddenly, LORD WESTERBY arrives: he is out of breath.

WESTERBY:	(*Excited*) What on earth happened? Is anyone hurt? Can I be of any assistance ... (*He stops: staggered*) Why, Mr Temple!

TEMPLE: (*Looking up quietly: equally surprised*) Lord
    Westerby!
FADE UP of music.

END OF EPISODE SIX

EPISODE SEVEN

THE DECIDING FACTOR

FORBES:	(*Struggling to get out of the car*) Temple, where are you?
TEMPLE:	(*Also struggling to free himself*) I'm over here … I fell off the seat when the car hit the kerb. (*Still struggling*) It's lucky for me I did.
FORBES:	Are you all right?
TEMPLE:	Yes. (*He opens the car door*) What about you?
FORBES:	I caught my shoulder on the back of the seat, but it'll be all right. Can you get out?

FADE UP background noises of excited voices; the sound of a police bell ringing.

TEMPLE:	Yes. Yes, I can manage. (*Quietly*) Dawson's dead …
FORBES:	Where did the bullet hit him?
TEMPLE:	(*Softly*) You can see for yourself.
FORBES:	(*A moment*) Poor devil! (*Quietly*) We'd better get him out of here.
TEMPLE:	Yes. I'll push the front seat back.
FORBES:	That's made it much easier.

TEMPLE starts to move the front seat.
Suddenly, LORD WESTERBY arrives: he is out of breath.

WESTERBY:	(*Excited*) What on earth happened? Is anyone hurt? Can I be of any assistance … (*He stops: staggered*) Why, Mr Temple!
TEMPLE:	(*Looking up quietly: equally surprised*) Lord Westerby!
WESTERBY:	God bless my soul! Fancy meeting you of all people! (*Turning*) Peter, it's Mr Temple!
MALO:	(*Amazed*) What? I say, what an extraordinary thing!
FORBES:	(*With authority*) Did you see what happened?

WESTERBY: Well, yes, but it happened so quickly! We were on the other side of the road. (*To TEMPLE*) As a matter of fact, Temple, we've only just left the restaurant. We were walking back to our hotel.

MALO: (*Faintly bewildered*) But what happened? I thought at first the chappie on the motorbike was trying to stop you, then I realised that you were in a Police car and I just couldn't make head or tail of it.

FORBES: Didn't you see him fire the shot?

MALO: Fire the shot?

WESTERBY: What do you mean? I thought he simply forced you off the road and on to the pavement?

TEMPLE: (*Quietly*) He shot the driver.

WESTERBY: (*Softly*) Good God, Temple!

MALO: (*Suddenly*) That must have been what we heard, sir! I thought it was the car back-firing.

TEMPLE: (*Watching MALO*) No, it wasn't the car, Mr Malo. Now, would you mind giving me a hand? I want to try and get the poor fellow out of the car.

WESTERBY: Yes. Yes, of course! Come along, Peter!

MALO: (*A little nervous*) Oh! Oh, I can see now that he's been ... shot ... (*Uneasy*) Oh, dear! How unpleasant. How very unpleasant.

FADE UP of music.

FADE DOWN of music.
A door opens.

VOSPER: (*Briskly*) There's no sign of Doyle, sir!

FORBES: Are you sure?

VOSPER: Quite sure, sir. I've just had two reports
             through from Trafalgar Square and one from
             Admiralty Arch.

The telephone rings.

FORBES: Yes, all right, Vosper! (*He changes his
             mind*) No! No, wait a minute! (*He lifts the
             telephone receiver*) Hello?

OPERATOR: Your call to Dulworth Bay. Inspector
             Morgan's on the line, sir.

FORBES: Thank you.

MORGAN: (*On the other end: sleepy: faintly irritated*)
             Hello? Who is this?

FORBES: Is that you, Morgan? This is Forbes!

MORGAN: Oh, good evening, sir!

FORBES: Morgan, listen! I want you to check on Tom
             Doyle. Find out if he's still in Dulworth
             Bay. If he's not, then I want you to ...

MORGAN: (*Interrupting him*) But he is, sir! At least he
             was an hour ago!

FORBES: How do you know?

MORGAN: I had a drink with him, sir – in The Feathers.

FORBES: Oh! All right, Morgan – that's all I want.

TEMPLE: (*Suddenly*) No, wait a minute! Ask him
             about Miss Maxwell.

FORBES: Mr Temple's here, he'd like a word with
             you. (*He passes the phone to TEMPLE*)
             Here we are.

TEMPLE: Thank you. (*On the phone*) Hello, Inspector!
             Any news of Miss Maxwell?

MORGAN: I saw her this morning for a few minutes,
             but she still won't talk.

TEMPLE: M'm. Any sign of her coming out of the
             hospital?

MORGAN:	If all goes well, she should be out in a day or two, sir. Dr Stuart seems quite optimistic.
TEMPLE:	I see.
MORGAN:	Are you coming down here again, sir?
TEMPLE:	Yes, I shall most likely be coming down tomorrow. Perhaps you'd book me a room.
MORGAN:	Certainly. Let me know what time you're arriving, and I'll pop in and see you.
TEMPLE:	Yes, all right, Inspector.
MORGAN:	Goodbye, sir.
TEMPLE:	Goodbye! (*He replaces the receiver*)
FORBES:	Well, it certainly wasn't Doyle that telephoned you! That call was a trap, Temple, and by God we marched straight into it!
VOSPER:	How do you know it wasn't Doyle, sir? Couldn't he have telephoned from Dulworth Bay?
TEMPLE:	Yes, but he didn't. It was a local call. (*Suddenly*) Inspector, you know Lou Kenzell, the man we interviewed this afternoon?
VOSPER:	Yes?
TEMPLE:	I want to see him again. Do you know where we can get hold of him?
VOSPER:	Yes. He's got a place in Shepherd's Market, sir. Whether it's genuine or not, I don't know. (*Puzzled*) Why do you want to see Kenzell again?
FORBES:	Temple's changed his mind about Kenzell …
VOSPER:	Oh?

FORBES: He thinks he's pretty deeply involved in this
            business. He also thinks he murdered
            Walters.
VOSPER: What – Lou Kenzell?
TEMPLE: Yes.
VOSPER: What makes you think that?
TEMPLE: It's just a feeling: a hunch if you like.
VOSPER: Yes, but you must have a reason for it.
TEMPLE: When I grabbed hold of Kenzell and
            threatened to throw him down the escalator,
            I noted the brilliantine he was using. It had a
            particularly pungent smell.
VOSPER: Well?
TEMPLE: I noticed that smell tonight when I got back
            to the flat. I noticed it in the hall and
            particularly in the bathroom where Walters
            was found.
FORBES: (*Interested: quietly*) Did you? Did you, by
            Jove! (*Suddenly, nodding*) You're right,
            Temple! Vosper – get hold of Rogers,
            Brook and Martin!
VOSPER: Very good, sir!
FOTBES: We'll have a talk to our friend Mr Kenzell.
            We'll see what sort of an alibi he's got.
            (*Grimly*) And it better be good!
FADE UP of music.

FADE DOWN of music.
FADE UP the sound of a car which draws to a standstill.
*The sound of car doors opening and closing: the car engine
switched off.*
FORBES: (*Quietly*) Which is the flat?
VOSPER: It's on the top – Number 7. The one with the
            big window.

FORBES:	(*Nodding*) Right. (*Confidentially*) Now listen! Rogers and Martin take the entrance into the Mews. Brook, you watch the street entrance.
BROOK:	Very good, sir.
FORBES:	You'd better come inside, Vosper, and plant yourself on the staircase.
VOSPER:	Yes, sir.
TEMPLE:	(*To VOSPER*) Have you been in this block before?
VOSPER:	Once: a long time ago.
TEMPLE:	Is there a lift?
VOSPER:	No, just a staircase.
FORBES:	Are you ready, Temple?
TEMPLE:	Yes.

FADE Scene.

FADE UP of FORBES: he is talking softly to VOSPER.

FORBES:	Is that the door?
VOSPER:	Yes, sir.
FORBES:	All right; you stay here, Vosper. If you hear anything unusual you know what to do.
VOSPER:	Yes, sir. And watch him.
FORBES:	Don't worry, we shan't take any chances.

TEMPLE and FORBES continue up the staircase. As they reach the flat door the sound of a Viennese Waltz can be heard playing on a portable gramophone.

| FORBES: | (*Quietly*) That's a gramophone, isn't it? |
| TEMPLE: | Yes. |

TEMPLE knocks on the door.
A pause.
The knock is repeated.
After a moment the gramophone stops playing.
A pause and then the door is unbolted and opened.

KENZELL: (*Annoyed*) Who is it? What do you want?

FORBES: We want to see you, Mr Kenzell.

The door opens.

KENZELL: (*Surprised*) Oh! Oh, it's you! What do you two want at this time of the night? It's a bit late for a social call, isn't it?

TEMPLE: We called earlier this evening but unfortunately you were out.

A moment.

KENZELL: Well – there's no law against going to the cinema, is there?

TEMPLE: (*Pleasantly*) No, of course not. May we come in?

KENZELL: (*After a momentary hesitation*) Yes, of course.

TEMPLE and FORBES enter. The door closes.

FORBES: (*Looking about him*) It's quite a nice place you've got here.

KENZELL: I'm glad you like it. Can I offer you a drink?

FORBES: (*Slowly*) No. No, I don't think so, Mr Kenzell, thank you.

KENZELL: Well, supposing we get to the point – what is it you want?

FORBES: Mr Temple is under the impression that you were not telling the truth this afternoon. He's of the opinion that you were instructed to steal the diary not by Carl Walters but by a certain Mr Curzon.

KENZELL: (*Angry: deliberately*) I was asked to steal that diary by Carl Walters, he paid me two hundred pounds to steal it! If I've told you that once I've told it to you a hundred times!

TEMPLE: (*Calmly: deliberately*) And I still don't believe you, Mr Kenzell.

211

KENZELL:	No?
TEMPLE:	No. I think that Curzon told you to steal the diary, he told you that if you failed and were unlucky enough to be caught then you had to pass the blame on to Walters. He also told you that it was a hundred to one that I'd made a copy of the diary and that it was at my flat. That's why you went to my flat, Mr Kenzell, that's why …
KENZELL:	What are you talking about? I've never been to your flat! I don't even know where it is!
TEMPLE:	(*Shaking his head: quietly*) I don't believe you. You went to my flat tonight. You went there, found Carl Waters already searching for the diary and deliberately murdered him.
KENZELL:	(*Apparently amazed*) You believe that I murdered Carl Walters?!
TEMPLE:	I do.
KENZELL:	But this is preposterous! Ridiculous! I tell you I've been out tonight – I've been to the cinema.
FORBES:	Alone?
KENZELL:	But of course! Is there any objection to my going to the cinema alone?
FORBES:	None, but unfortunately it doesn't provide you with a very good alibi.
KENZELL:	When one is innocent one does not require an alibi, Sir Graham. (*Quite simply*) I'm telling you the truth. I went to the cinema this evening. I left here at about six o'clock and returned at about a quarter past nine.
TEMPLE:	Where did you go? What did you see?

KENZELL: I went to the Forum on the Tottenham Court Road. I saw Hamlet. (*With sarcasm*) Would you like me to prove it by telling you the plot?

TEMPLE: That won't be necessary. Did you see the entire film?

KENZELL: No. I've already told you. I left here at about six o'clock and was back in the flat at a quarter past nine. I couldn't possibly have seen the entire film, Mr Temple.

FORBES: (*To TEMPLE*) It's a very long film.

TEMPLE: (*Suddenly*) Oh, you mean the Laurence Olivier film – the one in technicolour?

KENZELL: Yes. (*Suddenly realising*) Well, I don't know whether it's in technicolour or not but …

TEMPLE: (*Quickly*) Why don't you? You're supposed to have seen this picture!

KENZELL: Well …

FORBES: (*Quickly*) Temple, look out! He's got a gun! Be quick!

TEMPLE strikes out and catches KENZELL on the jaw.

KENZELL: (*Hurt: falling*) Oh!

There is a thud as Kenzell hits the floor.

A moment.

TEMPLE: Have you got the revolver?

FORBES: Yes. (*Staring down at Kenzell*) You certainly hit him.

TEMPLE: I hope I didn't overdo it! (*Stooping and getting hold of KENZELL*) Let's put him in that chair.

FORBES: I'll give you a hand!

FORBES and TEMPLE lift KENZELL off the floor and prop him in an armchair.

KENZELL: (*Moaning*) Oh … Oh …

TEMPLE: Come on, Kenzell! Wake up!

213

KENZELL: (*Still moaning, dazed and bewildered*) Oh! Oh, my head! Oh! …

TEMPLE: Pass me that syphon of soda water! (*He takes the syphon*) Thanks. (*To KENZELL*) Now come on, Kenzell! Pull yourself together! (*Shaking KENZELL*) Come on, Kenzell! (*A moment*) All right, you've asked for it!

KENZELL continues to groan and TEMPLE squirts the soda water full in his face.

KENZELL: (*Suddenly dazed*) Oh! Oh! Oh!!! Oh!!!! Oh!!!! (*He is gasping for breath*)

TEMPLE: (*Putting down the syphon*) Better?

KENZELL: (*Dazed*) What happened?

TEMPLE: We were just in the middle of a nice conversation and you passed out on us.

KENZELL: But something him me!

TEMPLE: Nothing to speak of. (*A moment*) Just out of curiosity, my friend – was Carl Walters the only person you murdered, or did you murder Baxter?

KENZELL: (*Tensely: desperately*) I don't know what you're talking about! Leave me alone! Oh, my face! My face …

TEMPLE: Kenzell, don't you realise that nothing you can say, nothing you can do, can save you now?

KENZELL: (*Frightened*) What do you mean?

TEMPLE: (*Quietly*) You know what I mean. You murdered Walters and you've got to pay the price for it. Now if you've got any sense, you'll tell us exactly   …

KENZELL: I'm not talking! I'm not saying anything! Leave me alone! Do you hear what I say?

214

	Leave me alone! For God's sake leave me alone! (*He is nearly hysterical*)
FORBES:	(*Calmly: official manner*) All right. Get your things.
KENZELL:	Where are you taking me?
FORBES:	(*Aside, confidentially to TEMPLE*) Tell Vosper I want him, Temple.
TEMPLE:	(*Softly*) All right.
KENZELL:	(*Desperately*) You heard what I said, where are you taking me?!
FORBES:	You will be charged with the murder of Carl Walters and then taken … (*Suddenly*) Temple, look out! He's going for the window!!! Stop him!!!!
KENZELL:	(*Desperately: pushing FORBES aside*) Out of the way! Get out of my way!
TEMPLE:	Kenzell! Kenzell, don't be a fool!!!!
FORBES:	Oh, my God!
TEMPLE:	(*A warning cry*) Kenzell!!!!

With a wild hysterical shriek KENZELL hurls himself through the window, the shriek continues as he falls to the mews below.
Quick dramatic FADE UP of music.

FADE DOWN of music.
FADE UP background noises of a large railway station.
FADE to inside of a railway carriage.

STEVE:	We must have been early, darling!
TEMPLE:	(*Looking at his watch*) I make it nearly a quarter past. We certainly ought to be leaving soon.
STEVE:	What time do we get to Dulworth Bay?
TEMPLE:	Just after five. Would you like this magazine, Steve?

215

STEVE: No, thank you. (*Thoughtfully*) Paul, I've been thinking about this business – about the Curzon case. There's an awful lot I don't understand.

TEMPLE: There's quite a lot I don't understand, darling.

STEVE: Yes, but take last night for instance. Who telephoned Charlie?

TEMPLE: Why Kenzell did. Unfortunately, Walters was watching the flat. He knew that we were dining at Marietta's and as soon as he saw Charlie leave, he assumed that the coast was clear and broke into the flat.

STEVE: But why did Walters want the diary?

TEMPLE: For the same reason that Curzon wanted it. Steve, you remember that plane that crashed at Dulworth Bay?

STEVE: Yes?

TEMPLE: Well, there was a man on board that plane called René Duprez. It's my belief that Duprez was a member of a diamond smuggling organisation and that he was actually in the process of bringing diamonds over here when the plane crashed.

STEVE: Go on …

TEMPLE: By a remarkable coincidence the plane crashed at Dulworth Bay, the very spot which Duprez was making for.

STEVE: But why was Duprez going to Dulworth Bay? (*Suddenly*) Oh! You mean to contact Curzon?

TEMPLE: Exactly! But Curzon was a bit slow off the mark, he didn't find the diamonds.

STEVE: Who did?

TEMPLE: (*Slowly*) Mr Baxter found them.

STEVE: Baxter!

TEMPLE: Yes. Baxter was an unimportant member of the gang but as soon as he found the diamonds, he realised that he was in a pretty strong position. He hid the diamonds, made a note of their whereabouts in a diary, and tried to contact Curzon.

STEVE: But why should he do that?

TEMPLE: Obviously with a view to doing a deal with him. You see it's one thing having the diamonds and another getting rid of them. So far as Baxter was concerned, Curzon was the answer to the distribution problem.

STEVE: But if Baxter was a member of the gang, he must have known Curzon.

TEMPLE: Not necessarily. It's my guess that Baxter always received his orders through an intermediary and was completely unaware of the identity of Curzon.

STEVE: (*Thoughtfully*) I can see now why he wanted Tom Doyle to look after the boys. He knew that he was playing a dangerous game and didn't want to take any chances.

TEMPLE: Exactly.

STEVE: Paul, who was that on the motor bike last night?

TEMPLE: It was Kenzell. Vosper found the uniform in the bedroom. That wasn't the only thing he found either. He found a photograph of René Duprez.

STEVE: You think that Duprez, Kenzell, Baxter and Carl Walters were all members of the same gang?

TEMPLE: I'm not so sure about Walters. Walters was in the diamond racket and he was after the diary but I'm not at all certain that he was actually a member of the organisation.

217

STEVE: Paul, who do you think is behind all this? Who do you think is Mr Curzon?

TEMPLE: (*Thoughtfully*) Well, it might be Lord Westerby, it might be Peter Malo, it might be Dr Stuart …

The carriage door slides open.

STUART: Did I hear you mention my name, Mr Temple?

TEMPLE: (*Pleasantly*) Why, hello, Doctor! What are you doing here?

STUART: I fancy we're all here for the same reason! Because we want to get to Dulworth Bay.

TEMPLE: Yes, but I didn't know that you were in London?

STUART: I came down this morning on the early train. I make an occasional trip now and again. It breaks the monotony if nothing else.

STEVE: I shouldn't exactly call Dulworth Bay monotonous!

STUART: No? Well, maybe not. Maybe not.

The train starts to move.

TEMPLE: You've only just caught it.

STUART: My word, yes! Do you mind if I put this case over in the corner, Mr Temple? (*He reaches over with his case*) Ah, thank you! (*Seating himself: with a sigh*) Ah, that was quite a near thing! Been too bad if I'd missed it. I'd have missed my surgery.

TEMPLE: (*With a newspaper*) I suppose you'd read about that friend of yours?

STUART: Friend? Which friend do you mean, laddie?

TEMPLE: Haven't you seen the papers?

STUART: No. I left Dulworth Bay far too early for newspapers and I've been too busy today to bother about 'em.

TEMPLE: Then you don't know about Mr Walters?

STUART: Walters? (*Suddenly*) Do you mean Carl Walters?

218

TEMPLE: Yes.

STUART: No. What's happened to the laddie?

TEMPLE: He's been murdered!

STUART: Murdered! Why man you're joking!

TEMPLE: (*Passing STUART the newspaper*) Read it for yourself.

A long pause during which DR STUART reads the newspaper and the train gathers speed.

STUART: (*Quietly: amazed*) Is this true?

TEMPLE: Perfectly.

STUART: (*Stunned*) But I can hardly believe it! In your flat! Why – man – it's incredible!

TEMPLE: How well did you know Carl Walters?

STUART: I met him about six months ago. He came to the hospital one morning with a nasty gash on his hand. I did what I could for the laddie and since it was just about lunchtime, he insisted on taking me down to The Feathers for a bite to eat. He seemed a very amiable sort of chap I thought. He never came to Dulworth Bay without looking me up.

TEMPLE: Have you any idea what his business was?

STUART: Well, he did tell me once that he owned one or two amusement arcades but whether it was true or not, I don't know. He was a great one for a leg pull you know.

TEMPLE: Was he a friend of Lord Westerby's?

STUART: I couldn't say, I'm sure. (*Innocently*) But you can easily find out by asking his Lordship.

TEMPLE: M'm.

STEVE: How's Miss Maxwell, Doctor?

STUART: Oh, she's a hundred-per-cent better. I'm amazed at the recovery she's made. It's nothing short of a miracle.

219

TEMPLE: I suppose it won't be long before she's leaving hospital?

STUART: His Lordship telephoned through last night. He seems very anxious to get the lassie home as soon as possible. I expect we shall move her at the end of the week, if not before.

TEMPLE: She's Lord Westeby's niece, isn't she?

STUART: So I believe. She's a very fine-looking woman. (*With a suggestion of a sigh*) I wish I had a niece like that.

TEMPLE: (*Smiling*) Doctor, I don't know whether you remember it or not, but you once told me that you'd been responsible for bringing the Baxter boys into the world.

STUART: Well?

TEMPLE: In other words, you knew Mr and Mrs Baxter before they came to live in Dulworth Bay?

STUART: I knew Mrs Baxter before she was married. (*Thoughtfully*) Her name was Lydia Steel and a fine-looking woman she was too.

TEMPLE: What sort of a person was Philip Baxter?

STUART: (*Suddenly with an amused note of exasperation*) Mrs Temple, your husband's just about the most inquisitive person I've come across! And I've known some inquisitive people in my time!

STEVE laughs.

TEMPLE: (*Completely unabashed*) What sort of a person was Philip Baxter?

STUART: He made a great deal of money very early in life and retired. He was good-looking, indolent, and I'm glad to say passionately fond of his two boys.

TEMPLE: What did he make the great deal of money out of, do you know?

STUART: He was a stockbroker. He had one or two lucky gambles and got away with it.

TEMPLE: M'm. I see.

STUART: You sound as if you don't believe it, Mr Temple?

TEMPLE: I don't. You see, I'm not only inquisitive, Doctor. I'm sceptical.

FADE UP the sound of the train.

CROSS FADE into music.

FADE DOWN of music.

FADE UP of TEMPLE washing his hands and face: he is making a great deal of noise.

STEVE is unpacking.

STEVE: I don't know why you didn't have a bath and have done with it!

TEMPLE: (*Through the soap and water*) What's that, darling?

STEVE: I said, I don't know why you didn't have a bath and have done with it?!

TEMPLE: You don't know why I what?

STEVE: (*Shouting*) I said, I don't know why you didn't have a bath and have done with it!

TEMPLE: (*Quite unperturbed*) I didn't feel like a bath.

STEVE: You've splashed water all over the place!

TEMPLE: (*Drying himself*) As a matter of fact, I don't like that bath! Last time we were here it left a very definite impression on me. I swore I'd never use it again.

STEVE: It's to be hoped we're not going to be here for very long!

There is a knock on the door.

TEMPLE: Come in!

The door opens.

STEVE: Darling, you're in your shirt sleeves!

221

TEMPLE:	That's all right!
MORGAN:	Am I disturbing you?
TEMPLE:	Oh, hello, Inspector! Come in!
MORGAN:	(*Closing the door behind him*) Good evening, Mrs Temple!
STEVE:	Hello, Inspector! Do sit down – if you can swim as far as the chair!
MORGAN:	(*Laughing*) What's been going on here?
STEVE:	You might well ask!
TEMPLE:	Good gracious me, what a hiatus, just because I've been having a wash! I always wash on Fridays. It's an old family custom.
MORGAN:	Perhaps it's just as well.
TEMPLE:	What do you mean?
MORGAN:	You've been invited out to dinner.
TEMPLE:	Not Westerby?
MORGAN:	Yes. I happened to bump into him this afternoon. I told him that you were coming down to Dulworth Bay and he asked me to deliver the invitation. I gather you saw him last night after the Walters affair?
TEMPLE:	Yes.
MORGAN:	He seemed rather surprised that you didn't tell him you were coming down here.
TEMPLE:	I didn't know. I only made up my mind on the spur of the moment.
MORGAN:	If it's not a rude question, Temple, why have you come down to Dulworth Bay? I should have thought there was plenty of excitement in Town without coming down here.
TEMPLE:	(*Still drying himself*) I came to Dulworth Bay for a very good reason, Inspector.
MORGAN:	And what's that?

TEMPLE:	Because I'm pretty convinced that Mr Curzon's here and Curzon's the bird I'm after. (*A change of manner*) What time is Westerby expecting us, do you know?
MORGAN:	He said eight o'clock.
TEMPLE:	Oh, we've plenty of time.
MORGAN:	I checked up on Doyle. Doyle was here all right, he couldn't possibly have telephoned you – unless of course it was a trunk call.
TEMPLE:	It wasn't.
MORGAN:	I don't know what's happened to Doyle, Temple. He seems to have changed. When I first met him, he seemed such a steady, reliable sort of chap. Now he's moody and arrogant and, so far as I can see, seems to be drinking like a fish.
TEMPLE:	Is he spending a lot of money?
MORGAN:	Well, he's certainly spending quite a bit and goodness only knows where he's getting it from. It almost looks to me as if someone's giving him money in order to stop him from talking.
TEMPLE:	When did you last see Doyle?
MORGAN:	I saw him this morning.
TEMPLE:	Did you tell him about the telephone call?
MORGAN:	No. I simply asked him what he did with himself after I'd left him last night.
TEMPLE:	What did he say?
MORGAN:	He said he had three or four more drinks and then walked back home. I know he was telling me the truth because several people saw him. In any case he couldn't possibly have got up to London in time to have made the phone call.

TEMPLE:	No. No, of course not.
MORGAN:	(*Quietly*) I had a chat with Sir Graham this morning. He told me about the diary and your theory about the Baxter place.
TEMPLE:	Have you started work?
MORGAN:	Yes, I've got two men up there now.
TEMPLE:	Good.
MORGAN:	I'll let you know the moment we find anything.
STEVE:	I gather Miss Maxwell's getting better?
MORGAN:	Yes, she's much better. As a matter of fact, she's more herself again. But she still won't talk. I suppose you've no idea why she wanted to see you that morning, Temple?
TEMPLE:	Yes, I've a pretty good idea. But I wish she'd confirm it.
MORGAN:	You know, Temple, we don't seem to have got very far with Miss Maxwell, do we? Don't you think it might be rather a good idea if someone else had a talk to her?
TEMPLE:	(*Faintly surprised*) Well – who for instance?
MORGAN:	(*After a moment: quietly*) Mrs Temple.
TEMPLE:	(*Thoughtfully, impressed*) Yes. Yes, that's not a bad idea. Not at all a bad idea, Inspector.

FADE UP of music.

FADE DOWN of music.
FADE UP the sound of a car as it draws to a standstill.

TEMPLE:	I can't park the car by the hospital, Steve. I'll have to wait for you here.
STEVE:	Yes, all right, Paul.

STEVE bangs the car door.

224

TEMPLE: I say, be careful, Steve! This thing doesn't belong to me, I've only hired it!

STEVE: (*Laughing*) Sorry, darling!

TEMPLE: Good luck!

STEVE: Don't expect too much! After all, if a woman won't talk, she won't talk!

TEMPLE: You don't have to tell me, Steve – I've been married to one for ten years! Do the best you can.

STEVE: All right. See you later.

The car door closes.

FADE scene.

FADE UP of STEVE knocking on a bedroom door.

DIANA: (*Calling from within the room*) Come in!

The door opens and closes.

STEVE: (*Pleasantly*) Hello!

DIANA: Oh, hello! The Matron said that you wanted to see me. (*Her manner is a little cold but not unfriendly*)

STEVE: Are you feeling any better?

DIANA: Yes, I'm much better thanks.

STEVE: How long have you been out of bed?

DIANA: I got out this morning, for the first time. It was quite an effort.

STEVE: I'll bet it was Dr Stuart says: (*Imitating the Doctor*) You've got the constitution of a horse.

DIANA: Well, as long as he didn't say I looked like one!

STEVE: On the contrary, he was very complimentary. May I sit down?

DIANA: Yes, of course. I'm sorry. (*With a little more warmth*) No, don't sit near the window you'll find it rather draughty. Sit over here.

STEVE: Oh, thank you.

A moment.

DIANA: (*Making conversation*) How long have you been down here?

STEVE: We arrived this afternoon.

DIANA: Are you staying long?

STEVE: It rather depends. Two or three days at least, I should say. Oh, by the way, we're dining with your uncle tonight.

DIANA: Oh, are you? He'll be awfully pleased, although I expect he'll bore your poor husband to death. David's frightfully sweet but he can be the most crashing bore.

STEVE: I expect his secretary will brighten up the party. (*Laughing*) I'm told he does the most incredible impersonations.

DIANA: (*Lightly: yet faintly surprised*) Who told you that?

STEVE: (*Simply*) Well, doesn't he …?

DIANA: Yes, but …

STEVE: (*Lightly, dismissing the matter*) I just forget who told me – it was probably Mr Malo himself.

DIANA: (*Seriously*) Mrs Temple, why are you and your husband so determined to get to the bottom of this affair? Don't you think it would be far more sensible of you both if you just forgot the whole business and went back to London?

STEVE: Is that what you want us to do?

DIANA: (*Earnestly*) Yes. Yes, I do indeed, Mrs Temple.

A moment.

STEVE: Miss Maxwell, I'm going to say something to you which you may not like, but nevertheless I'm going to say it.

DIANA: Well?

226

STEVE: Don't you think you owe my husband an explanation? After all, he did save your life you know.

DIANA: (*A note of tenseness in her voice*) I'm grateful to Mr Temple for what he did – terribly grateful, but … (*She stops*)

STEVE: But you haven't the slightest intentions of helping him, is that it?

DIANA: (*Suddenly*) There's nothing I can tell Mr Temple that he doesn't already know.

STEVE: I think there is. Why, for instance, are you frightened of Mr Malo?

DIANA: (*Quickly: aggressively*) I'm not frightened of Mr Malo!

STEVE: You sounded very frightened of him the night that you asked my husband to meet you.

DIANA: I was rather hysterical that night and not very sure of myself. I behaved very badly. I'm sorry.

STEVE: That wasn't the only night you behaved very badly, Miss Maxwell.

DIANA: What do you mean?

STEVE: Have you forgotten your telephone conversation. (*A moment*) You made an appointment to meet my husband at a café in Soho. You didn't turn up, instead he saw a girl called Doris White.

DIANA: I'm getting rather bored by this conversation, Mrs Temple. Do you mind?

STEVE: (*Rising*) I've no wish to bore you, Miss Maxwell. That's the last thing I should like to do.

DIANA: No, wait! I'm sorry. That was extremely rude of me and I apologise. (*After a moment*) Mrs Temple, when I telephoned your husband that night, I was desperately worried about certain things and I wanted to talk to him about them.

227

Later, I changed my mind. When you came down to Dulworth Bay however and I met your husband I formed the opinion that I'd been rather stupid about things and I decided there and then that the best thing I could do was to take him into my confidence. Please believe me, I was quite sincere about it – that's why I made the appointment to meet him on the yacht.

STEVE: Yes, but you changed your mind again?

DIANA: (*Quietly*) Yes.

STEVE: Why? Supposing there hadn't been an attempt on your life – would you still have changed your mind?

DIANA: No, I should have kept my promise.

STEVE: Then it really boils down to the fact that you're frightened, doesn't it?

DIANA: Yes, I am frightened. Desperately frightened. And I don't intend to take any more chances!

STEVE: (*Rising*) Well, if you do change your mind again, Miss Maxwell, let me know.

DIANA: I'm sorry not to have been more helpful. (*A faint suggestion of sarcasm*) It really wasn't a very bright idea to send you here, Mrs Temple.

STEVE: Oh, I don't know. You told me about Mr Malo.

DIANA: What do you mean?

STEVE: About his being able to do impersonations.

DIANA: (*Surprised*) But you already knew that!

STEVE: (*Sweetly*) Did I? Did I, Miss Maxwell?

FADE UP of music.

FADE DOWN of music.
FADE UP the sound of a car that is travelling at an average speed.
TEMPLE is driving.

228

Together with the sound of the car FADE UP of STEVE talking:

STEVE: ... It was simply a guess of mine about Malo doing impersonations but to my utter amazement she confirmed it.

TEMPLE: I think you did very well, darling.

STEVE: Anyway, it's pretty obvious that it was Malo that impersonated Doyle.

TEMPLE: Yes.

STEVE: You know, if Malo weren't such a weak sort of character, I'd almost feel inclined to believe that he was Curzon.

TEMPLE: You don't think he is?

STEVE: No, darling, I don't. I think Westerby's our man, I've thought so from the very beginning. I've got a sort of intuition about Westerby.

TEMPLE: (*Laughing*) That good old intuition! (*Peering*) We turn left here, don't we?

STEVE: Yes, turn left then straight down the lane.

The car slows down and turns the corner.

TEMPLE: (*Suddenly*) Hello, there's Doyle!

STEVE: Where? Oh, yes! (*The car slows down to a standstill*) What are you going to do?

TEMPLE: I'm going to give him a lift. (*He opens the car door and calls*) Hello, there! Hello, Tom!

TOM DOYLE strolls across to the car. His manner is drunken and, at first, faintly surly. He is very unsteady on his feet.

DOYLE: What do you want? (*Recognises Temple*) Oh, it's you. Thought you'd gone away! Thought you'd gone back to London.

TEMPLE: (*Smiling: pleasantly*) We did go back to London, Tom – but we've come back again.

DOYLE: Why? What d'you want to come back here for?
           Rotten hole. Stinks.
STEVE: Well, you're a bachelor! If you don't like it why
           don't you move?
DOYLE: It's impossible. Absolutely impossible. Plenty of
           money down here. Loads of money. Don't want
           to move when there's plenty of money. (*A
           moment*) Silly.
STEVE: (*Quietly, aside*) He's drunk, Paul.
TEMPLE: Yes. (*To DOYLE*) It sounds as if business is
           good, Tom. You must be doing a roaring trade!
DOYLE: Business is ro-tt-en.
TEMPLE: But I thought you said there was plenty of
           money?
DOYLE: There is if you've got your head screwed on.
           Got to have your head screwed on though. Got to
           have your head crewed on and your eyes open.
           Must have your eyes open. Abso ... Absolute ...
           Must have your eyes open.
TEMPLE: (*Smiling*) Jump in – we'll give you a lift home.
DOYLE: Thank you. (*He slips on the step of the car*)
STEVE: Oh, do be careful! Have you hurt yourself?
DOYLE: No.
DOYLE climbs into the car and bangs the door.
TEMPLE: Are you all right?
DOYLE: Yes, I'm all right.
STEVE: I say, mind my hat!
DOYLE: It's a nice car. Beautiful car. (*Sprawling across
           the back seat*) Plenty of room ...
STEVE: (*Quietly, to TEMPLE*) Go on, Paul!
TEMPLE changes gear and the car moves away.
FADE scene.

FADE UP of the car drawing to a standstill.

DOYLE is snoring in the back of the car.

TEMPLE: Come on, Tom! Wake up!

DOYLE: (*Opening his eyes*) What?

TEMPLE: I said, wake up! You're home!

DOYLE: Oh! Oh ... (*He begins to stir*)

TEMPLE: Can you manage?

DOYLE: Yes, of course I can manage. (*Endeavouring to extricate himself*) There's no room in this car, that's the trouble! No room ... It's hopeless. You want to sell it – get rid of it. Give the blo ... Give the thing away. It's hopeless ...

TEMPLE: (*Laughing*) Come on, Tom! (*He opens the car door*) Can you manage to get out?

DOYLE: (*Climbing out of the car*) Yes ... just about. (*He is out of the car*) There we are!

TEMPLE: Are you all right?

DOYLE: Of course I'm all right. How much is that? (*He takes coins from his pocket*) How much do I owe you?

TEMPLE: Oh, we'll forget that, Tom!

DOYLE: We certainly won't forget it! I've got the money, I'll pay! Insist on paying. Absolutely insist! Here's five-bob – keep the change.

STEVE: (*A little nervous: to TEMPLE*) Take it, darling.

TEMPLE: (*Amused*) All right. (*He takes the money*) Goodnight, Tom.

DOYLE: (*Turning away*) Goodnight. (*To himself*) Too dear. Far too dear ... Extortionate ...

TEMPLE changes gear and the car moves away.

TEMPLE: (*To STEVE*) Do you want one of the windows open?

STEVE: No, I don't think so, darling. He was well away, wasn't he?

FADE UP of the car.

231

Slow, gradual, FADE AWAY of the car.
FADE scene.

FADE UP the opening of a door and voices: STEVE,
TEMPLE and LORD WESTERBY:

WESTERBY: Now, Mrs Temple, I feel quite sure that you'd like a glass of port. (*He takes the decanter*)

STEVE: No thank you, Lord Westerby.

WESTERBY: I assure you I can recommend this, Mrs Temple. It's a really delightful wine. Can't I persuade you to change your mind? No? Well, I'm sure you'll have a glass, Temple?

TEMPLE: Thank you.

WESTERBY: Do sit down, Mrs Temple. (*Pouring wine from the decanter*) You know, it's an extraordinary thing whenever I see a bottle of port, I always find myself thinking of that play of Arnold Bennett's – Mr Prohack. Do you remember it?

TEMPLE: (*Amused*) What makes you think of Mr Prohack?

WESTERBY: (*Chuckling*) I don't know. That's the extraordinary thing about it. I think there was a line somewhere in the play – in the first act, I believe – about buying a bottle of port from the local grocers. (*Amused*) All I know is that as soon as I see a bottle of port – Bang – Mr Prohack!

TEMPLE: (*Taking a glass*) Thank you.

WESTERBY: Well, I'm sorry you won't join us, Mrs Temple. Will you have a liqueur?

STEVE: No, thank you. (*Laughing*) I'm sorry to keep on saying no!

WESTERBY: Not at all. It's rather a delightful surprise to find a member of the younger generation so abstemious.

STEVE: Thank you for the 'younger generation'.

TEMPLE laughs.

WESTERBY: Oh, by the way, Temple, before I forget. I read a book the other day that I'm sure would interest you – The Psychology of Crime by Professor Stern.

TEMPLE: Yes, I've read it.

WESTERBY: It's first-class, isn't it?

TEMPLE: I particularly liked the chapter on Psychonosology.

WESTERBY: Oh, brilliant! Are you quite comfortable over there, Mrs Temple?

STEVE: Yes, quite – thank you.

WESTERBY: (*Pleasantly*) I understand you saw my niece this evening?

STEVE: Yes. I'm so glad she's getting better. I saw an amazing difference in her.

WESTERBY: Yes, I expect you would. (*Turning*) Will you have a cigar, Temple?

TEMPLE: No, thank you.

WESTERBY: (*To STEVE*) You don't mind, Mrs Temple, if I …?

STEVE: (*Laughing*) No, of course not.

WESTERBY: (*Preparing his cigar*) I'm sorry my secretary couldn't join us this evening. (*Smiling*) He's quite a character you know. Was on the stage for a number of years. Did impersonations and things (*He lights his cigar*) He's not a frightfully good impersonator, but he's jolly amusing. Always makes Diana laugh. (*Casually*

233

	examining his cigar) She's rather fond of Malo. (*Looking up*) Are you sure you wouldn't like a cigar, Temple?
TEMPLE:	Yes, quite sure, thank you.
WESTERBY:	(*Making himself comfortable*) I was rather intrigued, on reading that book of Stern's to come across a reference to what he calls – the deciding factor. In other words, the unimportant little clue which, in the final stages of an investigation, can mean so much. Frankly, I'd always thought that sort of thing was exaggerated. You know what I mean, the detective finds a matchstick, picks up a hairpin, overhears an apparently harmless conversation. After reading that book of Stern's however, I'm not so sure.
TEMPLE:	If the case is an important one you mustn't overlook anything, Lord Westerby, however trivial it may seem.
WESTERBY:	Yes, in theory I can understand that, but I mean – well – in practice surely it doesn't always work out that way? For instance, have you ever come across anything like that? A small, unimportant thing which can, and does in fact, prove a deciding factor?
TEMPLE:	Yes. I came across something like that tonight.
WESTERBY:	(*Sitting up*) Tonight? You mean to do with the Curzon Case?
TEMPLE:	Yes.
STEVE:	(*Puzzled*) What, darling?
TEMPLE:	Oh, it was just an apparently unimportant little thing. Something you said as a matter of fact, Steve.

STEVE: (*Very surprised*) Something I said?

TEMPLE: Yes.

WESTERBY: (*Smiling*) I'm most intrigued, Mr Temple.

TEMPLE: On the way here, in the car, I asked my wife if she would like one of the windows down.

WESTERBY: Well?

TEMPLE: (*After a moment*) She said no.

FADE UP of music.

END OF EPISODE SEVEN

EPISODE EIGHT

CURZON

238

FADE UP of PAUL TEMPLE speaking.

TEMPLE: If the case is an important one you mustn't overlook anything, Lord Westerby, however trivial it may seem.

WESTERBY: Yes, in theory I can understand that, but I mean – well – in practice surely it doesn't always work out that way? For instance, have you ever come across anything like that? A small, unimportant thing which can, and does in fact, prove a deciding factor?

TEMPLE: Yes. I came across something like that tonight

WESTERBY: (*Sitting up*) Tonight? You mean to do with the Curzon Case?

TEMPLE: Yes.

STEVE: (*Puzzled*) What, darling?

TEMPLE: Oh, it was just an apparently unimportant little thing. Something you said as a matter of fact, Steve.

STEVE: (*Very surprised*) Something I said?

TEMPLE: Yes.

WESTERBY: (*Smiling*) I'm most intrigued, Mr Temple.

TEMPLE: On the way here, in the car, I asked my wife if she would like one of the windows down.

WESTERBY: Well?

TEMPLE: (*After a moment*) She said no.

WESTERBY: (*Puzzled*) She said no?

TEMPLE: Yes.

WESTERBY: (*With a little laugh*) Well, was that significant?

TEMPLE: Very significant.

WESTERBY: (*Faintly amused*) Do you know what he's getting at, Mrs Temple?

STEVE: I haven't the slightest idea.

WESTERBY: (*Still amused*) He simply asked you if you would like the window down and you said no?

STEVE: Yes.

WESTERBY: (*Chuckling*) This is all far too mysterious for me, I'm afraid.

TEMPLE: There's nothing mysterious about it at all. It's really quite simple.

WESTERBY: (*Still amused*) Providing you know the answer.

STEVE: Well, I just can't see why you should attach the slightest importance to the fact that I ... (*She stops speaking, softly*) Oh ... (*A sudden realisation*) Oh!

TEMPLE: (*Quietly, almost an aside*) You see what I mean?

STEVE: Yes ... (*Stunned*) Yes ...

WESTERBY: (*Surprised*) Why you look quite pale, Mrs Temple! Can I get you a drink?

TEMPLE: (*Slowly, watching STEVE*) Have a glass of port, darling. Lord Westerby was right. (*Still holding STEVE's gaze*) It's really excellent.

WESTERBY: (*Faintly concerned*) I think you'd better have something, Mrs Temple.

STEVE: (*After a moment*) I think I should like a glass of port, if I may.

WESTERBY: Why, yes, of course! (*Crosses to background; at the cocktail cabinet*) You know, Temple, I'm rather intrigued by this business. It seems to me that if you consider the fact that Mrs Temple didn't want the ... (*He stops speaking as the door opens*)

240

MALO:	May I come in? (*MALO is a little overwrought and faintly out of breath*)
WESTERBY:	(*Surprised*) Why, Peter! What on earth's the matter with you?
MALO:	I've had trouble with my car. The blasted battery went phut and I had to swing it.
WESTERBY:	You look to me as if you've had a fight or something.
MALO:	I feel as if I've been dragged through a hedge backwards. (*Angry*) That wretched car!
TEMPLE:	(*Quietly*) You've cut your face, Malo.
MALO:	Where? (*He feels his face*) Oh. Oh, it's nothing.
WESTERBY:	Peter's helpless with a car! If it doesn't spring to life the moment he presses the starter he flies into an absolutely panic!
MALO:	I certainly flew into a panic tonight. I was so angry I could have kicked the blasted thing!
STEVE:	(*Smiling*) Are you sure you didn't?
MALO:	What do you mean?
WESTERBY:	(*Laughing*) Come over here to the mirror, Peter, and take a look at yourself!

A moment.

MALO:	I say, I do look ghastly, don't I? (*Shocked*) Good Lord!
TEMPLE:	(*Laughing*) What did you do, climb under the car and examine the exhaust pipe?
MALO:	I did everything – except start the confounded thing!
WESTERBY:	I think you'd better have a drink, Peter. What would you like?
MALO:	Whisky, sir – please.
WESTERBY:	Here's your port, Mrs Temple.

STEVE:	Oh, thank you.
WESTERBY:	You'd better help yourself, Peter.
MALO:	Thank you, sir.
WESTERBY:	Just before you arrived, we were having rather an interesting conversation. Mr Temple was telling me that he'd made a very important discovery.
MALO:	What kind of a discovery?
WESTERBY:	(*After a momentary pause*) To do with the Curzon Case.
MALO:	(*A note of irritation in his voice*) I don't believe there is such a person as Curzon! If you ask me, it's all a lot of damn nonsense!
TEMPLE:	I'm sorry to disappoint you, Mr Malo.
MALO:	(*Looking up, quietly*) What do you mean?
A tiny pause.	
TEMPLE:	I know the identity of Curzon.
MALO:	(*Dropping his glass*) What!
WESTERBY:	(*Staggered*) Temple, are you joking?
TEMPLE:	No, I'm not joking.
MALO:	Well, if you know the identity of Curzon why the devil don't you do something about it?!
TEMPLE:	(*Seriously*) I intend to do something about it, Malo. (*A complete change of manner: lightly*) As a matter of fact I intend to give a cocktail party.
WESTERBY:	(*Staggered*) A cocktail party!
TEMPLE:	Yes, the day after tomorrow. You're both cordially invited.
WESTERBY:	(*After a moment: quietly, watching TEMPLE*) Cocktail parties aren't much in my line, Temple.

242

TEMPLE: (*Smiling at him*) That's only because you've never been to one of mine, Lord Westerby.

FADE UP of music.

FADE DOWN of music.
FADE UP of the sound of a car which is travelling at an average speed.
TEMPLE is driving.

STEVE: Don't go too fast, Paul.

TEMPLE: All right, darling.

A pause.

STEVE: Is that the Baxter place over there?

TEMPLE: It was the Baxter place, yes. That fire made an awful mess, didn't it?

STEVE: Frightful.

TEMPLE: Are you feeling any better?

STEVE: I'm all right now.

TEMPLE: You should have seen your face!

STEVE: I thought you were talking a lot of nonsense, darling, then it suddenly dawned on me what you meant.

TEMPLE: You went as white as a sheet.

STEVE: Well, I was so surprised! I was flabbergasted! Do you think Lord Westerby suspected?

TEMPLE: (*Thoughtfully*) I don't know.

STEVE: I suppose you told Sir Graham?

TEMPLE: Yes.

STEVE: And Morgan?

TEMPLE: I told Morgan tonight before you went to the hospital. He didn't believe me. He thinks I'm on the wrong track.

STEVE: (*Thoughtfully*) Paul, if he is Curzon – the person you suspect, I mean – then how do

243

	you account for the fact that Miss Maxwell telephoned you that night and ... (*She stops*)
TEMPLE:	Go on ...
STEVE:	That's funny, I thought I saw a light. I'm sure I ... (*Suddenly*) Paul, look! There's someone on the road! There's someone waving a light!
TEMPLE:	(*Puzzled*) Yes! That's odd!
STEVE:	(*Tensely*) You'll have to pull up, darling, he's in the middle of the road.

The car slows down and gradually comes to a standstill.

TEMPLE:	(*Surprised*) Steve, do you see who it is?!
STEVE:	It's Doctor Stuart!
TEMPLE:	Now what the devil does he want?
STUART:	(*Excited and faintly out of breath*) I'm sorry stopping you like this, sir, but would you be kind enough to give me a lift to ... (*Suddenly amazed*) Why, Mr Temple!
TEMPLE:	Hello, doctor!
STUART:	Why God bless my soul, you're just the man I want!
TEMPLE:	What's the trouble?
STEVE:	(*Quickly*) Has anything happened?
STUART:	(*Bewildered*) Aye, but I'm darned if I know what it is. Inspector Morgan seems to have met with an accident: he's over yonder in one of the bushes.
STEVE:	(*Astonished*) Inspector Morgan!

TEMPLE switches off the car engine.

TEMPLE:	Is he badly hurt?
STUART:	I'm afraid so. Frankly, I don't hold out much hope for the laddie.
TEMPLE:	(*Rather surprised*) But what happened?

244

STUART: I don't know. I was walking down the lane when I heard a noise. At first, I didn't know what the devil it was or where it was coming from. Suddenly I realised that it was coming from over yonder – from the bushes. When I went over there, I found the Inspector. He was in a terrible condition: moaning and groaning. It looked to me as if the poor devil had been having a fight with someone.

TEMPLE: (*Opening the car door: briskly*) Where is he – over there?

STUART: Aye – he's in one of the rhododendron bushes.

Start FADE.

STUART: I daren't move him before the poor fellow was bleeding so profusely.

FADE Scene.

FADE UP of INSPECTOR MORGAN: he is groaning and is obviously in great pain.

MORGAN: (*Weakly: a little frightened*) Who is that? Who is it?

STUART: Now take it easy, laddie. It's only me – Dr Stuart.

MORGAN: (*Tensely*) There's someone else with you! There's someone else! I can hear them. I can hear them walking about … (*Groans*)

TEMPLE: (*Quietly*) It's me, Inspector – Temple. We were on the way in to the village and the doctor stopped our car.

MORGAN: (*Weakly*) Temple …

TEMPLE: Yes.

245

MORGAN:	(*Relieved, yet dazed and confused*) Oh … Oh …
TEMPLE:	(*Kneeling down beside him: softly*) Now, Morgan, listen. What happened?
MORGAN:	I came down to the cottage. I was in the garden. I was in the garden searching for … for … (*He can hardly speak*)
TEMPLE:	(*Gently*) Yes, I know. I know, Morgan. You were in the garden and someone attacked you.
MORGAN:	(*Almost a hysterical note*) He thought I had the diamonds. He thought I'd found them. He came up behind me when I was looking in one of the flower beds and … and …
STUART:	Take it easy, laddie. (*To TEMPLE: quietly*) You mustn't ask him too many questions, Temple. I suggest we try and carry him back to your car.
TEMPLE:	Wait a moment! (*Tensely*) Morgan, did you see him? Did you see Curzon?
STUART:	(*Softly: apparently amazed*) Curzon!
MORGAN:	Yes … Yes, I saw him …
TEMPLE:	(*Tensely*) Well? Well – who was it?
MORGAN:	(*With a determined effort*) You were right. You … were … right … Temple. (*His head falls back*)

FADE UP of music.

FADE DOWN of music.
FADE UP background noises of a small dining room.
TEMPLE and STEVE are having breakfast.

TEMPLE:	Pass the marmalade, Steve.
STEVE:	Here we are …
TEMPLE:	Thank you …

246

STEVE:	Have you seen the Morning Post?
TEMPLE:	Yes.
STEVE:	It's not a very good photograph of Morgan, is it?
TEMPLE:	No, it's obviously an old one they had on the files. (*Depressed*) I feel awfully upset about last night, Steve. If only the poor devil had taken my advice, it might never have happened.
STEVE:	What did Sir Graham say?
TEMPLE:	He didn't say a great deal. He's coming down here with Vosper. They should be here in time for lunch.
STEVE:	Paul, I've been thinking about last night and about Peter Malo. It seems to me that his story about the car ... (*She breaks off: looking up*) Yes, what is it?
WAITRESS:	Excuse me, Madam – you're wanted on the telephone.
TEMPLE:	Are you sure it's for <u>Mrs</u> Temple?
WAITRESS:	Yes, sir. It's from the hospital, sir.
TEMPLE:	(*Quietly*) It's Miss Maxwell.
STEVE:	Yes. I wonder what she wants. (*She rises*) I shan't be long, darling.

FADE scene.

FADE UP of STEVE lifting a telephone receiver.

STEVE:	(*On the phone*) Hello?
DIANA:	(*On the other end: tense and nervous*) Is that you, Mrs Temple?
STEVE:	Yes, speaking.
DIANA:	This is Diana Maxwell.
STEVE:	(*Pleasantly*) Oh, good morning, Miss Maxwell.

DIANA: (*Quietly: tensely*) Mrs Temple, I've been reading in the paper about Inspector Morgan. Is it true? Is it true that he …

STEVE: (*Interrupting her*) It's true that he was murdered, if that's what you mean?

DIANA: (*Very softly: obviously under an emotional strain*) What happened? Who did it?

STEVE: I thought you said you'd read the papers?

DIANA: Was it … Curzon?

STEVE: Yes.

DIANA: Oh, it's horrible! Horrible! I can hardly believe that anyone could do such a thing! (*Suddenly*) Mrs Temple, I want to have another talk to you. I've got to see you. Come round to the hospital this morning. Please, Mrs Temple!

STEVE: What is it you want to talk to me about?

DIANA: I want to tell you why I telephoned your husband that night. I want to tell you everything … everything I know about … the … Curzon Case.

STEVE: But you've said that before, Miss Maxwell. You seem to have made quite a habit of it.

DIANA: This time I promise you, I'll keep my word. (*A note of desperation in her voice*) Please, Mrs Temple!

STEVE: (*After a moment*) I'll talk to my husband about it. If I'm coming, I'll be there in half an hour.

FADE UP of music.

FADE DOWN on music.

A door opens and closes.

TEMPLE: (*Quietly*) Good morning, Miss Maxwell.

DIANA: (*Surprised*) Oh! Oh, Mr Temple! I didn't expect to see you!

TEMPLE: So I gathered.

DIANA: I just hadn't the nerve to send for you again, that's why I asked for Mrs Temple.

TEMPLE: Nevertheless, it was me you wanted to see, wasn't it?

DIANA: Yes.

TEMPLE: Do you still want to see me, or have you changed your mind?

DIANA: (*After a moment*) No. No, this time I haven't changed my mind.

TEMPLE: Well, that's something anyway! May I sit down?

DIANA: Yes. Yes, please do.

A moment.

TEMPLE: I gather you know what happened last night? You know that Inspector Morgan was murdered?

DIANA: Yes.

TEMPLE: Have you any idea who murdered him?

DIANA: Your wife said – and the papers say – that he was murdered by Curzon.

TEMPLE: Yes. (*Slight pause: watching DIANA*) Who is this notorious Mr Curzon? Do you know?

DIANA: (*After a moment: obviously distressed*) Yes.

TEMPLE: You think it's your Uncle – Lord Westerby – don't you?

DIANA: (*Distressed*) I know it's my uncle! I know he's Curzon! I know he's Curzon because … (*She stops*)

TEMPLE: (*Gently*) Suppose you start at the beginning, Miss Maxwell. Supposing you tell me about the Baxter boys, about René Duprez, about the diamonds, and about why you telephoned me that night and arranged to meet me at the Tabriz. You did telephone me, didn't you?

DIANA: Yes.

TEMPLE: Were you in Town?

DIANA: Yes, my uncle lied when he said I spent the evening with him. But please, let me begin at the beginning. About three months ago, I discovered that my uncle, together with Peter Malo and Mr Baxter, were actively engaged in a diamond smuggling organisation. When I discovered this, I went straight to my uncle and told him that I intended to inform the police. He appeared to be desperately frightened, and he told me that the leader of the organisation was a notorious criminal called Curzon and that if I reported the matter to Scotland Yard Curzon would simply take the law into his own hands and liquidate both my uncle and Peter Malo.

TEMPLE: Go on …

DIANA: About six weeks after I spoke to my uncle, a plane crashed near Dulworth Bay – you probably remember reading about it?

TEMPLE: Yes.

DIANA: There was a man on board the plane called René Duprez. Durprez was a member of the Curzon organisation and was actually in the process of bringing diamonds over here when the plane crashed. Both my uncle and Peter Malo endeavoured to find the diamonds, but they failed, eventually they were discovered by Philip Baxter. Baxter hid the diamonds, made a note of their whereabouts in a diary, and then contacted my uncle. He told my uncle that he was prepared to sell the diamonds to him – at a price. Both my uncle and Malo were indignant; they insisted that the diamonds belonged to the group. The row with Baxter went on for some considerable time and then suddenly, to my horror, the Baxter boys disappeared. I was convinced that my uncle was responsible for this and that he was in fact the notorious Curzon, I went to Town, telephoned you, and arranged to meet you at the Tabriz.

TEMPLE: Why didn't you meet me?

DIANA: Because when I left the telephone box, I bumped head first into Peter Malo!

TEMPLE: Had Malo been following you?

DIANA: Yes. I told him that in view of this new development with the Baxter boys, I intended to meet you and tell you the whole story. And then suddenly … a rather remarkable thing happened …

TEMPLE: He convinced you that Westerby had nothing whatsoever to do with the Baxter boys, that he was <u>not</u> in fact responsible for their disappearance.

DIANA: (*Surprised*) Yes! … As soon as I realised that he was telling the truth I decided to go back to Dulworth Bay. (*Quietly*) The next day I read about the murder of Doris White.

TEMPLE: Was Doris White a friend of Peter Malo's?

DIANA: Yes, it was Malo that told her to impersonate me and go down to the Tabriz. Malo was afraid that if no one turned up at the restaurant you'd get interested in the Baxter case and discover about Westerby and the Curzon organisation. He told Doris to supply you with false information and throw you off the scent.

TEMPLE: But she never got that far – the poor girl was murdered. Why?

DIANA: Because my uncle heard that I'd made an appointment to meet you and he wanted to make

251

sure that if I did meet you, I shouldn't talk. Unfortunately, he knew nothing about Malo's arrangement with Doris and murdered the wrong girl.

TEMPLE: Was Malo under the impression that you'd already contacted me – before the telephone call, I mean?

DIANA: Yes, I think he thought that I'd written to you. As a matter of fact, that's why he searched your suitcases.

TEMPLE: And what about the Draper boy?

DIANA: As soon as my uncle knew that you'd made up your mind to come down to Dulworth Bay he decided that the best thing that could happen was for you to concentrate on the disappearance of the Baxter boys. He instructed Malo to add to the mystery by kidnapping Draper. I discovered this and swore to report the whole matter to Scotland Yard unless the boy was returned.

TEMPLE: And what about the fire at the cottage, and the tree that collapsed, and the attempt on your life? Was Malo responsible for those?

DIANA: He was responsible for the fire, but he couldn't have had anything to do with the tree and I'm quite sure that he hadn't anything to do with the attempt on my life.

TEMPLE: You think your uncle was responsible for that?

DIANA: (*Softly*) I'm sure of it.

TEMPLE: And you're equally convinced that he's the notorious Mr Curzon?

DIANA: Aren't you?

TEMPLE: (*Suddenly: a change of manner*) Miss Maxwell, I wonder if you would do me a favour? You know that yacht of yours?

252

DIANA: Yes?

TEMPLE: Well, I want to borrow it for a little while.

DIANA: (*Surprised*) Borrow it?

TEMPLE: Yes. (*With a laugh*) But don't get the wrong impression. I don't want to go on a cruise if that's what you're thinking! I simply want to give a cocktail party and it struck me that on board your yacht might be a very good place to hold it.

DIANA: Well, you can use the yacht with pleasure. Am I invited to your party?

TEMPLE: (*Quietly: shaking his head*) No. No, I'm afraid not.

DIANA: (*Taken aback*) No? Why?

TEMPLE: (*Quietly: seriously*) When are you supposed to be leaving here?

DIANA: According to Dr Stuart I can leave tomorrow.

TEMPLE: Well, take my advice – never mind what Dr Stuart says – stay where you are. Stay here for at least the next forty-eight hours.

DIANA: (*Surprised*) But why?

TEMPLE: Because a lot can happen in forty-eight hours, Miss Maxwell.

FADE UP of music.

FADE DOWN of music.

FADE UP the noise of a rowing boat: it is approaching the yacht.

The boat reaches the yacht and TOM DOYLE lifts the oars out of the water.

DOYLE: Well, here you are, doctor! This is the yacht. I don't see any sign of Mr Temple though.

STUART: No, and I'm dashed if I do!

DOYLE: What makes you think you'll find Mr Temple on board?

STUART: (*A little puzzled*) Well, I was told to meet him here. He sent me an invitation. Said it was going to be a party.

A pause.

STUART: Well, I don't know what to say, I'm sure.

DOYLE: It'll cost you another five shillings if I take you back.

STUART: Five shillings! Why man, you've got to go back in any case!

DOYLE: (*Impatiently: faintly surly*) Come on, doc! Don't argue the point – what's it to be?

STUART: (*Puzzled*) Well, I really don't know what ... (*Suddenly*) Why, there's Mrs Temple over there! (*He puts his hands to his mouth*) Hello, there! Hello, Mrs Temple!

DOYLE: Steady, man! Don't turn the boat over!

STUART: (*Shouting*) Mrs Temple!!!!

STEVE: (*Suddenly noticing STUART: calling down*) Oh, hello, doctor! I didn't see you!

STUART: (*Calling*) How do we get up?

STEVE: The ladder's been moved, it's over the other side!

STUART: (*To DOYLE: faintly excited*) Ye'd better go round the other side, laddie!

DOYLE: You sit still, mate, or you'll find yourself under the ruddy rudder!

STEVE: (*Calling from the yacht, further away*) It's over here!

STUART: (*Calling back*) We're coming!

FADE UP of the boat moving.

FADE scene.

254

FADE UP of DR STUART, TOM DOYLE and STEVE on the deck of the yacht. TOM DOYLE and DR STUART have just climbed over the side.

STEVE: (*Pleasantly*) You're late, doctor! We thought you weren't coming!

STUART: I was called out to a maternity case at the last minute and ... (*Suddenly irritated*) Look, will you give this laddie five shillings, I just haven't got any change at the moment.

DOYLE: I've never known you when you have had any! What the devil do you want with it?

STEVE: (*Amused*) Come along to the cabin, doctor! Come on, Doyle, I'll get Mr Temple to pay you.

FADE.

FADE UP of scene inside the cabin.
LORD WESTERBY is talking he is obviously faintly annoyed.
The door opens while WESTERBY is speaking.

WESTERBY: Now look here, Temple. Please don't think I'm impertinent, but you must have had a reason for inviting us here tonight. You must have had a very good reason, so if you don't ...

TEMPLE: (*Quickly, turning towards the door: briskly*) Ah, so here you are, doctor! I thought you were never coming.

STUART: Unfortunately, I was detained.

TEMPLE: (*Quickly, glibly*) Well, you're here anyway and that's the main thing! What would you like? A glass of sherry? Whisky and soda? Gin and ... Oh, by the way, I don't think

255

you've met Sir Graham Forbes. Sir Graham's an old friend of mine. (*Introducing them*) Sir Graham, this is Dr Stuart.

STUART: (*Slowly*) How do you do, sir?

FORBES: Good evening, doctor.

TEMPLE: (*Suddenly, surprised*) Why, hello, Doyle! I didn't expect to see you here!

STEVE: Mr Doyle wants five shillings, darling – the doctor hasn't any change.

TEMPLE: Oh! Well, you might as well have a drink while you're here, I'm sure you won't say no to a glass of beer!

DOYLE: Well – thank you, sir. (*To WESTERBY*) Good evening, m'Lord.

WESTERBY: (*Curtly*) 'Evening, Doyle.

MALO: (*Irritated*) Mr Temple, we've been here, on this yacht, for exactly three quarters of an hour and you still haven't told us …

TEMPLE: (*Pleasantly, interrupting MALO*) Haven't told you what, Malo?

WESTERBY: Dammit man, you haven't told us why you invited us here!

TEMPLE: But you know why I invited you here. I invited you here because I wanted to give a cocktail party.

FORBES: I'm afraid Temple has a weakness for parties, Lord Westerby. Especially this kind of party.

WESTERBY: What do you mean, sir? Especially this kind of party?

FORBES: When Temple was investigating the Gregory affair, he took the liberty of

	inviting to his flat all of the possible suspects.
WESTERBY:	Well?
FORBES:	(*Slowly*) Well, tonight, he's invited here – to this yacht – all the possible suspects in The Curzon Case.
MALO:	Are you suggesting that Curzon is here – that he's actually here on the yacht?
FORBES:	That's precisely what I'm suggesting, Mr Malo.
MALO:	But don't be crazy, old boy! There's only four of us here. Lord Westerby, the doctor, Doyle and myself!
DOYLE:	(*Ugly*) Here just a minute! Don't count me in on this! I wasn't invited anyway.
TEMPLE:	(*Politely*) But you're very welcome, Mr Doyle!
DOYLE:	That's as maybe – but I'm not staying! (*He turns and tries to open the door. It is locked*)
WESTERBY:	What's the matter, Doyle?
DOYLE:	(*Trying to open the door*) Why the door won't open! It's locked!
MALO:	Locked!
WESTERBY:	What do you mean?
DOYLE:	(*Angry, turning on TEMPLE*) What's the idea? Why is the door locked?
TEMPLE:	(*Calmly*) Well, obviously either to stop someone from getting in or to stop someone from getting out.
STUART:	(*Quietly, slowly*) Mr Temple …
TEMPLE:	(*Turning*) Yes, doctor?
STUART:	There's two things I'd like at the moment. One is a long whisky and soda, the other – a short explanation.

257

TEMPLE laughs.

The sound of a syphon.

FORBES: Well, here's your whisky and soda, doctor. I
                 think perhaps Temple had better give you
                 the explanation.

WESTERBY: (*Angry*) Well, someone had certainly better
                 give us one otherwise …

TEMPLE: (*Interrupting WESTERBY*) I saw your niece
                 yesterday morning, Lord Westerby – she
                 told me rather an interesting story.

WESTERBY: What do you mean? (*Suddenly*) And whilst
                 we're on the subject of my niece, why
                 haven't I been permitted to see her during
                 the past two days?

STUART: (*Calmly*) Don't you know why?

WESTERBY: No, I don't!

STUART: (*Quite calmly*) The lassie doesn't want to
                 see you. She gave explicit instructions that
                 under no circumstances were you to be
                 admitted: could I have a little more whisky
                 in this soda, Sir Graham, it's a wee bit on
                 the anaemic side!

WESTERBY: (*Highly indignant*) Are you trying to tell me
                 that my niece deliberately …

STUART: (*Interrupting WESTERBY*) I'm not trying to
                 tell you anything, m'Lord! It's Mr Temple
                 that's trying to tell you something, but you
                 won't let the poor devil get a word in
                 edgeways!

MALO: (*Rather nervous: a little frightened*) What
                 exactly did Diana tell you?

TEMPLE: She told me about the aeroplane crash,
                 about René Duprez, about Philip Baxter

	and the diamonds and about the notorious Mr Curzon.
MALO:	I – I don't know what you're talking about!
TEMPLE:	I think you do. However, let me refresh your memory. Philip Baxter, Lord Westerby and yourself were actively engaged in a diamond smuggling organisation controlled by a man called Curzon. When Baxter found the diamonds which René Duprez lost in the aeroplane crash he contacted Westerby for the simple reason that he was under the impression that Westerby was the leader of the organisation – that he was in fact Curzon.
WESTERBY:	(*Angrily*) Look here, Temple, what is all this nonsense? Diamonds! What diamonds! What the devil are you talking about?
FORBES:	(*Quietly*) Would you like to see them, Lord Westerby?

There is a pause.

MALO gives a sudden, quick gasp of astonishment.

STEVE:	They're very lovely, aren't they, Mr Malo?
WESTERBY:	(*Stunned*) Where did you find them? (*Suddenly: intensely angry*) Where did you find them?
FORBES:	We found them in a tree – in a nest – not so very far from where Dr Stuart found Inspector Morgan. It's a pity you didn't manage to get hold of the diary, Lord Westerby, because if you'd found the diary it's almost a hundred to one, you'd have discovered the diamonds.
MALO:	(*Suddenly, turning on WESTERBY*) You fool! You damn fool, Westerby! I told you

259

	we had to get that diary! I told you that at all costs ...
WESTERBY:	(*Very angry, silencing MALO*) Shut up! Shut up, Malo! (*Tensely, almost desperately*) Temple, listen! What you say is true. I was mixed up in the Curzon affair − so was Malo − so was Baxter. I wanted those diamonds and I tried to get them from him. I did my damndest to get them. But I'm not Curzon − no matter what you say, Temple − I'm not Curzon.
TEMPLE:	(*Quietly*) Philip Baxter thought you were Curzon. He was so sure of it that he got frightened, sent for Tom Doyle and told him to take care of the boys. When Doyle went to the cottage that night, he saw you there: He saw you and Carl Walters talking to Baxter.
WESTERBY:	That's a lie!
TEMPLE:	Is it a lie, Doyle?
DOYLE:	(*Suddenly*) No. No, it isn't!
WESTERBY:	(*Amazed: turning on DOYLE*) You mean to say that you saw me at the cottage talking to Baxter?
DOYLE:	Of course I did! If I didn't see you then why the 'ell should I say I did!
FORBES:	But if I remember rightly, Doyle, you contradicted yourself. In your first statement you said that it was Westerby at the cottage then, at a later date when Mr Temple questioned you, you said that it wasn't!
DOYLE:	Well − I − changed my mind.
FORBES:	(*Forcefully*) Why did you change your mind?

DOYLE:	(*Suddenly: extremely angry*) Why the 'ell do you think I changed it? Because Westerby made it worth my while, that's why! He gave me a hundred quid and told me that if I kept my mouth shut there'd be a 'ell of a lot more.
FORBES:	Was that the only money he gave you?
DOYLE:	No, it wasn't. He gave me the hundred quid the day after I made the statement an' two hundred an' fifty a couple o' days ago. That was the night I got drunk, the night I saw Mr and Mrs Temple.
WESTERBY:	(*Intensely angry*) It's a lie! It's a wicked lie! (*He moves to strike DOYLE but FORBES and DR STUART grab him by the shoulders*)
STUART:	Steady, laddie.
WESTERBY:	(*Desperately*) I never gave him a penny! I never asked him to contradict his statement! I never even knew about the statement! Temple, you've got to believe me! If you don't believe me then I'll swear to God, I'll …
TEMPLE:	(*Quite calmly*) But I do believe you, Lord Westerby.
DOYLE:	(*Softly*) What do you mean?
TEMPLE:	Doyle, you remember the night that Baxter sent for you – the night that you went to the cottage?
DOYLE:	Yes?
TEMPLE:	Well, it's my bet that you didn't see anyone that night except Baxter. Baxter told you that he was frightened of someone and that he wanted you to look after the boys. You

knew that Baxter was a member of the Curzon organisation and you suspected that he was in fact under the impression that Westerby was Curzon. Later, when you made your statement to the police, you fostered this idea by throwing suspicion onto Westerby. After you'd made your statement however you had another idea – quite a smart idea, Doyle. You pretended to change your mind. You gave us the impression that you were not at all certain whether you'd seen Westerby at the cottage or not.

DOYLE: Why should I do that?

TEMPLE: Because you knew perfectly well that it would make us more suspicious of Westerby than ever. Morgan, in fact, was convinced that you'd been got at by Westerby and that your original statement was the truth. From the very beginning you've endeavoured to foster this impression. Soon after you contradicted your statement you started to throw money about, act drunk, in fact convey the impression that you'd been bribed by Westerby.

WESTERBY: (*Astonished*) Temple, are you suggesting that Doyle is actually mixed up in this business, that he's …

DOYLE: Good God, Temple, you must be crazy! If I'd had anything to do with this business, do you think that Baxter would have sent for me? Do you think he'd have asked me to take care of the boys?

262

TEMPLE: Baxter wanted to protect his boys from
                     Westerby. He was convinced that Westerby
                     was Curzon and that sooner or later
                     Westerby would try and kidnap the boys in
                     order to secure the diamonds. It never so
                     much as entered his head that you yourself
                     were mixed up in the Curzon organisation.
                     He certainly never dreamt, not for one
                     moment, that in trying to hide the boys from
                     Westerby he was in fact actually handing
                     them over to Curzon.

WESTERBY: (*Staggered*) What!

STUART: (*Amazed*) Why man, are you suggesting that
                     Doyle is Curzon?

TEMPLE: (*With authority*) That's precisely what I'm
                     suggesting, doctor!

*Suddenly, quickly, a chair is overturned, and STEVE utters
a wild shriek.*

FORBES: Temple, look out!

DOYLE: (*With tremendous authority, desperately*)
                     Stand back! Do you hear me? Stand back!
                     Don't move!

WESTERBY: What's he got?

STUART: What the devil is it?

DOYLE: If anybody moves, I'll throw it straight into
                     the centre of the room! (*Retreating*) Now,
                     I'm warning you … I'm warning you, don't
                     move!

FORBES: (*Quickly*) What is it? What's he got,
                     Temple?

STEVE: Paul, what is it?

DOYLE: (*Desperately*) Tell them what it is! Go on,
                     tell them!

TEMPLE: (*Quietly: watching DOYLE*) It's what they
               call a Lenton. It's like a Mills bomb only
               fifty times more powerful. (*Grimly*) If he
               pulls the pin, we've had it!
DOYLE: And I warn you I shall pull it if anybody
               moves!!!!
MALO: (*Terrified*) My God, don't be a fool! Don't
               be a fool, Doyle!!!! Doyle, listen to what
               I'm saying! Don't pull the pin, don't …
DOYLE: (*Shouting at MALO*) Shut up!!!! (*Silence. A
               pause*) Now who's got the key to the door?
               (*Tensely*) Who's got it?
FORBES: (*After a moment*) I have.
DOYLE: Give it to Malo! Go on, give it to him! (*A
               pause:tensely*) O.K. Now open it! Go on,
               Malo, open the door!

MALO inserts the key in the lock and opens the door.

DOYLE: Now give me the key …

*Suddenly DOYLE dashes through the door, slams it behind
him, and locks it. Immediately, there is consternation in the
cabin. Temple has already reached the door and is
endeavouring, unsuccessfully, to open it.*

TEMPLE: He's locked it!
FORBES: (*Quickly*) Look out! Stand back! I'm
               blowing the lock off!!!!

*SIR GRAHAM fires his revolver at the lock – two or three
rapid shots – and then kicks open the door.*

STEVE: There he is!
STUART: He's climbing over the side!
TEMPLE: (*Suddenly*) No, don't fire, Sir Graham.

Before TEMPLE finishes speaking SIR GRAHAM fires.

WESTERBY: You've hit him!

There is a quick gasp of pain from DOYLE.

TEMPLE: Look out! He's dropped the bomb!

WESTERBY: My God, the pin's out!

TEMPLE: Get down! Get down on the deck, Steve!!!!

There is a tremendous explosion as the bomb goes off: this is followed by a wild scream from PETER MALO, and the sudden rush of water as the yacht keels over.

STEVE: (*Desperately*) Paul, the boat's turning over! It's turning over!

TEMPLE: Hand on, Steve! Hang on, darling!

FADE UP the noise of the yacht turning over and the sudden influx of water.

FADE UP the noise of water.

FADE.

FADE UP of TEMPLE and STEVE swimming in the water. They are both fairly exhausted.

TEMPLE: Are you all right?

STEVE: Yes ... Where's Sir Graham?

TEMPL: He's over there ... near ... the fishing boat ... Steve, are you sure you can make it?

STEVE: Yes ... (*Breathlessly*) Yes, I'll be all right.

TEMPLE and STEVE continue to swim.

TEMPLE: Good girl! Keep going, darling!

STEVE: Is – Is Sir Graham in the boat?

TEMPLE: Yes. Yes, I think he's made it ...

TEMPLE and STEVE continue swimming.

TEMPLE: All right?

STEVE: Yes ... Yes ... Don't worry!

A pause.

TEMPLE: We're nearly there ... Keep going, Steve! Keep going! (*Pause*) That's it! Now get hold of the boat with one hand and ... that's it, darling?

FORBES: (*Exhausted, leaning out of the boat*) Give me your hand! (*Taking STEVE's hand*) That's it! (*Straining*) Come on, Steve! Try ... and ... push

265

... Temple! (*Straining, in an attempt to pull STEVE out of the water*) That's it! That's the idea, Temple! She's ... nearly ... out ... Good girl! Good girl, Steve! That's the idea ... (*Sir Graham is pulling STEVE out of the water and into the fishing boat*)

FADE UP of music.

Slow FADE DOWN of music.

TEMPLE: Would you like another drink, Sir Graham?

FORBES: (*Hesitatingly*) No, I don't think so, Temple, thank you. (*He looks at his watch*) I suppose I really ought to be making a move.

TEMPLE: Nonsense, it's early yet!

STEVE: (*Thoughtfully*) Paul, I've been meaning to ask you ...

TEMPLE: (*Laughing*) Here we are, Sir Graham! Off we go again!

FORBES laughs.

STEVE: Why didn't you invite Doyle to the party?

TEMPLE: Because I thought it was a much better idea to get Dr Stuart to bring him along. That was all nonsense about the doctor not having any change. I fixed it up with him beforehand.

FORBES: Well, there was a time, quite frankly, Temple, when I suspected the doctor.

TEMPLE: Yes, but once you accepted Doyle's story about the boys you must have realised that it was purely a coincidence that the doctor happened to be in the lane that afternoon.

STEVE: The thing I don't understand is this. Once Doyle – alias Curzon – got hold of the boys why didn't he simply threaten Baxter and demand the diamonds?

266

TEMPLE: Because Doyle didn't actually know that Baxter had the diamonds. When Baxter found the diamonds, he contacted Lord Westerby believing of course that Westerby was Curzon.

STEVE: Who murdered Baxter?

TEMPLE: Malo did. Malo was quite determined to get the diary and equally determined to throw suspicion on to what he believed to be an innocent, yet nevertheless likely, suspect. (*Amused*) He picked on Doyle. That was the reason why he impersonated Doyle over the telephone that night. I made one mistake, however. I thought Lou Kenzell was working with Curzon when in actual fact he was hand in glove with Malo.

FORBES: But what made you suspect Doyle?

TEMPLE: Well, I first suspected him when he changed his story and tried to give the impression – rather successfully I must confess – that he'd been bribed by Westerby. Unfortunately for Doyle he over-played the part.

FORBES: What do you mean?

TEMPLE: The night Steve and I dined with Westerby we gave Doyle a lift home in the car. As soon as he saw me pull up, he pretended he was drunk. He tried to give the impression that he'd been drinking all night, that he'd plenty of money, and that – thanks to a mysterious benefactor – he could do more or less just what he wanted.

STEVE: But, darling, he was drunk! He was as tight as a Lord!

TEMPLE: (*Laughing*) That's just the point, Steve – he wasn't!

STEVE: I don't understand.

TEMPLE: Do you remember when he got out of the car?

267

STEVE: Yes.

TEMPLE: After he'd gone, I asked you if you wanted one of the windows open and you said no.

STEVE: Well?

TEMPLE: If Doyle had been drunk – really drunk – you'd have wanted a window open all right! But you didn't want a window open for the simple reason that there wasn't the smell of beer or a smell of whisky or …

FORBES: (*Astonished*) By George, I wouldn't have spotted that!

TEMPLE: I didn't spot it either, not until Steve refused to have the window down. Then I suddenly remembered that she simply loathed the smell of beer! Then suddenly it dawned on me that there hadn't been a smell of beer in the car – or alcohol of any sort for that matter! And then I realised that …

FORBES: That Doyle wasn't drunk, that he was simply putting on an act!

TEMPLE: Exactly.

FORBES: Well, I still think it was pretty smart of you, Temple. I certainly shouldn't have spotted it.

STEVE: Is Doyle going to get better, Sir Graham?

FORBES: Yes, I think he will but I'm very doubtful about both Westerby and Malo. They're in a pretty bad way I'm afraid. (*Rising*) Well, that's the end of the Curzon Case, Temple.

TEMPLE: Yes, and I must confess I've found it one of the most interesting … (*As the door opens*) … What is it, Charlie?

CHARLIE: I'm just off to the Palais. Anything you want before I go?

TEMPLE: No; but don't be late. Remember we're leaving early tomorrow morning.

CHARLIE: Yes, sir.

STEVE: Have you packed?

CHARLIE: Everything's oke ... umpedore.

TEMPLE: I see you're wearing one of my ties, Charlie?

CHARLIE: Yes, Mrs T. said it would be O.K.

TEMPLE: I trust it's quite satisfactory?

CHARLIE: (*Fingering his tie*) Not bad. Not bad at all.

TEMPLE: (*Dismissing CHARLIE*) All right, Charlie – and remember what I said – don't be late!

CHARLIE: O.K. Goodnight all!

STEVE: (*Laughing*) Goodnight, Charlie!

The door closes.

FORBES: I suppose you're both off to the country tomorrow? You lucky devils.

TEMPLE: Yes, Steve and I are going up to Bramley Lodge for two or three weeks.

STEVE: We're both dying to see Timothy – it's his birthday on Saturday.

FORBES: Yes, well, take it easy up there. Remember you've had a pretty strenuous time these last few days.

STEVE: Don't worry, we'll take it easy all right.

TEMPLE: (*Emphatically*) I'm certainly going to take it easy, make no mistake about that!

STEVE: Me too! (*Very pleased with herself*) From now on, Sir Graham, I'm going to sit back with my feet on the mantelpiece and, as Sam Dodsworth would say, think of nothing more important than ...

TEMPLE: (*Staggered*) I say, just a minute, old girl! That's my line!

STEVE: Oh, no! Not this time! (*Emphatically shaking her head*) Not this time, darling!!!!

They start to laugh.

FADE Up of closing music.

THE END

Francis Durbridge, the author of "Paul Temple and the Curzon Case," recalls a strange incident that happened about six months prior to his beginning to write his new serial. The incident serves as a prologue to the story.

The Superintendent Convinced Him
by Francis Durbridge

I have a friend who writes book reviews, essays, plays – in verse of course – and an occasional novel. He very rarely goes to the cinema, refuses to listen to anything except the Third Programme, and positively loathes detective stories. He does not like Paul Temple. In fact, to be brief, the only reason that he is a friend of mine is that his wife makes the most delicious omelettes, listens to the Light Programme, reads every thriller she can lay her hands on, and is, in short, a person of impeccable taste and considerable charm. She also likes Paul Temple.

Well, about six months ago, this friend of mine (whom I will call Elliot because, after reading one of his novels, I feel quite sure that he would like to be called Elliot) telephoned and asked me to call round and see him. As soon as I saw Elliot, I knew that he was upset about something. His face had a hang-dog expression, and he was barely toying with an omelette.

When I was seated, he said: "I've had the most extraordinary experience and as a writer of popular fiction I think you ought to know about it." I didn't care very much for the way he said "popular," but being an amiable sort of fellow, I made no comment.

He turned towards the armchair. "You know I've always been rather cynical about your stuff," he said. "I've never really believed all that nonsense you write about a master

271

mind being the head of a criminal organisation. But now, quite frankly, I've changed my mind."

I could tell by the way he spoke that it wasn't a leg-pull, so I simply nodded and told him to tell me his story.

"I went down to Marlow this morning," he continued, "and on the train I got chatting to an acquaintance of yours – Superintendent Bailey of Scotland Yard. As soon as he knew that I was a friend of yours he started talking about Paul Temple, detective fiction, and all that sort of nonsense. Anyway, to cut a long story short, I told the Superintendent that in my opinion the sort of characters you detective writers create simply don't exist."

I asked Elliot what the Superintendent said.

"That's just the point," said Elliot, and I could see he was very puzzled. "The Superintendent didn't agree with me. He told me about a confidence man named Waverley. For five years, according to the Superintendent, Scotland Yard had been searching for Waverley. One day he's in Bradford posing as a textile manufacturer, two or three months later he's a flourishing theatre manager in the West End of London, a year later he's a retired colonel in Cheltenham."

I nodded. "Isn't that precisely the same sort of character as Dr Belasco?" I said. "And when I told you about Dr Belasco you simply ridiculed me."

"I know," said Elliot, "but I still can't believe it, it seems fantastic!"

I said: "The trouble with you, Elliot, is that you have no imagination. When I talk about a master criminal I don't mean a man with six voices and twenty-seven disguises but a man who can conceal his true identity behind an ordinary everyday personality. Now take Curzon, for instance, the principal figure in my new Paul Temple serial. No one knows the identity of Curzon until the very last episode. It

272

might be Lord Westerby, or his secretary Peter Malo, or Tom Doyle, or Dr Stuart, or even ..."

"Yes, but that's just the point!" exclaimed Elliot. "I don't believe that's possible, at least – I didn't believe it was possible until this morning."

I said: "Well, obviously the Superintendent's a better man than I am. I've been trying to convince you that it's possible for the last ten years."

Elliot exclaimed: "I still don't think you understand! I don't think you realise what's happened!"

"Of course I realise what's happened," I said. "Your vanity's been hurt. You've suddenly realised that there's more to this detective stuff than you thought. It isn't quite so divorced from real life as you imagined!"

Elliot shook his head. The poor fellow really did seem perplexed.

"It isn't just a question of what I thought or even what the Superintendent said," he ejaculated. "It's what happened!"

"What happened?" I repeated. "What *did* happen?"

Elliot said: "When we got to Marlow, they arrested the Superintendent. He wasn't a Superintendent at all. His name was Waverley!"

Printed in Great Britain
by Amazon

22209300R00162